FROM LOMPOC WITH LOVE

A JAMES FLYNN ESCAPADE

HARIS ORKIN

Black Rose Writing | Texas

ISBN: 978-1-68513-703-8
LIBRARY OF CONGRESS CONTROL NUMBER: 2025944500
PUBLISHED BY BLACK ROSE WRITING
www.blackrosewriting.com

Printed in the United States of America
Suggested Retail Price (SRP) $20.95

From Lompoc with Love is printed in Book Antiqua

*As a planet-friendly publisher, Black Rose Writing does its best to eliminate unnecessary waste to reduce paper usage and energy costs, while never compromising the reading experience. As a result, the final word count vs. page count may not meet common expectations.

Author Photo Credit: Laura Burke

Other Titles by
HARIS ORKIN

YOU ONLY LIVE ONCE

GOLDHAMMER

ONCE IS NEVER ENOUGH

LICENSE TO DIE

THE SPY WHO HATED ME

Praise for

FROM LOMPOC WITH LOVE

"Imagine Ian Fleming after three double cappuccinos and a hit of laughing gas. Hair-raising and hilarious. More, please!"
—R. Lee Procter, author of *Prosperity, Pennsylvania*

"Our favorite delusional wannabe spy finds himself caught between a beautiful Russian sleeper agent, a dangerous Russian oligarch, and an alphabet soup of international spy agencies. Haris Orkin's best work yet!"
—Cam Torrens, award-winning author of the Tyler Zahn suspense mysteries

"Haris Orkin brilliantly channels Ian Fleming through the prism of Monty Python, dazzling the reader with charm, humor, and action as he leads this engaging international crew of heroes and villains in exciting escapades around the globe."
—Tom McCaffrey, bestselling author of the Claire Saga

"James Flynn is debonair, deadly and delightfully deranged as he undertakes his latest adventure in *From Lompoc With Love*."
—Gary Gerlacher, bestselling author of the AJ Docker series

"Haris Orkin has created a hero for our time. A certifiable nutcase. The world needs more like him. Highly recommended."
—Karen K. Brees, Amazon #1 bestselling author of the MI6 Agent Katrin Nissen WWII series

"Bravo to the author's delightfully twisted imagination and to everybody's favorite deranged, lion-hearted, goofball hero…James Flynn."
—Gojan Nikolich, award-winning author of *Tiger Season*

*I dedicate this book to the love of my life,
my beautiful, brilliant, ever-so-patient wife.*

FROM LOMPOC WITH LOVE

"The moment you doubt whether you can fly, you cease forever to be able to do it."
—**J.M. Barrie, creator of *Peter Pan***

Chapter One

Flynn held tight to a handrail as the cable car lurched away from the tiny town of Stechelberg. His stomach dropped. His heart lifted. His chest tightened. Human brains are wired to be wary of high places. Fear of heights is a normal biological response in most mammals. Not that Flynn didn't feel it. He just controlled it. Compartmentalized it. Used it to stay sharp and vigilant. He could tell by the faces of his fellow passengers that not everyone enjoyed the sensation.

Caitlyn caught his eye and smiled. She too enjoyed the adrenaline rush as the cable car roared towards the Schilthorn. Next stop, Gimmelwald, then onto Mürren, and finally Birg, the last stop before the last leg to the top of the summit. The towering peak of the Bernese Alps overlooked the valley of Lauterbrunnen.

Last year, a thug named Kalishnik shot Caitlyn in the head. She arrived in Interlaken fighting for her life, but with the help of an expert team of surgeons and the staff at the Burkhalter Center for Neurology and Rehabilitation, she overcame most of the symptoms of her traumatic brain injury. To Flynn she seemed back to her old self, though she still suffered from PTSD nightmares.

Flynn had his own PTSD symptoms to contend with. He'd been dealing with them for years. His most recent physical wound was largely healed. The bullet tore a path through his left thigh, but missed his femoral artery. An inch or two either way and neither Caitlyn nor he would be traveling to the top of the world today. Daily hikes on the *Wanderwegs* around Interlaken helped eliminate Flynn's irritating limp.

Caitlyn wanted to commemorate their one-year anniversary in Switzerland by doing something they hadn't done before. Hence, the Schilthorn. The train ride from Interlaken to Stechelberg had taken forty-five minutes, and they couldn't have picked a more beautiful day. The sky was a bright, cloudless blue. The pine-scented air crisp and bracing. A pristine dusting of snow topped the massive mountains surrounding the valley. The temperature would plunge the higher they climbed, so they'd dressed in layers. Insulated Patagonia winter jackets with hoods made up the last layer.

Dusty Sage for her.

Blue Heather for him.

Something seemed so familiar to Flynn about this cable car ride. The scenery reminded him of another time. He couldn't recall the particulars, but he did remember the surrounding mountains and the angle of the climb. He touched Caitlyn's hand. "Are you sure we haven't been here before?"

"I am firing with a few less brain cells, but I think I'd remember. Does it look familiar to you?"

"Perhaps it's just déjà vu."

"Or maybe you're remembering a past life."

Flynn smiled at that and Caitlyn smiled back, but not for very long. Her grin faded and her forehead wrinkled with worry. Flynn squeezed her hand. "You okay?"

"I'm worried about Bettina."

"Because she's traveling to Russia?"

"Putin loves murdering journalists. Since he's been in power, he's killed over three hundred. And that's just the ones we know about. Twenty-three have been convicted as spies and sentenced to life in prison."

Wind buffeted the cable car and caused it to rock. Flynn grabbed a grip strap to steady himself. "Bettina knows what she's doing."

"Does she? She's traveling to one of the most notorious penal colonies in Russia. A former gulag deep inside the Arctic Circle. It's where Putin sends his enemies to die."

"She's just there to interview Ivanov. They have no reason to lock her up."

"Who says they need a reason?"

"It's important for the book."

"The book about you and Ivanov and what you did to take him down?"

"Not just me. You too."

"No, *not* me. I told you this already. I was working for the agency. You know she can't write about me or anything I did."

"That's between you and her."

She shot Flynn a look. "If she writes about me, the CIA has to vet it before it can be published."

"It's an important story."

"Aren't you tired of being so damn famous? What if they make a movie out of it? You'll be even more goddamn famous."

"If I was still working for His Majesty's Secret Service then yes, that might be an issue. But that's part of the reason I resigned. It's difficult to be an effective secret agent when you're as well-known as I am."

Exasperation clouded Caitlyn's eyes. She opened her mouth to say something, but must have thought better of it because she looked back out the window at the astonishing view. Glancing past her, Flynn noticed someone staring at them from the opposite side of the cable car. A large man. Hulking and tall. When Flynn met his glance, he quickly looked away. He had a broad, meaty face and cold, dark eyes set too close together.

Flynn knew a killer when he saw one.

The man kept glancing in their direction. He clearly wanted to approach them, but the car was crowded, and it made more sense to kill them once the doors opened. He wore a heavy wool overcoat, his hands buried deep in the pockets. Flynn suspected one hand held a weapon with a silencer. Once they arrived at Gimmelwald, the man would make his move.

Flynn leaned closer to Caitlyn and whispered, "Do you see the man across the way?" When Caitlyn started to turn, he stopped her with a gentle hand on her cheek. "No, don't look directly at him. Glance past him and use your peripheral vision."

"Excuse me?"

"The brawny chap in the gray overcoat. The one who looks like a contract killer for the Russian mob."

Caitlyn sighed and pretended to check out the incredible vista and passed her gaze surreptitiously over a large tourist taking a picture with his smartphone. She returned Flynn's whisper. "More fat than brawny, I would say."

"You don't think he seems suspicious?"

"He's not even looking at you."

"Not now, but he was. He was staring quite intently, in fact."

"Maybe he recognizes you."

"Ivanov might be in prison, but he has allies and he has resources. He could easily hire a contract killer to get his revenge."

"So, who's the large lady next to him?"

"She could be part of the hit team."

"She's pushing a stroller."

"Which may hold a Benelli combat shotgun instead of a baby."

"*Really?*"

"Look. Now she's looking at me too."

"Because you are looking at *them*."

"Better safe than sorry is all I'm saying."

"You're being ridiculous."

Flynn patted his pockets, hoping to find something he could use as a weapon. "I knew we should have come armed."

"Would you please relax?"

"Our enemies never rest. Neither should we. When the doors open, follow my lead."

■　■　■

When Caitlyn first met Flynn, he was a patient at one of the most notorious forensic psychiatric hospitals in California. It housed serial killers, spree killers, and other various violent maniacs judged not guilty by reason of insanity. Those considered too sick and violent for even a supermax prison ended up at Hornitos. Previous to that institution, Flynn spent twenty years at a private mental health facility in Pasadena. City of Roses. Flynn believed his hospital was actually the headquarters of His Majesty's Secret Service and that he was an international superspy with a license to kill. As crazy as Flynn was, he was nothing if not heroic. Together, he and Caitlyn brought down a doomsday cult, and foiled a plot by Russian oligarch Oleg Ivanov to extort every major economy on earth.

Flynn was now a world-renowned hero and semi-reluctant celebrity. She hoped checking him out of the hospital and bringing him to Switzerland might lead him down the road to sanity, or at least some semi-recognizable version of reality. For a while, it did. Helping Caitlyn recover from her traumatic brain injury seemed to center him. He hiked with her every day in the hills above Interlaken. They dined in quaint restaurants and cafés. They paddled kayaks on Lake Thun. Their new life together was healthy and restorative, calming and predictable. Maybe too calming and predictable.

Flynn needed a certain amount of excitement to keep his synapses snapping. Caitlyn sensed him growing restless, and then Bettina O'Toole-Applebaum came to visit. A well-known journalist and writer for Rolling Stone, Bettina had participated in some of Flynn's earliest adventures. The stories she wrote about him helped ignite her career, and that shared history sent Flynn back into the past, even deeper into his delusion. Lately, he seemed increasingly more paranoid and less connected to the actual world. He started seeing enemies everywhere and believed their lives were in danger.

As the cable car approached Gimmelwald station, Caitlyn worried what Flynn might do. If he tried to hurt the fat tourist, she'd have to get between them. She saw no other option. Flynn had taught himself how to fight by watching martial arts movies, and practicing those moves in his hospital room. Caitlyn had an actual black belt in Shotokan karate. She'd competed in tournaments in college. She later studied Krav Maga and Jeet Kune Do, and learned how to shoot at the CIA training facility known as *The Farm*. Eventually, she was assigned to the Special Activities Center, the covert action and paramilitary operations division of the CIA.

Flynn had courage and kept himself in incredible shape, but he was no match for Caitlyn. Not in a one-on-one fight.

The cable car crested the top and came to a rocking stop at Gimmelwald station. Flynn leaned close and whispered, "Here we go."

The doors slid open with a hydraulic hiss and the crowded car emptied. Flynn kept his eyes on the brawny guy and the lady with the baby. They exited first. Caitlyn tried to keep herself between them and Flynn. But then they turned. The man aimed his eyes at them and pulled something from his pocket. The woman reached into the stroller.

Caitlyn tensed.

Shit. Is Flynn right?

She confronted the woman first, since she might have the more powerful weapon. Caitlyn took two fast strides in her direction, preparing to strike her in the throat and crush her trachea before disarming her and turning the weapon on the man. She stopped a split second before impact when she realized the man held a smartphone and the woman cradled a fat, bald little baby.

"Would you mind if we took a selfie with you and Mr. Flynn?" He had a thick German accent.

The woman with the baby stepped closer. "We are big fans."

Flynn gaped, gobsmacked. "A selfie?" He offered them both a smile. "I suppose that would be all right."

The man put his phone on a selfie stick and stood next to Flynn with his arm around him. The woman with the baby stood next to Caitlyn and smiled up at the camera.

"Everyone say *Käsekuchen!*"

And everyone did.

Everyone but the baby.

Chapter Two

The summit of the Schilthorn sits nearly 10,000 feet above sea level. It looms over the tiny village of Mürren and offers panoramic views of the surrounding mountains, including the Jungfrau, the Mönch, and the Eiger. The revolving restaurant at the top, Piz Gloria, was named after the mountaintop hideout of Ernst Stavro Blofeld as portrayed by Telly Savalas in the 1969 film On Her Majesty's Secret Service. *The producers found the restaurant partially constructed and offered to help pay to complete it in return for its exclusive use as a setting for the movie. Once filming was finished, the owners kept the Piz Gloria name and leveraged the publicity to help boost business.*

Caitlyn had no idea Piz Gloria was a monument to *On Her Majesty's Secret Service*. As they strolled the windblown deck around the restaurant, she spotted life-size cutouts of various characters from the film. She never saw the movie, but had to assume Flynn had. The look of confusion on his face was profound. There were cutouts of the actor who played Bond in various outfits, as well as Telly Savalas as the villain, and a young Diana Rigg as the film's love interest.

The film clips in the boutique museum helped Caitlyn understand the story somewhat. Though Flynn watched them in complete slack-jawed wonderment. He didn't comment on the life-size cutouts or on the film clips, but Caitlyn could tell they hit him hard. She hesitated to bring them up if Flynn wasn't going to. Did he understand what he was seeing? Or did he suspect he was suffering from some kind of psychotic break?

There were signs that pointed to the various villages, mountains, and glaciers both below and across the valley floor. But Flynn paid no attention to the scenic panorama, focused as he was on the life-size cutouts. He stood directly in front of a cutout of Bond. The actor aimed a pistol at some unseen assailant and wore a tweed sports coat.

Flynn approached a cutout of Telly Savalas and stared into his 2-D face with a deep and abiding hate. Caitlyn tried to steer him away. "This monster took everything from me," Flynn mumbled. "Everything,"

"You hungry?"

Flynn had no answer to that as another cutout caught his attention. One of the actress Diana Rigg. In the film, she played Contessa Teresa di Vicenzo, the great love of Bond's life. Tentative and terrified, he gingerly approached. Tears filled his eyes as he caressed the cold metal skin of the cutout. Caitlyn's heart hurt for him. He was so profoundly broken. She didn't know what to say or do, so she waited him out, hoping he might come to his senses.

He rested his forehead against the cold metal. "She was everything to me," he whispered.

She squeezed his hand and gave him a tug, pulling him along. "How about a drink?"

Flynn nodded. "I could use one."

"So could I."

As they entered the restaurant, another life-size cutout of Bond stopped Flynn again. This one wore a tuxedo. Caitlyn detected a flash of fear in Flynn's eyes. "I know I've been here before."

A string quartet in the corner played something classical as Caitlyn pulled Flynn over to the semi-circular bar. The bartender, a slender middle-aged Swiss gentleman, offered Caitlyn a friendly smile. "What can I get you?"

"Champagne for me."

"Bollinger?" offered the bartender.

Caitlin nodded. "Sure."

"And for you, sir?"

"A vodka martini."

The bartender smirked. "Shaken and not stirred?"

"Why, yes," Flynn said. "Is there something funny about that?"

"No, sir," chortled the bartender and got to work mixing Flynn's cocktail.

Flynn turned to Caitlyn. "Wonder what that's all about?"

Caitlyn shrugged and pretended to have no idea.

They paid for their drinks and Caitlyn directed Flynn to a table where the floor-to-ceiling windows allowed an unobstructed view of over two hundred mountain peaks. The restaurant's décor was more utilitarian than elegant. They served a selection of traditional Swiss specialties like fondue, raclette and rösti, but also a few international dishes as well.

Caitlyn ordered a split of champagne, hoping it might help loosen Flynn up. She then ordered a cold Schilthorn platter as an appetizer for the table, the salmon escalope for herself, and the *Geschnetzelte Kalbsleber* for Flynn. Piz Gloria was more about the view than the food, however, not that Flynn paid attention to either one. The cutouts and film clips sent him spiraling to somewhere deep in his troubled subconscious. Caitlyn reached across the table to squeeze his hand, hoping she could bring him back to the present. "Hey? You okay?"

Flynn stared at the head of a stuffed mountain goat looming over Caitlyn. "I'm fine."

"You don't seem fine."

"I haven't thought of my first wife for quite some time." Flynn's eyes glistened. "Before I met you, she was the love of my life. Like you, she understood who I was and what I did. Her father led the Unione Corse."

"The Corsican Mafia?"

"He, too, lived a life of danger. But unlike most organized crime figures, he lived by a code. A code I could respect. And when push came to shove, he did the right thing. If not for him, I'd likely be dead."

She took a bite of salmon. "This is really good. Do you want to try some?"

"I'm sorry, but I just don't have much of an appetite."

Flynn pushed away his plate and looked off across the restaurant. Something caught his attention. An immediate change overcame his demeanor. The sadness and fear faded as his eyes grew hard and resolute. He stopped slumping and sat up straight.

She turned to see what he was looking at and he grabbed her by the hand and squeezed it hard. "Don't turn around."

"*Seriously?*" She turned around anyway and at first couldn't tell what set Flynn off. All she saw were families enjoying lunch, elderly tourists marveling at the view, and young couples staring into each other's eyes. "Who do you think is—"

"Three strapping men. They're not looking now, but they were before you decided to tip our hand and turn around."

Caitlyn faced Flynn. "They're probably just more fans looking for a selfie."

"Or a GRU death squad dispatched by Vladimir Putin to take us off the board."

Sadness sat like a cold lump in Caitlyn's stomach. Suddenly, she had no appetite either. She hoped to help Flynn find his way back to sanity, but after a year, she now knew that hope was nothing but a fantasy. Flynn's psychiatric nurse back in L.A. had warned her. So did the psychiatrist she consulted with here. He told Caitlyn that decades of delusional ideation were difficult, if not impossible, to break.

The truth was Flynn *had* confronted and defeated multiple evil geniuses with insane plans to take over the world. People everywhere saw Flynn as some kind of mad hero standing against the forces of evil. So, what if he was crazy? The general public had no problem buying into his delusion. Maybe they assumed all heroes were a little nuts.

Caitlyn finally understood that shattering Flynn's delusion would also shatter his sense of self. That made their relationship untenable. Tears blurred her vision as she looked across the table. "Let's just go home."

"They're getting up."

"Let's just go."

"They're coming for us."

"James, please…"

Flynn searched the room, desperate for a way out. He settled on something and stood, reaching out with his hand. "Follow me, if you want to live."

∎   ∎   ∎

Flynn grabbed a knife off the table and hid it up his sleeve. He darted across the crowded restaurant, colliding with a waiter carrying a massive tray of food. It crashed and clattered, but he kept moving. He didn't look back to see if Caitlyn was behind him. He knew she'd follow his lead. The three assassins made their move as well. Flynn caught a glimpse of them at the edge of his peripheral vision.

The string quartet included a cello, and that was why Flynn moved for the bandstand. He once escaped a cadre of killers by sliding down a mountain in a cello case. That particular case held a Stradivarius, and the cellist who owned that priceless instrument rode down the mountain with him. The musicians abruptly stopped playing as Flynn grabbed the cello case with a quick, "Sorry."

"Flynn!" Caitlyn followed right behind him. "*What the hell are you doing?*"

He held the case close as he charged down the stairs and found himself in some strange dimension where frozen images from his past surrounded him. His memories played like short film clips, bombarding him from all sides. The smiling villain who murdered his spirited and beautiful wife. He watched the memory of her tragic murder, all in living color. He hurried on. Frantic footsteps rushed behind him. Flynn pushed forward through a set of hydraulic doors.

The ice-cold air shocked his system. In his haste to escape, he left his Blue Heather Patagonia jacket draped over the back of his chair. He had no gloves and no wool cap. He hoped Caitlyn had at least grabbed hers before chasing after him.

"Flynn! Stop!" Caitlyn shouted.

Flynn hurried down the metal staircase. Cable guardrails lined either side of a trail that connected to another steep staircase that led to yet another trail. As he charged down the winding path, a fierce wind caught the cello case and nearly ripped it from his grasp. Deep snow covered the steep slope below.

"Flynn!" Caitlyn sounded closer now. He stopped to turn. She nearly collided with him. "What the *hell* are you doing?"

He saw the three strapping men pounding down the stairs above. All three reached into their pockets. It was now or never. He snapped open the cello case and laid it flat on the snow at the top of the slope. He sat inside of it even as Caitlyn tried to pull him out. "No, no, no!"

Flynn tugged hard and Caitlyn fell in next to him. The added weight slid the case forward and Flynn held on as they skittered down the slope. An icy wind blew back his hair as they picked up speed. The angle was nearly vertical. A double black diamond run. Flynn remembered the previous cello case slid forward like a sled and was easier to steer. This one acted more like a snow saucer and before he knew it, they were hurtling backwards down the mountain.

At the top of the slope, the GRU death squad weren't holding guns, but phones as they videotaped Flynn and Caitlyn's downward trajectory. They didn't follow on skis. They didn't have assault rifles. There were no helicopters with M-60 machine guns or shooters on snowmobiles. Piz Gloria slowly faded away in the distance as they rocketed faster and faster down the slope.

Trees rushed by on either side. Flynn rocked back and forth in an attempt to turn their makeshift sled around. They slammed into something solid, nearly bouncing them both out of the case. Instead, they flew into the air and landed hard, facing sideways as they careened down the precipitous incline.

"We gotta get out of this thing!" Caitlyn screamed.

Flynn saw her point. They appeared to be closing in on a stand of trees. Both sides of the slope disappeared. If they went off either edge, they'd likely plummet into some bottomless crevasse, never to be found again.

The last time he rocketed down a ski slope in a cello case, he used the Stradivarius itself as a crude rudder. Now, he had nothing to steer with. Less than nothing. Usually, Flynn's instincts in the face of danger were flawless. Not today. He'd been inactive too long, living a soft and uneventful life. He'd lost his edge and now both of them were going to pay the ultimate price.

Caitlyn grabbed Flynn by the hair and wrenched his head back. "When I say jump, jump. *JUMP!*"

Caitlyn jumped.

Flynn didn't.

She held onto his arm even as he dragged her down the hill. Finally, she lost her grip and tumbled away. Flynn grew numb as he roared forward, eyes welling up from the cold. He hoped to find a gap in the trees, but steeled himself for impact. The case banged into a mogul, bounced into the air, and hit the next mogul even harder.

Flynn went flying. Less like Superman and more like a live chicken tossed from a plane. The cello case was long gone, but Flynn continued to fly. He caught a branch across the chest, flipping him backwards. He crashed through the hard crust of a snowdrift and came to a dead stop. He stayed motionless, just in case he broke something. With a tentative wiggle of a foot and then a leg, he pushed himself to a sitting position. His buttocks were frigid and somewhat damp due to all the snow crammed down the back of his pants.

He heard the crunching of snow behind him and turned. Caitlyn loomed over him.

She did not look happy.

Chapter Three

The remote arctic settlement of Kharp was founded during the construction of the Salekhard-Igarka railway in 1961. A work camp housed the prisoners laying the tracks. Eventually, it became a permanent prison constructed out of quarry stone for those deemed most dangerous to the Soviet state. Two more prisons were eventually constructed around the periphery of Kharp. Polar Wolf, Polar Owl, and Polar Bear housed political prisoners, murderers, rapists, and serial killers. Since Putin came to power, he has filled all three to capacity with those he perceives as his enemies. Every morning, prisoners gather outside for roll call in thirty below zero weather. They aren't allowed to stamp their feet or rub their hands together to stay warm. If any one prisoner moves, the entire group is soaked to the skin with a water cannon.

Kalishnik stayed at the best hotel in Kharp. It was also the *only* hotel. Most people stayed thirty miles away in Salekhard. Mainly because the Hotel Kharp offered only slightly better accommodations than what inmates experienced in the prisons. At least, guests weren't locked naked in steel boxes, shocked with cattle prods, or beaten with rubber truncheons. Though they did have to suffer through the stale and rancid buffet breakfast served in the filthy lounge off the lobby.

Kalishnik only came to Kharp to visit with his longtime employer, Oleg Ivanov. The former oligarch was locked away in Polar Owl. Normally, prisoners there weren't allowed visitors, but palms were greased and guards were paid to look the other way. Not even Putin could do away with the corruption endemic in the Russian prison system.

As Kalishnik finished his tea, an attractive Black woman had the audacity to sit down at his table across from him. She held out her hand as if expecting Kalishnik to shake it, but he just stared at it until she withdrew it.

"Do you speak English?" She spoke with an American accent.

Kalishnik considered feigning ignorance but wondered why a buxom Black woman from America would sit across from him in the crappy breakfast room of a shitty motel near a Russian prison in the Arctic Circle. "A little."

"My name's Bettina O'Toole-Applebaum and I'm a journalist from America."

Kalishnik stared at her silently.

"I know you work for Oleg Ivanov, and I assume you're here to visit him."

"What do you want?"

"I write for a number of well-known magazines in America, but I'm currently working on a book about Mr. Ivanov, and how he ended up in prison here. I'd like to interview him and get his side of the story."

"No."

"Perhaps you could ask him when you see him?"

"No."

"I know he hasn't been painted in the best possible light by the media, and I'd like to rectify that."

Kalishnik knew that Ivanov wouldn't trust her or want to talk to her. "No."

"All right, well, I'll be here for a few more days. Think about it. If you decide to ask him *and* he wants to talk to me, just leave a message on this number." She slid a card across the table to him.

Kalishnik looked at it but didn't touch it. He stood up and walked away and left the card where it lay.

.   .   .

Bettina O'Toole-Applebaum had visited some dangerous and horrible places over the years, but Kharp took the prize when it came to ugly. She flew from San Francisco to Astana, Kazakhstan, with a stopover in Istanbul. From there she took a train to Omsk and flew to Salekhard in an ancient puddle-jumper. The last leg of the journey involved a train from Salekhard to Kharp. She checked into the Hotel Kharp. It lived up to its name.

Her door didn't close all the way, and there was no security chain. A weird stain covered a quarter of the bedspread, and she worried the sheets were infested with either lice or bedbugs. A clump of hair clogged the bath drain, and four inches of brownish standing water filled the bottom of the tub. Old cigarette smoke and some kind of caustic disinfectant made her eyes water. The phone had a dial tone, but looked fifty years old and was probably tapped. Bettina marched back to the front desk to demand another room, but no other rooms were available. As the only hotel in Kharp, they had no competition and no reason to improve anything.

On her first day in Kharp, Bettina went to Polar Owl and waited six hours in the bitter cold to talk to someone who spoke minimal English. They told her no visitors were allowed and two guards escorted her away from the front gate.

She discovered Kalishnik in the breakfast room the next morning. He had to be there to visit Ivanov. Clearly, *some* visitors were allowed. She figured Ivanov still had enough cash to open doors, so she approached Kalishnik with her offer. Over the years she'd interviewed gangbangers in L.A., Mexican cartel bosses, and enforcers for the Italian, Armenian, and Russian mafias. But Kalishnik stood in a class by himself. Their brief conversation chilled her to the bone. She figured she'd stay in Kharp one more day just to see if Ivanov would talk. If not, she'd be glad to get her ass out of town on the first available train.

■ ■ ■

Kalishnik hated the cold. He had lived in the UK with Ivanov because that was where Ivanov insisted on living, but winter in London beat winter in Moscow, and the south of France bested them both. He grew accustomed to that Mediterranean climate and living on Ivanov's mega-yacht. Before Flynn blew it up. The warm, dry weather eased his achy joints.

The former Spetsnaz commando had suffered many injuries, bullet wounds, and broken bones over the years. They throbbed and tormented him in the cold and damp. As a former champion boxer, his hands hurt the worst. He wore a long, woolen peacoat, a lambswool scarf, heavy leather gloves, and a stocking cap to keep the heat from escaping the top of his head. The bitter wind bit into his skin and chapped his lips as he stood in line at the gate to Polar Owl.

Everyone admitted as a visitor paid for the privilege, and Kalishnik, using Ivanov's money, paid more than most. A younger guard led him through the prison past high corrugated steel walls and fences topped with brutal coils of razor wire. Guard towers with heavy machine guns kept a constant vigil. Not that anyone would dare try to escape. Even if they made it over the wall, where would they go?

Kalishnik passed prisoners without jackets standing outside in a courtyard, shivering in the cold. One man rubbed his hands together for warmth, which elicited an angry shout from the guard taking the roll call. Another guard blasted the group with a fire hose, buffeting them about and soaking them to the skin.

Kalishnik kept walking.

His escort led him into one of the cell blocks. Inside, it wasn't much warmer or less damp. The screams of tortured prisoners echoed through the halls. Passing by one door, a man handcuffed to a chair cried for mercy as a hulking guard electrocuted him with a cattle prod. The sharp stench of shit and piss overpowered the reek of rusted metal, damp cement, and acrid sweat.

One heavy, locked door led to another long hallway, and another locked door, and yet another endless corridor. The prisoners in their bare cells with their metal cots topped with thin mattresses and threadbare blankets looked emaciated, exhausted, and defeated.

Another door led to yet another cell block, but this one welcomed him with the scent of baked goods, cinnamon, and fresh-cut flowers. These larger cells had art on the walls, shelves with books, thicker mattresses, and warmer blankets on wider beds. Some had televisions and couches and space heaters. Kalishnik followed the guard escorting him to a large steel door at the end of the corridor.

Another massive guard stood watch outside. Unlike the others, this door didn't have a window into the cell. The guard knocked and, a moment later, the door creaked open. A breathless and beautiful young woman in a bra and panties stood framed in the entryway. She took a step back to reveal Ivanov lying face down and naked on a massage table.

Ivanov glanced up at Kalishnik and nodded. He raised his finger as if to say, "Give me a moment." The masseuse struggled to close the heavy steel door.

Kalishnik stood silently next to the guard and, after twenty or so minutes, the sweaty female masseuse left with her portable massage table. Ivanov, now wearing a white terrycloth robe, sat in a motorized recliner and beckoned Kalishnik in, directing him to a plastic folding chair.

Kalishnik could still detect the woman's light citrus and floral perfume as he sat across from his employer. Once one of the richest men in the world, the former GRU agent made his fortune in cybersecurity with the world's most popular anti-virus and anti-spyware software until the FCC classified the company as a national security risk. From there he diversified into everything from real estate to mining to media, finance, and transportation. Though he made even more by creating software for ransomware gangs.

He'd given Putin a generous cut of those ill-gotten gains and created troll farms to spew Russian propaganda all over the world. But after so many years of paying Putin the lion's share of his profits, he decided to cut the president out completely and blackmail him along with the rest of the world. Ivanov's wife, Anya, however, enlisted the aid of a mental patient to expose her husband's plot and, in the process, took control of most of his fortune. But Oleg Ivanov didn't become a billionaire by being a *plonker*. He'd squirreled enough away in hidden accounts all over the world to keep him in the billionaire's club.

Kalishnik pointed around the room and then pointed to his ear.

Ivanov smiled. "I have the room swept for bugs daily."

"And you trust the ones doing the sweeping?"

"I do. Do you know why?"

Kalishnik shook his head.

"Because they hate Putin as much as I do. As do so many of my old friends in the military and the GRU. His foolish war has made him enemies everywhere. Sending ill-equipped soldiers to die in a meat grinder doesn't make for good PR. Everyone knows someone who has died there. He turned the world against us and destroyed our economy in the process…and for what? For some vision of a Russian empire that can never be what it once was? It is time for him to go. But it won't be some idealistic politician who defeats him. It will be someone who knows how to fight as dirty as he does."

Kalishnik nodded. When Ivanov was on a roll, the best course of action was to shut one's mouth and nod one's head.

Ivanov tapped out a cigarette and lit up. "Have you done what I asked?"

Kalishnik nodded. "We found a woman. She's part of the illegal program."

"Is she beautiful?"

"Very beautiful and very willing. Her brother died in eastern Ukraine. *Trudovske.*"

"And she understands the plan?"

"She does."

"Do you have a picture of her?"

Kalishnik took out his phone, opened the camera app, and found a picture. He showed it to Ivanov.

He nodded his approval. "She looks a little like that tall blonde movie star from South Africa. What's her name? The one in the *Mad Max* movie?"

Kalishnik shrugged and put away his phone. "What do you want to do about your wife?"

"*Ex*-wife."

"Do we need a plan for her as well?"

"For Anya, it's much less complicated. All she needs to do is die."

Kalishnik nodded. He started to stand up, stopped, and sat back down. "One more thing."

Ivanov lit a cigarette, took a puff, and blew the smoke up over his head. "What?"

"I wasn't sure I should say anything, but if I didn't, I worried you might be irritated."

"I'm already irritated."

"A journalist approached me at the shitty hotel here. She wants to interview you for a book she's writing. She claims she wants to tell your side of the story."

"Who is she?"

"Bettina O'Toole-Applebaum."

"An American?"

"A black one."

"Black? She has balls coming all this way."

"I already told her no."

"Tell her yes."

"What?"

"Yes."

"Yes?"

"*Yes*! I'm stuck in a fucking gulag in the middle of fucking nowhere. My enemies can say anything they want about me, but now I have a chance to change the narrative. Why wouldn't I take advantage of that?"

Kalishnik was incredulous. "So, you *do* want to talk to her?"

"But make it clear she needs to write something that will get the democratic governments of the world to lobby for my release."

"And what if she wants to write something else?"

"Like what? A hit piece?"

Kalishnik shrugged. "Maybe."

"Then I will have her killed."

"Should I tell her that?"

"Of course you should tell her that."

"So, when do you want to talk to her?"

"Before the GRU figures out she's here and either locks her up or deports her stupid ass."

"So tomorrow?"

"Tomorrow would be good."

Chapter Four

From the Secret Intelligence Service (MI6) website and recruitment portal:

We've protected the UK from overseas dangers such as terrorism, cyber threats, and regional instability since 1909. As an Intelligence Officer, you'll be central to our mission. Intelligence Officers gather, deliver, and use secret intelligence to keep the country safe. It's a fascinating and diverse role where you'll use everyday skills, including communication and empathy, to tackle extraordinary challenges. If you're from a Black, Asian, mixed-heritage, or ethnic minority and from a socially or economically disadvantaged background, this is your opportunity to bring your fresh perspective into intelligence, gain unique experience, and discover if a career with us is right for you.

Duncan Dankworth's stomach was rock hard. Not with muscle, but with painful bloating. He never should have eaten that Spotted Dick for dessert. The combination of dried fruit, suet, and sugary custard irritated his IBS. Stress worsened those symptoms, and the fact that his immediate superior's superior demanded an emergency meeting out of the blue filled him with tremendous gas. His cubicle was surrounded by a half dozen other cubicles, so he couldn't just let rip with a thunderous trump. His CIA counterparts always found it amusing to hear that trumping is UK slang for farting.

Dankworth did a summer internship with MI6 his senior year at university. He studied modern languages and linguistics with a concentration in Russian and French. He originally applied to the foreign office, but was diverted to the spy track via a letter offering him an interview for "alternative overseas opportunities." He went in for said interview, but expressed some reluctance until they assured him that he wouldn't be firing guns or leaping out of helicopters.

His dad was from Liverpool, and his mum was from India. They liked his mixed-race and working-class background and told him they thought he might bring a different viewpoint to intelligence work. Unlike many of his colleagues who were from the south of England and attended Oxford or Cambridge, Duncan had a regional accent. He grew up in Whickham near Newcastle on Tyne, went to a local grammar school, and attended a redbrick university.

Duncan completed the three-year Intelligence Officer Training Pathway to learn the language and methodology of his profession. Because of his background in linguistics and modern Russian, they encouraged him to work in the Russia House. They created a cover for him as a business analyst who worked for a UK-based financial services firm with offices in Moscow and St. Petersburg. Duncan eventually became a case officer, running Russian agents for three years, until his health became an issue. The stress of running covert agents in Putin's Russia caused his IBS to flare up and affect his work. Finally, MI6 brought him back to London to recover and become a mentor and trainer for Russia-bound case officers.

Duncan had never met his immediate superior's superior and couldn't help but wonder if he faced some sort of trouble. Happier and healthier back in London, he wanted to continue as a trainer and mentor, and eventually progress to operational manager. His IO salary wasn't lavish, but respectable. He appreciated the thirty days of annual leave, the excellent pension scheme, and the on-site gym, restaurant, and coffee bar. As an ethnic minority, he thought it unlikely they'd outright fire him, but even with all the recent diversity initiatives, he knew MI6 was still run by old upper-class white men and likely always would be.

His immediate superior's superior, however, wasn't an old white man, but a middle-aged white woman named Kathy. Peter, her thirty-something assistant, ushered Duncan into her rather large office (by MI6 standards). She even had a large window that looked out on the Thames, Westminster Abbey, and Big Ben. Petite and cheerful with short, wavy blonde hair, Kathy offered Duncan a warm smile and pointed to a chair across from her desk.

As one of four director generals at SIS, Kathy directed the intelligence operations of agents all over the world. Surprising, since the history of MI6 was rife with both racism and misogyny. Early on, women at MI6 were either secretaries or deployed as "honey traps" to ensnare or blackmail foreign agents with their feminine charms. In 1909, Vernon Kell, a co-founder of MI6's precursor agency, commented that his ideal recruit was "a man who could make notes on his shirt cuff while riding horseback." Women weren't considered upper management or field agent material. Though when asked about that glass ceiling, Vernon Kell famously said, "I like my girls to have good legs."

Duncan's few friends believed he worked as a foreign trade specialist for a large automobile manufacturer. No one beyond his close family knew who employed him. Even then, he could never discuss his day-to-day activities. He had to turn off his phone before entering the giant emerald-green fortress-like building at Vauxhall Cross. Once there, the phone remained locked away. He had a desktop computer, but limited access to the internet. The only contact with the outside world came via a landline.

Kathy settled her bum on the edge of her desk. "Tea?"

Duncan didn't want to worry about spilling tea, but he also didn't want to offend her hospitality. "Certainly. Thank you, Mum."

Kathy hit an intercom button on her rather complicated-looking phone. "Peter, could we have some tea, please?"

"Of course, Mum."

"Thank you." She turned her attention back to Duncan. "Seeing we've never met, I suppose you're wondering why I called you here today."

Surprised by her candor, he nodded. "Yes, Mum. As a matter of fact, I was a little concerned that I may have done something to offend."

Kathy laughed at that. "Don't be ridiculous. You've done excellent work for us."

That surprised Duncan. He assumed he was relatively invisible to the powers that be. "That's kind of you to say, Mum."

"Nothing kind about it. I'm simply stating the truth. And the truth is…we need you for a very important assignment."

"Mum?"

"An undercover Russian spy has contacted MI6. She claims she wants to defect and is offering us a whole raft of intelligence secrets."

"Is she based here in London?"

"No, she's in the United States. California, to be precise."

"California? Why didn't she contact the CIA?"

"One, because she doesn't trust them, and two, she will only defect and turn over the information to someone she believes works for MI6."

Duncan flushed with excitement, but the shot of adrenaline also exacerbated his IBS and filled his intestine with even more painful gas. "And so you want to send *me*?"

"Yes, but not exactly. The person she wants to surrender to is not actually an employee of MI6."

"I…I don't understand."

"There's a man who has gained quite a bit of notoriety over the last few years because he believes he works for His Majesty's Secret Service."

"But he doesn't?"

"No. In fact, he's actually a mental patient."

"Are you talking about James Flynn?"

"So, you know of his exploits?"

"How could I not?"

Her bright smile faltered. "Quite."

"Why would this Russian agent want to defect and turn her information over to a mental patient?"

"She claims she's in love with him."

"In love with James Flynn?"

"It's a tricky situation and we need you to manage it."

"Manage it how?"

"You need to convince Flynn to romance this woman and seduce her into handing over the intelligence."

"Is she mentally ill as well?"

"That is something you will need to access."

"Jesus."

"Of course, it's possible she's quite sane, and this is some sort of honey trap."

"But Flynn's not even an actual MI6 agent."

"No, but he's caused problems for the GRU in the past, and they may be looking for revenge. But if this is *not* a trap…this could be an intelligence coup of monumental proportions."

"And the CIA is okay with us taking the lead on this?"

"It's actually the FBI who has jurisdiction in this case. Once you arrive in California, you will liaise with the special agent in charge of counterterrorism in the Los Angeles office."

"Not counterintelligence?"

"Her name is Miranda Jacks. She knows Flynn personally and has had dealings with him previously." Kathy slid a folder across the table. "Everything you need to know is in this file."

Duncan flipped open the folder. A candid picture of the female Russian agent looked back at him. She was shockingly attractive. Tall and lean and very well-proportioned. Her long blonde hair framed the face of a supermodel. "She's quite beautiful, isn't she?"

"It wouldn't be much of a honey trap if she looked like Dame Edna."

"I suppose not." Duncan put down the picture.

"Flynn is currently living in Switzerland. Interlaken, to be precise. He's residing with a retired CIA agent. She has been briefed on the situation. However, she is hostile to Flynn's involvement, so she is the one you will need to convince."

"Are you sure I'm the best person for this assignment?"

"You're one of the finest young case officers we have at Russia House."

"It's just that…I…well…"

"*What?*"

"I have an entire network I'm running in Moscow."

"We'll have someone take charge of that for you. At least temporarily."

"It's just that I spent years cultivating the trust of so many of those agents. I worry that…"

"*I don't know what I'm doing?*"

Duncan blushed. "No, of course not, Mum."

"You will leave this evening for Interlaken. Go home and pack. We will send a car to take you to the airport."

Duncan's anxiety rose and he struggled to keep a wet fizzle from escaping his tightly clenched buttocks. "Understood, Mum."

"Good. And do me a favor, Dankworth. Try not to cock this up."

"You can depend on me, Mum."

"I certainly hope so." She motioned to the door. "Off with you now."

Duncan squeezed his arse tightly as he stood and stiffly moved for the exit. He nearly escaped unscathed, but as he passed through the door, a staccato series of bum cracks echoed off the walls, making his exit less than elegant. Rather than call attention to his faux pas, he left without a word, but did catch the shocked and disgusted face of Kathy's male secretary as he sat at his desk, fussing with some paperwork.

Chapter Five

Bettina O'Toole-Applebaum packed her bags. She couldn't wait to get on the morning train and leave this godforsaken place behind. The room was bad enough, but the town was even worse. Having grown up in California, she wasn't used to the bone-chilling cold of the Arctic Circle. She turned off the flickering overhead fluorescent light, sat in the rickety desk chair with the threadbare upholstery, and pulled her Mylar emergency space blanket tighter. She couldn't bring herself to sleep in the bed, and, after tonight, she wouldn't have to.

Just as she slipped off to sleep, a violent banging on the door caused it to creak open. A huge form filled the doorway, silhouetted by the faint light in the corridor. Kalishnik's basso profundo voice croaked out the word, "Da."

"Da?"

"He will meet you."

"When?"

"In morning. I will come get you."

He walked away without closing her door, and Bettina didn't sleep for the rest of the night.

■   ■   ■

Bettina didn't bother unpacking. She planned to leave town right after her interview with Ivanov. She would take the afternoon train to Salekhard, and put this place in her rearview mirror.

Kalishnik arrived at 9:00 a.m. and escorted her to the prison. The guards let him pass without a word. She followed him through what she could only describe as a medieval house of horrors. The Spanish Inquisition had nothing on United Russia. She made mental notes on every gruesome detail. The torture. The screams. The stench of piss and shit and sweat and fear. She'd toured prisons before, but nothing this horrific.

Ivanov's cell lay deep inside the prison, but his accommodations were far superior to those offered at the Hotel Kharp. Compared to most other prisoners, Ivanov and those who shared his cell block lived in relative comfort. Apparently, his wife hadn't taken all his money as he was still able to pay some hefty bribes. His breakfast looked far better than the one Bettina choked down that morning. He enjoyed eggs and bacon, a freshly baked croissant, and coffee that smelled like actual coffee. Her stomach growled audibly. She had to assume Ivanov heard it as well. But he didn't offer her any breakfast or even a cup of coffee. The oligarch regarded her with disdain and rotated his finger in a circular motion, indicating her turn to speak.

"Thank you for seeing me."

"Kalishnik mentioned you wanted to tell my side of the story." Ivanov spoke excellent British English with a slight Russian accent.

"I do."

"Perhaps I should explain the injustice I've suffered."

"Do you mind if I record you?"

"Not at all."

Bettina turned on her phone's voice recorder and set it in the center of the table. She opened a notebook. "Are you ready for my first question?"

"It's important you understand exactly what was done to me. That way you can write it the way I want it."

"I'm an independent journalist."

"Yes, I know. You have a reputation as a truth teller. You are very well-respected. People will believe whatever you write."

"Which is why I need to write the truth."

"Of course. But then there are many truths and many ways to shade it. Did Kalishnik tell you that if you write something critical of me, I will send him to kill you?"

Bettina felt a cold shiver. "No, he did not."

"He is a man of few words. Maybe nine words. Maybe fewer. He mainly speaks with his fists." Ivanov clenched his fists and grinned. "Do you understand what you need to do now?"

Bettina had no intention of whitewashing the man, but she always believed it was better to ask for forgiveness than for permission. "I understand."

"Good. Then this is the bottom line. Putin made me his political prisoner, and my wife was complicit in that injustice. He used her to bring me down because he wanted my fortune. He steals from all of us oligarchs. I wanted to push back and expose him for who he is. That is why I am now a political prisoner in the ice-cold asshole of the world. Tell my truth, and the world will bring pressure to bear. Perhaps he will trade me for a few of his spies. Perhaps not. But either way, we will expose him for the monster he is."

"Didn't you do his bidding for a number of years?"

"Not because I wanted to, but because if I didn't, I would die."

"So he gave you the same choice you gave me."

"Exactly. But in my case, I'm the aggrieved party. I only want what's best for the world. Putin only wants what's best for Putin."

Bettina nodded and wrote something in her notebook.

"What are you writing?"

"Just a note to myself."

"I'm all for a free press, but please don't push it."

"Understood."

"I certainly hope so. You're such a smart and attractive young woman. I would hate for anything… unfortunate to happen to you."

"As would I."

"Shall we begin?"

*   *   *

Ivanov eventually ordered coffee for both of them. He told her a long tale, most of which clearly wasn't true. He made himself the hero of his own story and made his wife the villain. He claimed she seduced a dangerous mental patient to do her bidding at the behest of Putin. Bettina had already interviewed Flynn and Caitlyn and Ivanov's wife, Anya, and knew the actual unvarnished truth.

As all good liars do, Ivanov used some of the truth and twisted the rest to match his narrative. He sounded convincing because he had convinced himself, but Bettina had interviewed many dangerous psychopaths over the years. The clinical name was antisocial personality disorder. Sociopaths and psychopaths share many of the same symptoms, but sociopaths are much more impulsive and erratic. Psychopaths are extremely organized and can fake an approximation of empathy and even compassion. They can pretend to be charming and charismatic, which explains serial killers like Ted Bundy and Svengalis like Charles Manson.

Ivanov spoke for nearly five hours, giving Bettina all she needed to paint him as the narcissistic asshole he was. She wasn't about to let Ivanov intimidate her. She would write about all of it, including his threats, and tell the FBI office in L.A. to keep an eye out for Kalishnik.

They spoke for so long, Bettina worried she might miss the last train out of Kharp. But Ivanov eventually talked himself out and abruptly ended the interview with a stern warning. "I know you've probably been threatened with death before, yet here you sit as healthy as can be. Don't confuse me with the others you've dealt with. I served in the GRU, and before that, the KGB. Like my previous sponsor, Putin, I have a long memory. Don't make the mistake of crossing me."

Kalishnik led her back through the house of horrors, into the frigid courtyard, and through the front gate, where two Federal Security Service officers waited. They arrested her on charges of espionage. Two guards emerged to take her back into the prison. Bettina put up some initial resistance, but a punch in the solar plexus took her to her knees. Her hands were cuffed behind her, and they wrenched her to her feet. The metal bit into her wrists and burned her skin with cold.

She always knew arrest was a possibility in Putin's Russia, but somehow thought her celebrity would shield her. She hadn't considered that Putin was a pariah now and seemingly comfortable with the hate directed at him from all around the world. With his nuclear weapons, stolen billions, and subjugated population, economic sanctions no longer moved him. As a journalist publicizing the plight of his enemy, Putin would see Bettina as a threat.

The prison guards dragged her back inside, past all the brutal beatings and electroshock torture, past all the shrieks of agony and hopeless sobbing, past all the rapists and murderers who smiled their creepy smiles as they undressed her with their eyes.

They locked her in a frigid cell with a tiny cot, a thin mattress, and a threadbare blanket. After three hours, she yearned for the relative warmth and security of her shitty hotel room. She had been disappeared off the face of the Earth. How would anyone know where to find her? She'd taken many chances in her career and flirted with danger and death so many times. She realized now she'd been very lucky. And now, that luck had run out.

Chapter Six

Interlaken means two lakes in German, and its history dates back to the early twelfth century. It began as a small settlement surrounding a monastery and sits on a flat alluvial plain between Lake Thun and Lake Brienz. In the intervening centuries, the town became a trading center known for its natural beauty. In the early 1800s, the paintings of Swiss landscape artist Franz Niklaus Konig brought even greater recognition. Many hotels and spas were built to lure tourists to the area. World War One brought an abrupt halt to that growth, but soon after the war, the location became a hub for those wanting to hike, climb, and ski the mountains of the Jungfrau region. Today, the area is celebrated for its cheese-tossing competitions, where contestants compete to see who can throw enormous wheels of Emmental, Gruyère, and Appenzeller the furthest.

MI6 supplied Duncan Dankworth with Flynn's address in Interlaken. The flat occupied the top floor of a newer building on the north shore of Lake Brienz and had last sold for 1.3 million Euros. *How do a mental patient and an ex-CIA agent have the money for such a swanky address?* He looked at the pictures on the rental website. The four-and-a-half room flat included a well-appointed open kitchen, two master bedrooms, and a private wellness area with a Swedish sauna and spacious Jacuzzi.

It irked him to have to work with a celebrated lunatic, but the fact that Flynn lived in luxury only irritated Duncan more. He would have preferred to approach the Russian agent in

California directly, but the powers that be apparently didn't trust him to try that strategy.

Duncan flew to Zurich and took the two-hour train ride to Interlaken. He was too annoyed to appreciate the beautiful scenery passing his window. Instead, he obsessively read over the file Kathy had handed him. He worked to keep calm and not irritate his IBS. He'd need his full focus if he hoped to convince Flynn to accompany him on the mission.

After arriving at Interlaken Ost, he took a cab to the lakeside address. He buzzed the flat and waited only a moment before the voice of a vexed female with an American accent answered. "Yes."

"Duncan Dankworth here to see Mr. Flynn."

"Take the elevator off the lobby. We're on the top floor."

The door buzzed and Duncan let himself inside, located the elevator, and, within minutes, stood in a luxurious living room with a floor-to-ceiling window that offered a stunning view of Lake Brienz and the surrounding mountains.

Flynn greeted him with a welcoming smile and a firm handshake. "James Flynn. It's very good to meet you." The man looked like his photos, but even more so. Tall and lean with broad shoulders, a charming smile, and manly crinkles around the eyes. Movie star handsome, as so many of the articles about him breathlessly and annoyingly pointed out. He had at least four inches on Duncan and thirty additional pounds of lean muscle mass.

"Duncan Dankworth, Mr. Flynn. I'm with MI6."

"Of course you are. And this is Caitlyn Valentine."

Duncan reached out his hand. "Ms. Valentine."

Caitlyn didn't bother to shake, but nodded curtly. She was just as striking as her photos. Slender and tall, wiry and strong. She wore jeans and a black turtleneck. Her hair hung longer than in the pictures, softening the angles of her face. A friendly sprinkle of freckles dusted her upturned nose—a charming counterpoint to her icy green eyes.

Flynn motioned to a sliding glass door that led to a wraparound deck. "Would you care to sit outside? It's a beautiful day."

Duncan nodded. "Why not?"

Flynn seemed so damn rational. Duncan could see why so many were fooled into thinking he wasn't completely crackers. "Would you like a cocktail or a glass of wine?"

"Not when I'm on duty."

Flynn smiled at that. "I hope you don't mind if I indulge." He looked at Caitlyn. "Darling?"

She shook her head.

Flynn insisted that Duncan take the chair with the best view and sat across from him. Caitlyn sat catty-corner. Anger radiated off her. Duncan decided he'd be better off talking to Flynn alone. "Ms. Valentine, you really don't need to be here for this."

"I disagree," Caitlyn said.

"And I concur," Flynn added. "Ms. Valentine is a veteran intelligence agent. She recently left the CIA, but currently works for a very prestigious private concern. Kroll."

"Which is why she needs to step away. What I'm about to reveal is highly classified intelligence."

"If that's how you feel, then perhaps you should leave. I trust Caitlyn implicitly, and if you can't trust her, then you can't trust me."

Duncan didn't trust Flynn at all, but Kathy was quite clear. This operation wouldn't work without him. "Fine. Let's read her in as well then."

Caitlyn shook her head. "Actually, let's not read either one of us in. I don't know what MI6 wants with Mr. Flynn, but whatever it is, I doubt it's in his best interest."

Flynn put his hand on hers. "Now, let's not be hasty, darling. Let's hear the man out."

Caitlyn sighed and shook her head. "Fine."

"What I'm about to say is quite sensitive, which is why I brought this handheld device." Duncan pulled something out of his briefcase that looked like a walkie-talkie with a touch screen and an antenna.

Flynn leaned in to examine it more closely. "Is that a bug detector?"

"It's actually a jammer that blocks all signals going in or out." Duncan flicked it on and set it on the table.

"Ingenious. I'm guessing Q had something to do with that device."

Duncan smiled politely. "Q?"

"The quartermaster at MI6."

"Of course," Duncan mumbled dismissively. "Tell me something, Mr. Flynn. Do you know anything about the illegals program?"

Flynn nodded. "The deep sleeper program created by Directorate S? Of course. They masqueraded as Americans and imbedded themselves in corporations, political organizations, and even the military."

Caitlyn narrowed her eyes. "I thought the CIA caught them all in 2010?"

"Apparently not," Duncan replied. "A female agent purporting to be part of that program contacted MI6 and offered to give up the rest of them. She claims there are nearly three hundred in total spread across the US and the UK, working inside defense contractors, university think tanks, and government agencies."

Caitlyn seemed much more interested now. "*Three hundred active sleeper agents?*"

"That's what she claims."

"What does Flynn have to do with any of this?"

"Nothing," Duncan said. "Except for the fact that the female agent in question will only meet with Flynn."

"Why Flynn?"

"She says she's in love with him."

Caitlyn snorted at that. "Seriously?"

Flynn, offended by Caitlyn's amused snort, pushed back. "Is that so preposterous? After all, it's happened before."

Caitlyn snorted again. "When?"

"Long before I met you. When I was a much younger man. A female Russian file clerk claimed to be in love with me and offered to steal a top-secret device if I spirited her out of the country."

Duncan raised an eyebrow. "What kind of device?"

"A cryptography machine used to decode highly secret Soviet spy communications."

Caitlyn grinned. "Oh, you mean—"

"Of course, she wasn't *really* in love with me. It was a trap created by an evil organization bent on revenge for what I had done to foil a previous plot. They sent her to seduce me. She pretended to be in love with me, and by the end of our time together…she was no longer pretending."

"We believe this too might be a trap," Duncan said.

Caitlyn nodded. "Where is this Russian agent located?"

Duncan pulled the file out of his backpack. He opened it to reveal the candid picture of her. "California. A place called Lompoc. One hundred and fifty miles north of Los Angeles."

Flynn nodded. "Home to Vandenberg Space Force Base." He reached for the picture.

"She's very attractive," Caitlyn commented.

"The better to draw me in," Flynn replied.

Caitlyn leaned back and regarded Duncan with growing suspicion. "If you believe it's a trap, why send in Flynn?"

"Because I've been known to turn beautiful enemy agents to our side," Flynn said. "If we play our cards right, perhaps we can run her as a double agent."

Caitlyn sighed. "Yeah, I don't think so."

Duncan nodded. "My superiors *do* think so. Which is why I'm here. They want Mr. Flynn to spring the trap."

. . .

Flynn shared Caitlyn's suspicions, but how could he say no to His Majesty's Secret Service? Caitlyn was fully recovered and no longer needed him the way she once did. In fact, since she accepted employment with one of the largest private intelligence agencies in the world, Flynn had felt rather useless. He worried his enemies were closing in, but Caitlyn chalked that up to boredom and paranoia. Caitlyn didn't want to believe it, but Flynn was sure those men at Piz Gloria were after him. He'd made many enemies fighting the enemies of freedom, and it could have been any of them.

Caitlyn didn't want him working for MI6 again, but what if this Russian really was infatuated with him? What if she *could* expose every agent in the illegals network? Who knows what deadly plots he might uncover? Who knows how many lives he might save?

Of course, Caitlyn's concern might be genuine. That last mission left them both badly injured. Caitlyn mainly worked from home now, but that didn't mean she was any safer. Her recent activities might have caught the attention of one of their many adversaries.

Duncan Dankworth tapped the picture. "Well, Mr. Flynn? Are you in?"

In his day, odd little fellows like Dankworth weren't recruited by MI6. But perhaps that was the point. No one would suspect such a soft, peevish little man of being a British agent.

A faint buzzing captured Flynn's attention. He noticed something off in the distance. A tiny speck moved across the water in their direction—in far too straight a line to be a bird or anything from the natural world. As the buzzing grew louder, Flynn suspected it might be a drone.

Flynn tapped Caitlyn's hand and pointed towards the drone. It caught her eye immediately.

She glanced at Dankworth. "Is MI6 keeping us under surveillance?"

"Excuse me?"

She pointed. "Is that one of yours?"

Duncan squinted into the distance. "One of my what?"

The drone closed the distance at a rapid clip. Flynn leaped to his feet. "Inside! Now!"

Caitlyn was already moving, but Duncan sat motionless, quite perplexed by Flynn's admonition.

"Excuse me?"

Flynn tackled Duncan and they fell through the open patio door. Caitlyn leapt in after them, jumping over both of them as the unmanned aerial combat vehicle buzzed closer. She drew a Glock 17 and blasted the automated kamikaze, clipping a wing and sending it crashing into the edge of the deck, detonating the explosive device it carried. Glass shattered, sending shards everywhere. Most of the force was directed downward, decimating the deck and obliterating their security deposit.

Flynn caught the terror in Duncan's eyes. That explained his inability to get up off the floor. Flynn grabbed him by the wrist and pulled him to his feet.

"Move, move!" Flynn shouted. "They're coming!"

"Who's coming?"

His question was answered by the breaching charge on the door. The explosion blew it right off its hinges. Three men entered with submachine guns and murderous intent.

■ ■ ■

The flying door clipped Caitlyn on the shoulder and spun her sideways, knocking the Glock from her hand. The three men who entered through the smoky haze looked familiar. With a start, she realized they were the same ones Flynn had fled from at Piz Gloria.

She dove to the floor, snatched up her Glock, and shot the first one in the forehead. The others ducked and dove for cover. Duncan Dankworth tried to crawl away and ran face first into the leg of an overturned chair.

Flynn ran as well. Right towards the danger. He tackled one man before he could riddle the fleeing Duncan with bullets. Flynn tussled with him on the floor, fighting for the gun. The weapon roared as bullets stitched across the ceiling.

The third assassin aimed his weapon at Flynn just as Caitlyn scissored his legs and brought the man down. He lost his gun and crashed on top of her. She looked to Duncan for help, but he clutched his injured face and struggled to stand up.

"Duncan!" she shouted.

He looked right at her and then crawled off through the breached doorway like a terrified infant.

"Bloody hell," Flynn shouted after him as he worked to disarm the killer trying to murder him. The hitman used his full weight to push the gun barrel towards Flynn's face. Flynn fought to restrain him as the gun edged closer.

Caitlyn had her own killer to contend with. He pressed his forearm down on her throat, intending to strangle the life out of her. She bucked and fought, but couldn't match his size or strength. The struggle stopped when she stretched to reach the knife sheathed to her ankle. A smug grin lit up his face when he figured she'd given up the fight. Pain and horror replaced it, however, when she drove her blade deep into his groin.

He screamed to high heaven as she tore and ripped and twisted. After the life left his eyes, she pushed him off with her knee, grabbed his gun, and aimed it at the asshole still wrestling with Flynn. She fired a quick burst. Flynn's assailant went limp, collapsing on top of him. Flynn rolled the hired killer off, climbed to his knees, and then his feet, wiping the spray of blood off his face.

"Dankworth!" Flynn shouted.

"Dankworth!" Caitlyn screamed. She wondered if Dankworth sold them out, but then she saw the top of his head peek around the edge of the door, his eyes wide with panic. "Where did you go?" she shouted.

Dankworth had no answer for her. Instead, he looked around the room to make sure the coast was clear and then made his way back inside.

"Why didn't you draw your weapon?" Flynn demanded.

"I don't have a weapon. Why would I have a weapon?"

"Because you're a secret agent! You're with MI6! What did you do with the gun they issued you?"

"No one gave me a gun."

"So you came here unarmed? Why didn't you use your martial arts training?"

"I have no training in martial arts."

An incredulous Flynn got in Dankworth's face. "You can't shoot. You can't fight. What exactly *can* you do, Dankworth?"

"I'm a case agent. Not a bloody commando."

"You didn't learn to fight in the military?"

"I was never *in* the military."

"Then why would they make you a double 0?"

Dankworth turned dark crimson. "Don't be a bloody idiot! There are no double 0's! It's fiction. A ridiculous fabrication for a series of ridiculous films."

"Yes, yes, I understand the designation is all hush-hush, but I'm one of the fraternity. You can tell me."

"Tell you what?"

"Why is MI6 recruiting agents who can't fight or shoot?"

"I have a PhD in modern languages and linguistics. I speak fluent French and Russian. Until this insane assignment, I was assigned to Russia House."

"I too have First in Oriental Languages. From Cambridge. So a proper education doesn't necessarily preclude the ability to fight and shoot. I joined the secret service just before the war."

"What war?"

"*The* war. I was accorded the rank of lieutenant in the Special Branch of the Royal Naval Reserve and left the service with the rank of commander."

Caitlyn finally jumped in to nip their insane conversation in the bud. "We need to get the hell out of here."

Dankworth looked around at all the bodies. "Shouldn't we wait for the police?"

"Absolutely not," Flynn replied. "I don't know how MI6 is training their agents nowadays, but, apparently, they haven't taught you anything."

Chapter Seven

"Then war broke out in heaven. Michael and his angels fought against the dragon, and the dragon and his angels fought back. But he was not strong enough, and they lost their place in heaven. The great dragon was hurled down – that ancient serpent called the devil, or Satan, who leads the whole world astray. He was hurled to the earth, and his angels with him."
   Revelation 12:7-9

Caitlyn had worried that Flynn was slipping deeper into his delusion with each passing day. Sledding down the side of a mountain in a cello case was undeniably crazy. He saw things that others didn't. Things that weren't there and some that were. But it wasn't paranoia if someone was really trying to kill you.

She so badly wanted to sleep as Lake Thun trundled by, but she couldn't allow herself that luxury. Not with all the threats arrayed against them. Her fear was that Oleg Ivanov would seek his revenge, but in the end, the danger came from a different direction entirely.

The assassins all wore the same St. Michael the Archangel medal on a silver chain. The Archangel was the patron saint of the military and the divine symbol of the Army of God. They'd plotted to bring on Armageddon, but Flynn and Caitlyn had stopped them.

The retired four-star Air Force general who'd led them was sentenced to life at a supermax prison in Colorado. But he still had many followers. Men who would give their lives for him.

Many who believed he was God's right hand, sent by the deity to fulfill the prophecy and lead them in the final battle between heaven and hell. General Jedidiah Anderson, descendant of one of the Confederacy's greatest military leaders, still commanded the Lord's mortal army on earth. Since his incarceration two years previously, he had sent no one after Flynn or Caitlyn.

Until now.

Until MI-6 tracked Flynn down and led his enemies right to them.

Duncan Dankworth sat across the aisle. His lip trembled as he clutched his stomach. He wasn't wounded in the attack, but appeared distressed, frazzled, and frightened. And angry. He didn't even bother looking out the window at the towering mountains. The alpine meadows. The quaint villages on the glorious *Wanderwegs*.

Caitlyn loved living in Interlaken with Flynn. She found a peace there she had found nowhere else, and she had hoped to live there forever. But forever was over. That life was gone. Danger had found them.

"What?" Dankworth glared at her.

"What do you mean, *what*?" Caitlyn glared back.

"Why are you staring at me?"

"Why do you think?"

"You seem angry with me."

"No shit, Sherlock."

"Why would you be angry with *me*?"

Flynn started to open his mouth and Caitlyn raised a finger to shush him. "Please let me handle this."

Flynn raised his hands as if to say, *fine*.

She pointed that same finger at Dankworth. "You led them right to our door."

"Me?"

"Did you even check to see if someone was following you when you left the train station?"

"Why would someone be following me?"

"Can you really be that clueless?"

Flynn finally jumped in. "Caitlyn, what's done is done. Besides, you know they were already onto us. They attacked us at Piz Gloria."

"Because MI6 gave our location to who knows who in the U.S."

"We don't know that for a fact."

"I think we do. The general has spies everywhere." She glowered again at Dankworth. This time he looked away, grimaced, and burped.

Flynn put his hand on Caitlyn's knee. "People who do what we do can never afford to get too comfortable. And much as I've loved our time here, we both knew it couldn't last forever. I have a job to do, and so do you."

"I think I should go with you to Los Angeles."

"You blow off this contract with Kroll and they might never work with you again. You made a commitment. You need to honor it. You can join me in a few days."

"James, please—"

"I'll be working with Miranda Jacks and the entire Los Angeles FBI office. Plus, there are all my former colleagues in Pasadena. Honestly, I'll have many people watching my back. More than we ever had here."

"He's under my protection as well," Dankworth added.

"Don't remind me."

Chapter Eight

The launch of the very first satellite by the Soviet Union in 1957 caused major panic in America's military-industrial complex. The Russians used intercontinental ballistic missile technology to launch Sputnik, which proved the Soviets now had rockets capable of raining atomic bombs on North America in a matter of minutes. The success of Sputnik spurred the creation of NASA and kicked off the space race. In 1958, the Strategic Air Command was tasked with creating a deterrent missile force. The army's Camp Cooke became Vandenberg Air Force Base, the main missile testing ground for the launching of satellites and experimental intercontinental ballistic missiles. Located in Santa Barbara County, the 98,000-acre base is eight miles north of Lompoc and sixteen miles south of Santa Maria. In 2021, Vandenberg Air Force Base became Vandenberg Space Force Base.

Kalishnik arranged to meet Harper Sinclair at Santa Maria's Chick-fil-A. Kalishnik loved Chick-fil-A. He found the freshly breaded boneless chicken breast to be perfectly crispy on the outside and thick and juicy on the inside. The toasted buttery bun and dill pickle chips added a delicious softness and tangy burst of flavor, which complemented the spices in the crunchy breading. He discovered Chick-fil-A on his first visit to the United States and made it a point to enjoy an original chicken sandwich on every trip since. No other fast-food restaurant had the same hold on Kalishnik. He enjoyed the occasional Double-Double at In-N-Out, but he craved Chick-fil-A.

After Ivanov was spirited off to Russia for his show trial, his wife, Anya, tossed Kalishnik out of their London flat. He considered moving to Moscow, but hated the weather and worried that the FSB might change their mind and decide to arrest him as well. Instead, he decamped to a hotel in Lisbon and lived there under an assumed name.

Harper Sinclair ordered the grilled chicken sandwich, a far inferior offering. Slim as she was, Kalishnik assumed she rarely ate fast food. He thought their meeting would be more anonymous in Santa Maria as it had a much larger population than Lompoc. Plus, Lompoc didn't have a Chick-fil-A. He took a bite of his sandwich and washed it down with some Dr. Pepper.

Most sleeper agents appeared perfectly average. Bland. Plain. Not strikingly ugly or particularly beautiful. They were chosen to be unremarkable. Virtually invisible. Not Harper Sinclair. Kalishnik marveled at her attributes. How she carried herself. How she spoke English with no trace of a Russian accent. Instead, she had the accent Vivian Leigh used as Scarlett O'Hara in *Gone with the Wind*. He needed to speak English because Harper insisted on English at all times. Not that there was anyone else around. At three in the afternoon, they had the patio to themselves.

He set his Dr. Pepper down. "Can I ask you question?"

Harper nodded.

"How long you live in California now?"

"Fourteen years."

"You know Chuck Norris?"

She almost smiled. "Chuck Norris the movie star?"

"I'm big fan, and you live here long time, I thought maybe you meet him."

"California's a big place, cupcake."

"So that's no?"

"No."

Kalishnik nodded. "Ivanov is grateful you agree to help with his plan."

"I'm not doing it for Ivanov. I'm doing it for the money he promised me. And to screw over Putin."

"Because of your brother?"

"He was a proud soldier and Putin forced him to fight in that stupid war."

Kalishnik was surprised to see tears spring to her eyes. "I heard they executed him."

"Because he refused to obey orders. Orders that would've gotten him killed." Harper put down her sandwich. "Over four hundred thousand Russian soldiers have died there. More than three times the number of soldiers who died in Afghanistan. Putin needs to be stopped before he kills us all."

"Ivanov agrees with you."

"Like I give a damn." She pushed away her sandwich and took a sip of her drink. "Just tell me what he needs me to do."

"Tell me more about company you work for."

"Airtech Defense Systems. We design circuit boards for satellites and ICBM missiles. Boards that can withstand the rigors of outer space."

"And you give this intelligence to FSB?"

"I do. Though long term, they want me to create a back door so Russian hackers can take control of both the missiles *and* the satellites."

"And you will confess this to Flynn and MI6 intelligence."

"And the FBI."

"And then reveal the identities of all the sleeper agents currently in U.S."

"Yes."

"How do you know their identities? Ivanov wants to know this. Does not the FSB keep each sleeper agent separate from every other?"

"They do, but I'm a hacker, and it's hard to keep things hidden from me."

"So, you lure Flynn and seduce him with promise to reveal sleeper agents?"

"That plan is already in motion."

"And then you give him information and he hands it to MI6 and FBI, and sleeper agents are caught and arrested, and Putin is humiliated."

"You can't humiliate a psychopathic narcissist. Putin has no shame. But he will lose his entire U.S. and UK spy networks."

"Once that is done, Ivanov needs you to set up Flynn so I can eliminate him and leave evidence that points to Putin as killer."

"Isn't Putin *already* an international pariah?"

"There are some US politicians who admire him. Who repeat Russian propaganda and GRU disinformation. We don't know what Putin has on them, but connecting him to Flynn's death will create big problems for that *mudak*. Those politicians will no longer support him. People love that lunatic."

Harper studied Kalishnik's expressionless face. "When will I get my money?"

"When Flynn is dead, Ivanov will wire you ten million dollars."

Harper pushed away from the table and stood. "Are we done here?"

"Don't you want dessert? Chick-fil-A's Chocolate Chunk cookies are killer."

Chapter Nine

Instead of making slow, endless circles in the gridlock that ensnarled Los Angeles International Airport, Sancho left his Aston Martin DB9 Volante in one of the parking structures and waited for Flynn at baggage claim.

Flynn gifted Sancho the DB9 after their first terrifying adventure together. Sancho was an orderly at the time, and Flynn carjacked him in the parking lot at City of Roses. The private psychiatric hospital treated patients with addiction issues, depression, borderline personality disorder, and various forms of psychosis. Flynn fell into the severely delusional camp. Even so, he became a mentor and role model for Sancho.

While most patients wore threadbare T-shirts, sweatpants, and flip-flops, Flynn wore second-hand suits made by Armani, Brioni, and Hugo Boss. He exhibited endless *joie de vivre* and lived life like every day was his last. He helped Sancho find his confidence *and* his courage. If not for Flynn, Sancho never would have married Alyssa. If not for Flynn, he wouldn't have had the money to buy a house or finish his nursing degree. But Sancho was a father now. His family depended on him. He couldn't be there for Flynn the way he used to be. Luckily, Flynn now had a new sidekick.

Caitlyn Valentine.

Flynn's call surprised him. It was totally out of the blue. At first, he refused to tell Sancho the reason for his return to Los Angeles. When pressed, Flynn claimed he was on a secret mission. That immediately raised red flags. Sancho insisted on picking Flynn up at the airport. He invited him to stay with his family in Pico Rivera. Mainly, he wanted to keep an eye on him. Flynn on his own was trouble waiting to happen.

Flynn's flight on Lufthansa had already arrived at Tom Bradley International Terminal, but first he'd need to go through customs. At LAX, that could take a while. So, Sancho found a cement bench outside the terminal and braved the beeping horns and diesel exhaust from the nonstop traffic.

Sancho last saw Flynn in Switzerland. He brought the whole family. Caitlyn was still dealing with her injuries and Flynn devoted himself to her recovery. He claimed he had resigned from the Secret Service, and that gave Sancho hope that Flynn might eventually stumble his way back to reality.

Flynn burst through the double hydraulic doors, pulling a suitcase on wheels. A leather messenger bag dangled from one shoulder. "Sancho! It's been too long, old friend!"

Sancho rose as Flynn dropped his bags and shook his hand, pulling him close in a manly embrace. "Where's Caitlyn?"

"She's meeting with a client in New York City. She'll be along in a day or two."

"I gotta say, I'm a little surprised to see you here, *esé*. Life looked damn good in Interlaken."

"Until my enemies tracked me down."

"Enemies?"

"The Army of God."

"No shit?"

"We escaped unscathed, but our time there is done. MI6 needs my help."

"To do what?"

"It's a long story, but suffice it to say, it's time for me to get back into action."

Worry squeezed Sancho's heart. "I thought those days were over, *mano*."

"I thought so too, but the enemies of freedom never rest."

"Is the Army of God still after you?"

"Not at the moment."

"Good to hear." He grabbed Flynn's suitcase. "You ready?"

"Absolutely. I made a reservation at the Langham in San Marino."

"Don't be silly, bro. Save your money. Stay with us."

"I appreciate the hospitality, but I wouldn't want to put you out."

"We're family, *esé*. Besides, Alyssa's making a special dinner. You don't want to disappoint her."

"Definitely not."

"Okay then, let's go. We're gonna ride in style, bro. I brought the DB9."

"Good man."

"You want to borrow it while you're here? I mostly drive my Nissan and keep this baby in the garage."

"Thank you, Sancho."

"Of course, man. *Mi carro es tu carro.*"

■　■　■

Flynn had forgotten the insanity of L.A. traffic. Even at midday, the 405 was bumper to bumper. Aston Martin's engineers designed the DB9 for open highways or twisty mountain roads, not stop-and-go traffic on an L.A. freeway. Sancho grinned at Flynn and patted him on the knee. "I missed you, man."

"Likewise, my friend. How's life at headquarters?"

"Um…Good."

"So, you're still working with the team?"

"There's some new people, but a lot of the old crew is still around."

"I'd like to stop on the way, if that's okay."

"Stop at City of Roses?"

"I feel I should report to M. Let him know why the home office sent me to Los Angeles."

"I can tell him."

"But *I* can't tell *you*."

Sancho sighed. "Do you want to call him?" He pointed at his iPhone in the center console. "We can pull over. You can step out of the car."

"No, I better do this face to face."

"What if he's busy? What if he's in a meeting? I think we should call ahead and make an appointment."

"This is time sensitive. He'll understand. Besides, I need to see Q and what new technology he's dreamed up for me."

"I don't know, man."

"Well, I do. No arguments now. We're only twenty minutes away."

■ ■ ■

Soon after they arrived at City of Roses, Flynn made a beeline for M's office. M's gal Friday, Miss Honeywell, dropped her Hostess Ding Dong when she saw Flynn. "Well, look what the cat dragged in!"

"Honeywell, you look as scrumptious as ever."

Honeywell usually ignored Flynn's inappropriate compliments and rarely gave him the time of day. She worked for M's predecessor and had been with the service for many years. Now in her mid-fifties, the voluptuous African-American beauty offered no reaction to Flynn's flirtatious banter. "You made me drop my damn Ding Dong."

"Did you miss me?"

She raised an irritated eyebrow at Flynn and hit a button on the interoffice intercom. "Dr. Michaels, I have James Flynn here to see you."

"*James Flynn?*"

"Yes, sir."

"He's no longer a patient here."

"I understand that, sir. Should I send him in or should I send him on his way?"

Flynn sat on the edge of her desk. "Tell him I'm here on orders from MI6."

"Did you hear that, sir?"

"I did."

Flynn leaned closer to the intercom. "Sir, I'm sorry, but I can't leave here until I talk to you."

"Jesus Christ."

"Sir?"

"Fine. Send him in."

Flynn grinned and opened the door to M's office. "Thank you, Honeywell. By the way, I love what you've done with your hair."

She smirked and turned back to her computer. Flynn entered M's inner sanctum. Unlike his predecessor, M kept his office clutter free. The cold, impersonal décor matched his icy attitude. He glowered at Flynn through steel-rimmed spectacles. "Don't bother sitting. You won't be staying long."

"It's good to see you too, sir." Flynn took a seat in the chair across from M's desk. "Has the head office briefed you on my mission?"

"You're no longer officially a patient here, so I can't really talk to you. It's a liability issue. I hope you understand."

"Got it. Right. I've gone rogue, so you must officially disavow any knowledge of me. But unofficially, an MI6 agent by the name of Duncan Dankworth will be joining me here in L.A. tomorrow."

"Flynn—"

"Yes, I know. I normally work alone, but MI6 insisted that Dankworth join my mission. To be perfectly frank, I found the young man quite *un*impressive. Between you and me, he's about as helpful as a one-legged man in an arse kicking contest."

M sighed and pointed at the door. "Please close the door on your way out."

"Sir, I've always appreciated your no-nonsense attitude. You've always been tough but even-handed and I wanted to apologize for what happened the last time I was here."

M continued pointing at the door. "Don't make me call security."

"To be fair, at the time, I had no idea that Ms. Grossblatt was your wife."

M hit a button on his intercom. "Honeywell, get him out of here."

The door abruptly opened. Honeywell grabbed Flynn by the arm, pulled him to his feet, and dragged him out the door, slamming it behind herself.

Flynn smiled at Honeywell. "I guess that's that then. The man does not like to dilly-dally, does he?"

She handed Flynn off to Sancho, who quickly ushered him into the corridor. "Sounds like that went about as well as I expected," Sancho said. "You ready to book?"

"Not quite yet."

■　■　■

Sancho raced after Flynn as he poked his head into the activity room. Eighty-three-year-old Quentin played Parcheesi with bipolar Bob, schizophrenic Zipper, and three-hundred-pound Ty.

The anxiety-ridden ex-gangbanger grinned when he spotted Flynn. "Well, look who's in the house, yo! If it ain't Jimmy Flynn!"

"Good to see you, Ty."

Quentin, Flynn's old roommate, offered Flynn a curt nod. "Flynn."

Flynn referred to Quentin as Q. The self-styled genius believed he was the greatest inventor since Thomas Edison. Inventions he claimed to have created include the silicon microchip, the zipper, and the corn dog. Over the years, he supplied Flynn with all kinds of imaginary spy gear. Some he created himself. Some he ordered from Amazon. Everything from laser pens to explosive toothpaste to sonic blasters and military-grade putricants.

Mary Alice watched *The Great British Baking Show* with ninety-five-year-old Doris Frawley. Doris, a 1940s pinup girl and bit player in two Cecil B. DeMille religious epics, claimed that she gave birth to the anti-Christ in 1952 after participating in a sex-magick ceremony with L. Ron Hubbard and Jack Parsons, the founder of Pasadena's Jet Propulsion Laboratory.

Mary Alice, a big-boned, freckle-faced lady with dyed red hair and anger-management issues, offered Flynn a big, toothy grin. She jumped to her feet, rushed over, and threw her big freckly arms around him. "You're back! You came back!" She had an East Texas accent and the raspy voice of a three-pack-a-day smoker. "I knew you'd come back!"

"Good to see you too, Mary Alice."

Flynn politely tried to extricate himself. She grabbed him by both butt cheeks and pulled him closer. "Are you here to take me away from all this?"

"I wish I was, but I'm on a mission for his Majesty, and I'll be counting on all of you for your continued support."

"You know you can count on me, lover."

Sancho gently pried Mary Alice's arms off Flynn and tried to steer him out of the activity room. "Good to see you all, but James has people to see and places to go."

Mary Alice pushed Sancho to one side and grabbed Flynn by the shoulder. "You're not here to stay?"

"I'll be back, my dear, but for the moment, duty calls. Q? I'm hoping you might have some new technology in the works."

Q nodded and pulled himself to his feet with a nearby walker. "Follow me."

Flynn and Sancho followed Q as he shuffled back to his room. Rodney Shoop, his roommate, lay sound asleep in bed. His bushy, white Santa Claus beard rested on his belly as he snored away.

Q slid a cardboard box out of his closet, reached inside, and pulled out two objects. He laid them both on the bed. "In anticipation of your probable return, I created two new devices that might come in handy." He picked up a pair of plastic glasses with cardboard in place of where the lenses would be. Each side had concentric red circles topped with the word *X-Ray* on one side and *Vision* on the other. "These revolutionary x-ray spectacles will allow you to see through walls. See through clothes. See through flesh to the bones beneath."

Sancho couldn't help but roll his eyes. Clearly, they were the same X-Ray Specs his friend Paco ordered from an ad in the back of a comic book when they were kids.

Flynn put them on and held his hand up to the light streaming in the window. "Extraordinary."

Q handed him a keychain attached to a tiny can of pepper spray. "Guess what this is?"

"Pepper spray?" Sancho innocently asked.

"Hypno-spray. It's camouflaged as pepper spray, but actually contains a powerful psychotomimetic drug that creates an instantaneous susceptibility to hypnotic suggestion. In short, anyone you use it on will fall into a trance and do whatever you ask. They will tell you the truth. Even turn against their own."

Sancho laughed at that. "Seriously?"

Q sprayed a spritz directly in Sancho's face. The pain staggered him and took him to his knees. He screamed in agony and Q shouted. "You're a dog! You're a dog! Bark like a dog!"

"What the hell, Quentin! Jesus Christ!"

Q nodded. "Perhaps I need to use a bit more."

Before Q could aim and spray another dose, Sancho started barking. And howling. And growling.

Rodney woke up with a start. "What the heck??"

Through his blurry, teary eyes, Sancho saw Flynn smile with delight. "Incredible."

"You are no longer a dog!" Quentin insisted with a loud, booming voice. "You are back to being you. You are Sancho Perez! Psychiatric nurse at City of Roses."

Tears streamed down Sancho's face. "Jesus, dude."

Quentin handed the pepper spray to Flynn. "Quite remarkable, is it not?"

"Quite," Flynn agreed.

Snot flowed from Sancho's nose as intense pain continued to burn his mucous membranes. Flynn offered an arm, helped Sancho to his feet, and out of Quentin's room. The agony gradually diminished as Sancho stumbled his way down the corridor. He made a stop at the restroom to rinse his eyes and face with cold water. The tears finally stopped flowing and Sancho, though still in pain, could finally see. He made his way out, wiping his face as he collided with the head nurse at City of Roses.

Nurse Durkin stood six feet tall and tipped the scales at two hundred pounds. Most of it solid muscle. She stared at Flynn with a glare that could cut steel. "What is Mr. Flynn doing here? He is no longer a patient at this facility and not authorized to be on the premises."

"He came to see Dr. Michaels, but we're actually on our way out."

Flynn stepped closer and offered Durkin a charming smile. "Arabella, my dear, it's been too long."

She ignored Flynn and kept her scowl focused on Sancho. "Why are your eyes all bloodshot? What have you been doing?"

"Nothing we shouldn't be."

"Should I call security?"

"No need. I got it handled." Sancho caught the ambivalence on Durkin's face. Always a stickler for the rules, especially when it came to Flynn, she'd revealed her true feelings for him at Sancho's wedding. Like every other nurse at City of Roses, she couldn't resist his movie star looks and effortless charisma. Though she seemed to be doing a damn good job of resisting him at the moment.

"If he's not gone in the next ten minutes, my next call will be to the police."

"Come on, James, time to go."

Chapter Ten

The ancient Aztecs and Oaxacans are credited with creating the first mole sauce. There are seven different kinds of mole, only two of which use cocoa as a primary ingredient. Not to be confused with an enemy spy in an espionage organization, a small blind mammal that tunnels underground, or the kind of mole that dermatologists like to keep an eye on.

Alyssa made chicken mole negro, black beans, Spanish rice, and fresh pineapple salsa. Flynn enjoyed everything thoroughly, including the ice-cold Negra Modelo beer. Baby Miguel, now two and a half, grinned at Flynn, his face covered with mole sauce and studded with rice and black beans. He sat next to Flynn and periodically threw his spoon at him. The fifth time, the spoon bounced off Flynn's head.

Alyssa took it away from him. "Sorry, James."

"No worries." A baby-sized handful of rice and beans sticky with mole sauce splatted against Flynn's face. Baby Miguel grinned and laughed and Flynn gamely wiped his face and neck with a napkin. "I wouldn't have missed this for the world. Though I really don't want to be a burden, and I'm more than happy to stay at the Langham."

Sancho patted him on the hand. "I know that, dude, and I appreciate the gesture, but we can't have you spending your money like that. You're family."

Alyssa chimed in. "And we don't want to hear another word about it." Another tiny handful of black beans and rice smacked Flynn in the face.

．　．　．

Flynn slept in a sleeping bag that smelled of campfire smoke, on a squeaky air mattress on the floor across from Miguel's crib. Various toys from inside the crib periodically bounced off Flynn's head.

Miguel stood inside his crib, held onto the slats, and hopped up and down like a monkey. He wore a Mickey Mouse t-shirt and colorful rubber pants with little dinosaurs. "Up, up, up, up," he said.

"It's late, Miguel. Time to sleep. Lie down. Sleepy time."

Miguel just laughed and blew a raspberry.

Flynn rolled over and tried to ignore him. A surprisingly loud clunk reverberated as something heavy hit the floor. Flynn turned to see Miguel pulling himself to his feet, staggering in Flynn's direction. He lunged for Flynn, grabbing him by the face with both hands and squeezing his cheeks with insane baby strength.

Flynn lifted the toddler's little body into the air and set him back down in his crib. "I believe I'm too much of a distraction, little one. Time to go to sleep."

Flynn dragged the sleeping bag into the living room and tried to get comfortable on the couch. It was a little saggy and a little short, but finally Flynn drifted off.

A tiny hand slapped him in the face. Flynn opened his eyes.

Baby Miguel stood nose to nose with him. "Poo poo."

Something brown and gooey leaked from the dinosaur-bedecked rubber pants. Flynn's eyes watered with the stench. He considered waking Sancho and Alyssa but decided to let them sleep and change the soiled nappy himself.

How difficult could it be?

Flynn carried Miguel at arm's length back to his room and set him on the changing table. Peeling off the toddler's rubber pants, he discovered sticky, brown poo leaking everywhere. It looked very much like the mole sauce they had for dinner, but smelled a hell of a lot worse. Flynn found baby wipes and used a dozen of them, tossing them in a plastic-lined trash can. Miguel squirmed and wriggled toward the edge, and Flynn barely managed to keep him from rolling off the changing table.

He unfastened the Velcro and opened the disposable nappy to find even more caca. Flynn gagged like a cat hacking up a hairball and tried to understand how such a tiny person could produce so much doodoo. He had to hold Miguel in place as he searched for another nappy. Flynn stretched and reached and finally got his hands on one.

He lifted Miguel's feet to slide it under him. Urine erupted from the toddler's tiny tallywacker, spraying into the air and into Flynn's mouth. He spit and gagged before finally blocking the stream with the nappy. Miguel grinned. Flynn used the rest of the box of wipes to clean him off. Defusing suitcase nukes proved far easier than changing little Miguel's diaper.

He set Miguel on the floor and he tottered out of his bedroom, arms flailing, laughing and giggling. Flynn chased after and caught him halfway across the living room. He carried him back to his crib and laid him back down. "Okay, little one, I'll sing you a lullaby and get you back to sleep."

.   .   .

While in the bathroom for a late-night pee, Sancho heard what sounded like singing between the splashing. He crept across the tiny house and peeked in baby Miguel's room.

Flynn leaned over the crib and sang a French lullaby. His delusional *compadre* believed he spoke French. That his mother was Swiss and his father Scottish. That they perished in a climbing accident when he was ten. Flynn had lost his parents at age ten, but his father managed a muffler shop in Burbank, and his mother worked in a hair salon. None of his relatives would take him in. He ended up in the foster care system, bullied and terrorized for seven years.

Little Flynn had escaped into 1960s spy movies and, over time, created an imaginary persona based on the most famous of those characters. Someone who took no shit. Someone unafraid and in control. Someone women wanted to be with and men wanted to be. Eventually, that made-up identity became a full-fledged delusional disorder.

Sancho knew children bewildered Flynn. Yet, children can't help but ground you in reality. Sancho hoped some time with Miguel might help Flynn find his way back to his authentic self. Miguel began to snore and Flynn sang softer and softer. "*Fais dodo, t'auras du lolo.*"

■ ■ ■

Duncan Dankworth arrived in Los Angeles at 5:10 p.m. on British Airways flight 269. The tight seating in economy, inedible airline food, and twelve-hour flight time exacerbated his IBS. The tension from traveling always caused it to flare up.

It took him an hour to get through customs and another hour before he finally picked up his Kia Soul at Budget Rent a Car. He spent the next thirty minutes driving in circles around LAX before he finally found the correct on-ramp for the proper freeway. That was what they called them in California. Freeways. Not motorways. He needed to use the loo, but that would have to wait until he found his hotel.

Traffic in London was actually worse, but in London you didn't have to drive on the wrong side of the road. In addition, in London he usually had some idea of where he was going.

Google Maps indicated that the drive to his hotel should take thirty minutes. Instead, it took him an hour and a half of driving, lost and full of anxiety in rush hour traffic, before he finally pulled into the Best Western Royal Palace Inns and Suites.

It was hardly a palace. The blocky budget hotel squatted on Sepulveda, not far from the freeway, between Party City and The Sofa Club, in a seedy neighborhood ten minutes south of the Federal Building in Westwood. Too nervous to get back in the car, Duncan walked to the closest restaurant he could find. El Super Taco. They offered an interesting selection of tacos. Everything from pork stomach to beef tongue and beef head.

He decided to order something somewhat recognizable. A chicken burrito. He begged them to make it mild, but it still inflamed his IBS, and he spent all night cramping, tooting, and trumping.

The next morning, he drank a cup of burnt coffee and skipped the Royal Palace's breakfast buffet. The seven-minute drive to the Federal Building took him thirty minutes. He parked in the outdoor parking lot and climbed from his little Kia just as Flynn pulled in. The nutter drove a gleaming Aston Martin DB9. The throaty rumble of the six-liter V12 mocked the unimpressive whine of Duncan's four-cylinder Soul.

Flynn hopped out, nodded to Duncan, and glanced askance at his mode of transportation. "How was your flight?"

"Long. May I borrow your phone?"

"Excuse me?"

"I have a number for our defector, and I'd like to send her a text with your phone."

Flynn handed over his phone, and Dankworth sent Harper Sinclair a text. He then passed Flynn his phone back and Flynn read the text aloud. "This is James Flynn. I understand you're trying to reach me. I'll call you at this number in the next hour." Flynn raised an eyebrow.

"What?"

"A little on the dry side, isn't it?"

"So?"

"Shouldn't we be a little more charming?"

Duncan rolled his eyes. "They're waiting for us upstairs. You ready?"

"To save the world?" Flynn slapped Duncan on the shoulder, rocking him sideways. "Always."

Flynn headed for the Federal Building and Duncan followed, hanging back a bit to let out a little poot.

Chapter Eleven

Yuri Drozdov, former chief of the KGB's Directorate S, claimed it took seven years to train an "illegal." That was what he called the Soviet sleeper agents he planted abroad. He taught them to talk, think, and act like Americans (and Brits, Germans, or Frenchmen). The KGB would write a detailed biography and forge a birth certificate based on an American baby who passed away the same year they were born. They then trained for years to learn an accent local to the region where they supposedly grew up. Many attended elite universities and earned postgraduate degrees. They landed jobs with the military, defense contractors, university research institutes, and intelligence agencies. They communicated through dead-drops and other clandestine means. Weapons, communication caches, and even suitcase nukes were planted in Western democracies around the world in case the Cold War ever became a hot one.

FBI Special Agent in Charge Miranda Jacks considered Flynn a valuable resource. Though completely delusional, Flynn had foiled more plots and saved more lives than anyone she'd ever worked with. That included agents of the FBI, CIA, DEA, Secret Service, and every other intelligence and criminal investigative agency combined. He brought her cases that on the surface seemed absolutely insane. But in every instance, someone was plotting something horrendous. Maybe you need crazy to counter crazy in this crazy world.

Even as others dismissed Flynn as a headcase, she appreciated his twisted perception and off-kilter acumen.

Perhaps because she too had often been ignored, dismissed, and condescended to over the course of her career. Few Black women had risen as high in the ranks as she had. Miranda attributed part of that success to Flynn. She saw past his obvious flaws and understood what he brought to the table.

That didn't mean she accepted everything he said as the gospel truth. But in this case, a Russian agent reached out directly to MI6. She claimed to be in love with Flynn and wanted to speak to him and *only* him. Miranda suspected ulterior motives, as did MI6 itself, so they brought her in to work with Flynn. That it was a counterintelligence case and not counterterrorism meant that she also had to bring in Kurt Daniels, the head of counterintelligence for the Los Angeles field office.

Daniels had a contentious relationship with Miranda. Their spheres of influence often intersected, and Daniels didn't like that. He also made it clear he didn't like the idea of working with Flynn. If it were up to him, Flynn would be locked up in a loony bin and the FBI would handle this operation entirely on their own. But luckily, it wasn't up to him.

Burly and in his early forties, Daniels was one of the many Mormons recruited by the FBI. He saw his job as a primal battle between good and evil. Within the FBI, they were known as the Mormon Mafia. Daniels's aide was a younger, larger version of himself. Miranda's aide, Gloria Fuentes, had the same disdain Miranda had for their counterintelligence counterparts.

An FBI agent ushered Flynn into the conference room with a slight, tentative-looking man in an ill-fitting suit. That had to be Duncan Dankworth. From the name, she was expecting the usual smug upper-class tool Miranda had so often dealt with. But like the FBI, MI5 and MI6 were trying to diversify their ranks, and Dankworth seemed at least partly of Indian descent. As Dankworth was a Scottish name, Miranda suspected an Indian mother.

Introductions were made, and Kurt Daniels took control by addressing not Flynn or Miranda, but Dankworth. "We thank you for bringing this defection to our attention, but as the enemy intelligence agent is currently in California, this falls under the purview of FBI Counterintelligence."

"Understood," Dankworth said. "But the enemy agent in question approached MI6 directly, which is why we believe we need to take the lead."

"I'm sorry, but I've been instructed by my superiors to keep a tight rein on this operation. If this is going to happen, it's going to happen under our direction."

Miranda Jacks jumped into the conversation with a smile. "Then I guess it's not happening. According to MI6, the enemy agent in question will only meet with Flynn. Is that correct?"

Dankworth nodded. "Unfortunately, yes."

At this point, Flynn joined the conversation. "Agent Daniels, I do hope you realize I'm not actually a mental patient. That's my cover identity here in the states. Like Dankworth, I'm an operative for MI6. Though retired and recently reactivated on a temporary basis."

Daniels completely ignored Flynn and shot an angry glare at Miranda. "This is a case for counterintelligence, not counterterrorism."

"This won't be any kind of case if you turn this into a pissing contest," Miranda said. "Do you really want to tell your superiors that you blew the biggest intelligence coup in modern history?"

Flynn tried to calm the frayed feelings. "It doesn't really matter who claims credit as long as we get this done. Harper Sinclair requested me personally. Otherwise, I wouldn't even be here."

Daniels raised an eyebrow. "Who?"

"The Russian agent. Haven't you read the file?"

"Of course I've read the frickin' file."

Miranda sighed. Daniels always reacted belligerently when caught in a lie. *Of course the asshat hadn't read the file.*

Dankworth addressed Daniels. "I agree that Flynn being the main contact isn't optimal, but I'll keep a close eye on him, and you can keep a close eye on me."

That seemed to mollify Daniels, even though he harrumphed in frustration before nodding his assent. "Fine."

Miranda attempted to move things along. "I understand you have a phone number for her?"

Dankworth nodded. "We assume it's a burner. I thought we'd have Flynn call her while we're all here to monitor the situation. I texted her with Flynn's phone to let her know he'd be calling."

Flynn chuckled. "And what a tedious and utterly charmless little text it was. I'm surprised she even replied."

"But she did, didn't she?"

"With a thumbs up. Which I take to be sarcasm."

Dankworth sighed and looked at Daniels as if it say, *See what I have to deal with.* He glanced at Flynn. "Please call her and put it on speaker."

Flynn did so.

"Mr. Flynn, I presume?" The sultry female voice had a Southern drawl. More aristocratic than redneck. Miranda was impressed. Remarkable, considering her native Russian origins.

Flynn grinned to put a smile in his voice. "Am I speaking to Harper Sinclair?"

"You are indeed. But how do I know it's really you?"

"You don't, and you won't. Not until we meet face to face. But I do appreciate what you said in your note to me. And I hope I'm not being too forward, but I find *you* quite attractive, too. If you look anything like the picture you sent me."

"I guess you'll just have to trust me too," Harper said seductively.

"It's dangerous for both of us then."

"It's a dangerous world."

"I agree. No one gets out alive, so we must find our pleasures where we can."

Harper chuckled. "Somehow I do believe it's you."

"And I sense that you too are indeed…you."

Her voice got huskier. "When can we meet?"

"Whenever you would like. I am at your beck and call."

Miranda grinned at Flynn's effortless charisma. It amused her that both Dankworth and Daniels found Flynn's charm less than charming.

"How about tomorrow?" Harper asked.

"Pick the time and place and I'll be there."

"Do you know what an aebleskiver is?"

"Yes, of course. A Danish pastry."

"Meet me tomorrow for aebleskivers at The Solvang Restaurant in Solvang, California."

"What time?"

"One o'clock. I'll call in sick so we can have the afternoon to ourselves."

"I look forward to finally meeting you in person."

"Make sure you come alone."

"Of course."

"If anyone's with you or watching, I'll know, and that'll be the end of it." The phone clicked off as Harper hung up.

Dankworth looked at Daniels. "Where's Solvang?"

"Not far from Lompoc. It's a tourist area. She clearly wants to meet him in a crowded public place."

Dankworth turned to Flynn. "Of course, you won't be going alone."

"You heard what she said. I have to do this on my own."

Miranda shook her head. "I'm sorry, James, but we can't let you walk in there without a wire. But don't worry, we'll monitor you from a discreet distance."

Daniels balked at that. "There's no we, Miranda. Like I said, this is my operation."

"If Miranda isn't watching my back, then I'm out as well," Flynn said. "No offense, Daniels, but I don't trust you *or* Dankworth. Not like I do Miranda. She's saved my bacon more than once. All Dankworth has done is draw a target on my back. And Daniels, if you want to be the douchebag in charge, do it somewhere else."

"How dare you talk to me like that!"

"Tell your FBI bosses that if Miranda isn't running this operation, I'm done."

"You want me to pull the plug? I'll pull the damn plug!" Daniels shouted.

"It's not your plug to pull," Miranda said. "This assignment comes right from the top. If you want to call the attorney general and tell him the FBI is out, be my guest."

Daniels sputtered.

Dankworth acquiesced. "Fine. Agent Jacks can run the show. But I need to be there as well."

Miranda threw Dankworth a lifeline. "I'm okay with having you along for the ride, but you need to stay the hell out of my way." She locked gazes with Daniels. "I'd like you to run logistics from here."

"Now you're giving me orders?"

"Would you rather not be involved at all?"

Daniels's face turned magenta, threatening to explode, but Miranda knew he was out of options. He didn't outrank her, and without her participation, the operation wouldn't exist. If he blew up the operation out of spite, he might find himself running the FBI office in Homer, Alaska.

Daniels swallowed his pride and angrily sighed. "Fine."

Miranda smiled. "Good."

Chapter Twelve

Solvang's origins date back to 1804, when the Spanish built Mission Santa Inés, one of twenty-one missions built across the length of Alta California. The mission was abandoned after the American conquest of California in 1847, but in 1911, a new settlement was founded by a group of Danish Americans who wanted to establish a Danish community far from Midwestern winters. Solvang means "sunny field" in Danish. With all the Danish-themed architecture it became a popular tourist destination. Ronald Reagan's "Western White House" was nearby. He and Nancy would regularly show up in Solvang to eat aebelskivers and cast their votes back when he was president.

Flynn had traveled to many famous and glamorous places. London. Paris. Miami. Tokyo. Monte Carlo. But this would be his first time in Solvang, California. The drive on Highway 1 along the coast and through Santa Barbara was glorious. As Sancho's DB9 hugged the winding curves through the gently rolling hills of the Santa Ynez Valley, Flynn kept an eye on the two black SUVs tailing him. Miranda Jacks shared a ride with Dankworth and kept her distance as she drove. He trusted she'd keep Dankworth from doing anything *too* stupid. Flynn dressed for the day in a navy mesh-knit polo shirt, khaki-colored chinos, and chukka boots. He wore a wire and a tiny button camera so the FBI and MI6 could monitor his meeting with Harper Sinclair.

Being a Saturday, Solvang teemed with tourists. Flynn jockeyed for a parking spot with an angry blue-haired lady who not only got the better of him but gave him the finger. He finally parked a short distance away in a lot on the edge of town. As he made his way into the village, he found the streets swarming with gangs of elderly women. A few older males were dragged along by their wives, but most of the tourists were female. They shopped and laughed and drank tea and wine spritzers and ate ice cream and fudge and all manner of pastries. Flynn attributed some of their amped-up energy and belligerent behavior to all the sugar, caffeine, and alcohol flooding their brains and bloodstreams.

Flynn followed the directions on his iPhone and headed down a red brick sidewalk, passing shops that sold hats, snow globes, and a variety of other tourist tchotchkes, knickknacks, and bric-a-brac. Babies cried, toddlers screamed, and exhausted parents wilted while smiling performers, dressed in traditional Danish garb, danced to Danish folk music.

A bell rang on a horse-drawn trolley car. Flynn waited for it to pass. He glanced at the map on his iPhone, stepped off the curb, and a wobbly bicycle built for two nearly clipped him. He turned the corner on Copenhagen Street, and an elderly lady on a mobility scooter ran over his foot.

Flynn limped inside The Solvang Restaurant to find the place packed. It wasn't hard to spot Harper. For one thing, she pointed at him and waved. For another, she was the only woman in there who had yet to experience menopause.

Even prettier than she appeared in the candid picture, her long blonde hair framed a face that wouldn't be out of place on a supermodel. Flynn got her full measure when she rose to shake his hand. She wore jeans embroidered with camelias, and a blousy white ruffled shirt opened just enough to reveal a copper and turquoise necklace nestled in the modest swell of her cleavage.

"Harper Sinclair, I presume."

"Mr. Flynn. You do not disappoint."

"Neither do you, my dear. The photo you sent does not do you justice."

"I love the accent."

"Likewise."

"Well, I'm from Georgia. That's how we talk there."

"Which Georgia are you referring to?"

Harper laughed at that.

The waitress, a large blonde lady in late middle age, showed up with an order pad and a nametag that read Claire. "Do you two know what you want?"

Flynn went for the traditional Danish open-faced sandwich plate and a Carlsberg beer. Harper had the Jolly Green Salad and an iced tea. The waitress turned to go, stopped, and looked back at Flynn with a smile. "You look so familiar to me. Are you an actor?"

"I'm afraid not, Claire."

"Is that your real accent?"

"It is indeed."

She reached out and touched Flynn's hand. "I'll be right back with your beverages."

Harper smiled and shook her head. "I guess I'm not the only one."

"Only one what?"

She offered an ironic yet still seductive smile. "Women just love you, don't they?"

"It's a superficial infatuation. They fall for the me they see on the TV news. Not the actual me."

"Is that what you think I did?"

"I'm not suggesting anything untoward, but this is the first time we've met face to face."

"Is this you letting me down easy?"

"This is me getting to know you and you getting to know me. I'm sure every man you meet falls for you as well."

"They like what they see, but then most men are very shallow creatures."

"I don't disagree."

"The difference is that most men can't tell when they're out of their league. They act so surprised when a woman isn't attracted to them. In fact, some of them are quite offended. A few even get angry. That difference in perception can cause some real problems."

"I'm guessing with your training, you know how to defend yourself."

Harper smiled at that, reached across the table, and rested her hand on Flynn's. "I don't want this to get weird, so how about some straight talk? I know the only reason you're here is because I have something you want. And that isn't necessarily me."

"Well, let's not be too hasty."

"You don't have to pretend with me. We'll spend some time together and see what develops. If nothing happens, nothing happens. I'll still give you what you want."

The waitress returned with their drinks. Flynn lifted his pilsner glass. "To what might develop…"

Harper clinked her iced tea against Flynn's pilsner. There was more food than Flynn could finish, yet Harper insisted on ordering aebelskivers. They came in threes, and Harper ate two of them. Delicate and delicious puffed pancake balls filled with lingonberry jam and dusted with powdered sugar.

She paid for their meal, scraped back her chair, and stood up, licking a bit of jam off the corner of her mouth. "Did I get it all?"

"Almost."

She smiled and licked off the last of it, and Flynn found it quite sensual, but he assumed that was her intention. "You want to take a stroll?"

"Sounds delightful."

Harper led Flynn outside. As they headed down the red brick sidewalk, she touched his hand. "Did you arrange for someone to follow us?"

Duncan immediately came to mind. *Did Miranda set him loose? Not likely.* "Of course not."

"In the next few seconds, I'm going to turn and point out one of the windmills. If you use your peripheral vision, you'll see that three rather large men are following us. They are pretending to be tourists, but I'm pretty sure they are a GRU assassination team. These boys must be second-stringers. Otherwise, I probably wouldn't have spotted them."

She turned and pointed to the windmill. Flynn nodded and smiled and pointed at the very same windmill and made a comment that looked like it was about the windmill but wasn't. "They don't exactly blend in, do they?"

They all wore plaid shorts, white socks, white sneakers, and the same baggy red T-shirts with a windmill in a circle and the word Solvang emblazoned above. All three were over six foot two, and Flynn saw the bulge of a Belly Band holster under each shirt. One licked an ice cream cone. A second had fudge on his face. Powdered sugar decorated the nose of the third.

Harper nodded and smiled and led Flynn forward. She approached a bike-rental kiosk and quickly rented two cruisers. She hopped on one and pointed Flynn to the other. He quickly climbed on and saw the three GRU agents hurry in their direction, flattening toddlers and grandmothers alike.

Harper sped away and Flynn tried to follow. It occurred to him that he didn't remember ever riding a bike before. He tottered forward a foot or two before crashing over onto his side, scraping his elbow and smacking his head. Harper quickly turned around and wheeled back. "You don't know how to ride a bike?"

"Apparently not."

"Shit!" Harper pulled Flynn to his feet, but the GRU team was closing in. All three pulled their weapons, but there were still a lot of bodies between them. She hurried down the crowded sidewalk and Flynn followed close behind. She slid a Glock 17 out of her purse. "Do you have a gun?"

"No, but I have this."

"Pepper spray?!"

"Hypno-spray!"

Harper led them down one alley and through another. She ducked into a store that sold troll dolls. Flynn followed. The three assassins were no longer behind them, but Harper didn't slow down. She body-checked little girls and boys and their mothers, clearing a path to the back.

"My car's only a few blocks away," Flynn shouted.

"What street?"

"Mission Drive!"

Harper pushed through the back door into an alley, and Flynn hurried after her. Before long, they reached Solvang Park. Flynn finally had his bearings. "Follow me!"

Flynn put on Q's ingenious x-ray spectacles, hoping to see if the Russian agents were hiding behind something and waiting to pounce. He held up his hand and could see his bones, but in the bright light of day Flynn found it hard to see anything else. He tripped on something that barked and growled at him and stumbled over something else that shrieked like a banshee.

Harper caught him by the arm. "What the hell are you wearing?"

Flynn removed his x-ray spectacles to see a crying toddler sitting on the ground next to an upside-down ice cream cone. "Can't really say. Classified."

As she dragged him past the visitor center to the edge of the park, the three GRU agents stepped out from behind a hedge. All three aimed their pistols at Flynn and Harper. A trio of grandmothers stood between them, screaming in terror and pointing at their weapons. Harper raised her own gun, and, in that instant, a black SUV roared from the alley and slammed into all three GRU agents.

. . .

Miranda kept her foot on the gas and sent the assassins flying. Two guns went off. She prayed no innocent bystanders caught a bullet. She ran over one killer and slammed another into a wooden fence. She caught his shocked look an instant before her airbag deployed. Her ears rang with the bang of the inflatable restraint.

Miranda stumbled from the car, blinking from the cornstarch in her eyes. One Russian agent lay unconscious on the ground, and another, on his knees, raised his weapon. An elderly tourist smacked the gun out of his hand with a quad cane as a mob of other oldsters tackled him to the ground. The Russian stretched to reach for his gun, but another senior citizen drove a mobility scooter over his wrist.

A second black SUV squealed to a stop, and agents in FBI windbreakers piled out. They fought past the mob of angry elders to restrain and secure the Russian assassins. Miranda shouted orders, "There's a third suspect and he is armed and dangerous."

Agents spread out as local law enforcement arrived with their lights flashing and sirens screaming. Miranda held up her FBI badge as the sheriffs approached. "FBI! There's one more shooter! You need to find him!"

Miranda looked around for Flynn, Harper, and Duncan but didn't see them anywhere. "Flynn!" she shouted. "Duncan Dankworth!" *Did Duncan go after the third Russian?* That didn't seem likely, but maybe she'd misjudged him. Miranda caught her reflection in a car window, her face powdered white with cornstarch. A Black woman in whiteface. Perfect.

Chapter Thirteen

Flynn and Harper hopped in Sancho's Aston Martin and hit the road. He had to get Harper out of harm's way. He considered calling Miranda Jacks but now wondered if there was a leak at the FBI office in Los Angeles. Could they have a spy in their ranks? Or had the GRU been monitoring Harper's machinations and discovered her deceit? He looked over to see her staring at him.

"Where are you taking me?"

"Somewhere safe?"

"Can you be more specific?"

"Central California."

"Wouldn't we be safer to head to Los Angeles? It's easier to disappear in a big city."

"They would expect us to head south for just that reason, which is why I'm heading north."

"To San Francisco?"

"Or some destination in-between."

"This car isn't exactly inconspicuous."

"I agree."

Flynn pulled off the highway at Pea Soup Anderson's in Buellton.

"What now?" An irritated Harper glared at Flynn. "You have a hankering for pea soup?"

Flynn parked the Aston Martin and took some tools Sancho kept in the trunk. He used them to break into a 2005 Nissan Altima and moved his luggage from the Aston Martin to the

Altima. Harper had no luggage, as she probably didn't anticipate she'd need any when she left to meet Flynn that morning. He'd have to find a way to get Sancho his car back later.

Within minutes, they were back on the road. The Nissan's back seat was full of fast-food bags and empty soda bottles. Flynn detected the distinct aroma of cannabis baked into the upholstery.

Flynn merged onto the 101 north and noticed Harper smiling at him. "You have quite the skillset."

"I've picked up a few tricks over the years."

"The owner will probably report his car stolen, and when they find the Aston Martin, the FBI will put two and two together."

"And by that time, we'll be in another car."

"So, you have this all figured out."

"Not everything. For one thing, I don't understand your motivation here. After so many years in America, why did you suddenly decide to defect? Or are you simply trying to lure me into a trap?"

"You think that assassination team was there to kill *you*?"

"Who else would they be after?"

"*Who do you think?*"

"You?"

"Of course, me. If I were luring you into a trap, why would I have warned you? Why wouldn't I just kill you myself?"

"Perhaps you assumed the FBI was still listening, and you wanted to keep the fiction of your defection alive."

"Or maybe they were trying to kill us both."

Flynn nodded. "Let's go with that assumption. How did they discover you wanted to defect?"

Harper shook her head. "I don't know. I sweep my living area and all my communication devices daily. And not just to see if US intelligence is on to me. My own people are constantly watching me, too. So, I'm very careful. I can't say the same for MI6 or the FBI. If someone gave us away, it was likely one of them."

"Answer my first question, then. Why did you decide to defect?"

"For the same reason thousands of soldiers have deserted the Russian army. Nearly half a million have died in Ukraine. One of them was my brother."

Flynn glanced at Harper to see her fighting tears. "What was his name?"

"Anatoly."

"I'm sorry."

"Putin wants to restore the Russian empire. He sees himself as a modern-day Peter the Great. If he isn't stopped, he will instigate a war with NATO and millions more will die."

"So this is you putting a thumb in Putin's eye?"

"This is revenge for my brother. This is the destruction of his entire intelligence network in the US and the UK. I will give MI6 and the FBI what they want, but they need to protect me. And so far they have *not* impressed me."

Flynn bought them burner phones at a truck stop in Arroyo Grande. He hot-wired a late-model Ford Fiesta, and they hit the road after tacos and tamales at Burrito Loco. They both ditched their smartphones back in Solvang, but Flynn had Miranda's number memorized and called her from the burner.

She picked up on the third ring. "Miranda Jacks."

"It's me."

"*Flynn?* Where the hell are you?"

"Is this a secure line?"

"Of course it is."

"Someone tipped off the GRU. Are you sure that wasn't someone inside the FBI?"

"Are you kidding me?"

"The GRU could have cloned your phone for all you know."

"Just tell me where you are."

"It's safer for everyone if I don't."

"Jesus Christ."

"Just know that the package is safe."

"Are you talking about Harper?"

"Who?"

"Flynn, stop it. Just listen to me—"

"I better sign off before someone starts a trace."

"What? Wait! You blocked caller ID. I need your number."

"I'll call you back in a few hours."

"Flynn!"

Flynn clicked off. Harper laughed. "You don't trust anyone, do you?"

"I live in a world where trusting the wrong person can easily get you killed."

"I'm familiar with that world."

"I bet you are."

Flynn called Caitlyn from Morro Bay while Harper used the ladies' room. She didn't pick up, so he left her a cryptic message. "It's me. We need to talk."

Caitlyn called back almost immediately. "Are you okay?"

"I'm fine."

"Miranda called me and told me what happened."

"Yes, it turned into a bit of a cock-up."

"She's with you now?"

"She is. She believes that either MI6 or the FBI might have a spy."

"Wouldn't be the first time."

"If it was a trap and she wanted me dead, I would be."

"So, you still think she's sincere?"

"I don't know, but I intend to find out."

"And how do you intend to do that? The same way you tried to get information out of me?

"Is that jealousy I hear?"

"Hey, you're a grown-ass man. You want to bed a beautiful Russian spy? You don't need permission from me. But I would like you to tell me where you are."

"You know I can't do that."

"I know you can't trust MI6 or the FBI, but you *can* trust me. I won't tell a soul. I'll just be there to watch your back."

"I'm sure they have eyes on you, too. It's safer for everyone if you don't know."

"Flynn—"

"Be careful now. They may come after you to get to me."

"Just tell me where—"

Flynn clicked off as Harper climbed into the car.

"Who were you talking to just now?"

"Just checking messages. Miranda Jacks is very irritated with me."

"So am I. Are you going to tell me where we're going?"

Chapter Fourteen

Arthur Harold Beal bought a two-and-a-half-acre hillside lot in Cambria in 1928 and spent the next 50 years carving out the terraces with only a pick and shovel to create his own "castle on a hill." Known locally as Captain Nitt Witt, Beal worked as a trash collector in the 1940s and 1950s and made use of what other Cambrians threw away to decorate his homemade castle. Some of those parts are discards from Hearst Castle, where Beal was once rumored to be an employee. He used beer cans, abalone shells, washer drums, car parts, driftwood, old stoves, and countless other found objects to embellish and adorn what came to be known as Nitt Witt Ridge. Now an official California historical landmark.

Flynn booked them a room at Whitecap Lodge on Moonstone Beach. The rugged shore stretched just north of Cambria, where eight different motels offered a variety of ocean views. Beachy yet elegant, the Whitecap Lodge mixed modern and vintage elements of Scandinavian design and California bohemian culture. Flynn found it quite comfortable.

Their room had a fireplace, a panoramic view of the Pacific, and an outdoor soaking tub. Flynn could have booked two rooms but didn't. And Harper offered no objection. He had a job to do, and Caitlyn would have to get over her petty possessiveness. Of course, he understood her jealousy. He felt much the same way when she used her allure to charm her way into the confidence of Oleg Ivanov. But later, once the heat of emotion cooled, Flynn knew Caitlyn only did what she had to.

He took Harper to dinner at one of Cambria's most romantic restaurants. At least according to Yelp. Madeline's Restaurant and Wine Cellar served French and California cuisine in a quiet, elegant, candlelit atmosphere. Flynn ordered sauteed scallops over mushroom duxelles with lemon beurre to start, and Harper ordered a baby spinach salad with warm bacon vinaigrette. Flynn's main course was the seared elk chops with wild mushroom sauce. Harper went for the Louisiana Seafood Gumbo. They shared an excellent bottle of Pinot Noir and a chocolate truffle mousse cake for dessert. Then they took a sunset walk on the boardwalk above Moonstone Beach.

Since Harper had no change of clothes, she sported the same embroidered jeans and white ruffled shirt she wore at lunch. As the sun sank below the horizon, the temperature dropped precipitously. Cambria had to be thirty degrees cooler than Solvang. Flynn slipped off his leather jacket and draped it over her shoulders. She smiled and pulled it snug. "You're really going the whole nine yards."

"Am I?"

"Romantic dinner. Romantic walk along the beach. I told you. You don't have to pretend with me. I'm loving the attention, but only if it's genuine."

"I'm just seeing what develops."

"You don't believe me, do you? You think if *you* don't put out, *I* won't put out."

"I don't think any such thing."

"You really are a gentleman, aren't you?"

"My number one priority is keeping you safe. If you can give me what you have and I can get it to the FBI, Putin won't have a reason to murder you."

"First off, I don't have the files on me. I have the thumb drive hidden in a secure location. Secondly, Putin is all about putting the fear of God into anyone who would turn against him. He'd want to make an example out of me, no matter what. So, I need to know the FBI can put me into witness protection."

"If you went into witness protection, how would I ever see you again?"

She leaned closer, her lips brushing Flynn's ear. "I think you'd find a way. You're nothing if not resourceful."

A three-quarter moon rose over the ocean and Harper stopped to admire it. Flynn watched her in the moonlight. "How did you pick the name Harper?"

"While researching your country, I read lots of books. History. Biographies. Novels. *To Kill a Mockingbird* by Harper Lee was one of my favorites."

"What about Sinclair?"

"It's Scottish. The Clan Sinclair. They were knights. Warriors. Plus, it's the last name of another famous American author."

"Upton Sinclair."

"I think those names go well together. Don't you?"

"What's your real name?"

"Nadya Lipovsky. But that's not the real me. Not anymore. I'm Harper Sinclair and have been forever. I'm a quintessential Southern Belle. I even dream in English now."

They returned to their room and Flynn lit a fire in the fireplace. Harper stood next to him and started unbuttoning her blouse. "I need a shower. Would you care to join me?"

"I would, but I'm wondering if we should take things a little slower."

"Slower?" She smiled seductively.

"The anticipation of pleasure is a pleasure in itself. Do you know the German word *vorfreude*?"

"I do not."

"The joyful anticipation that comes from imagining future pleasures."

She shrugged and grinned. "Imagine away." She unbuttoned the last few buttons as she disappeared into the bathroom and shut the door. Flynn pulled out his burner and placed a call to Miranda Jacks.

She answered on the third ring. "Jacks."

"It's me."

"Where the hell are you?"

"I'll tell you, but you can't tell anyone else in your organization. I'm afraid you might have a traitor in the ranks."

"It's not us. It's probably MI6. They've been infiltrated more than once."

"So has the FBI."

"Do you have the files?"

"I do not. She didn't bring them with her to Solvang. She wasn't sure she could trust us."

"Did she tell you where they are?"

"Hidden in a secure location is all she would say. What she wants from you is protection from Putin."

Miranda sighed. "We've been contacted by the Russians. They want her back."

"Of course they do."

"In exchange for Duncan Dankworth."

"*Duncan Dankworth?*"

"They snatched him up in Solvang."

Flynn closed his eyes and sighed. "Of course they did."

"At this moment, he's on his way to Polar Owl. A Russian prison in the Arctic Circle."

"Polar Owl? That's where they're holding Oleg Ivanov."

"*And* Bettina O'Toole-Applebaum."

"*What?*"

"They arrested her when she went to interview Ivanov."

"On what charge?"

"Espionage. They're claiming she's a spy."

"That's ridiculous."

"Of course it is. But they're using her as leverage."

Flynn sighed and rubbed his eyes. Talk about a dog's breakfast. "They want Harper for Dankworth and Bettina?"

"That's the ask."

"What do your superiors want to do?"

"They want that list of Russian sleeper agents living in America."

"So, they don't want to make the trade?"

"They do, but I think they'll hold off making it until they have what they need from Harper."

"Bloody hell."

"Tell me where you are. I'll only bring agents I know and trust, and I won't file an action plan. We can put her into protective custody and keep her safe."

"Until your superiors trade her back to Putin."

"It's about priorities, Flynn. We can blow up Putin's entire espionage network and bring Bettina back home. I wish we could save Harper too, but we can't let perfect be the enemy of good."

"*Le mieux est l'ennemi du bien.*"

"*Exactement.*"

Flynn sighed. "Cambria, California. The Whitecap Lodge. Room 12."

■   ■   ■

Harper had just turned on the water when her super-mini smartphone began to vibrate. Only two and a half inches long, she kept it snug in her panties, hidden from Flynn. Only one person had the number. Kalishnik. She left the water running and answered with a whisper. "Yes."

"Where are you?"

"I'm with Flynn. The GRU sent a hit squad to eliminate me, and we barely made it out alive. If not for Flynn..."

"I'm sure they've been watching you."

"It wasn't me. I believe the GRU has someone inside MI6 or the FBI. Or both."

"*Blyat.* Have you turned over the information to the FBI?"

"Not yet. First, I need some assurances from them."

"Do you still need Flynn to make exchange?"

"I might."

"Do not fall for him. He can have that effect on people."

"Are you speaking from experience?"

Kalishnik scoffed. "Me? No. All I've ever wanted is to kill him."

Harper considered her options. "If Flynn was dead, I suppose I could borrow his burner and contact Miranda Jacks directly."

"Tell me where you are. I'll end his miserable life and make it look like Putin killed him."

"How do you plan to do that?"

"By killing him with standard Russian military sidearm. I will leave it at crime scene. Wiped clean. Now tell me where you are."

"Room 12. The Whitecap Lodge. Cambria, California."

"Can you keep him busy until I get there?"

"I can try."

Chapter Fifteen

The low-flow showerhead dribbled hot water down Harper's back. She rinsed off the day's grime and sweat and fear, but the guilt wouldn't wash away. She wasn't used to feeling remorse. They had trained it out of her at the Ministry of Defense Military Academy in Moscow. They were taught that whatever they did, they did for the greater good of Mother Russia. But then she began to see that Putin only did what he did for the greater good of Putin. That truth began chipping away at her indoctrination.

Then Putin invaded Ukraine, and her brother died in that stupid, useless war, and she knew that her entire life was a lie. Flynn didn't deserve to die, but she needed the money and support that Ivanov promised her. With that ten million, she could truly disappear and continue the fight. Much to her surprise, she found Flynn charming. A gullible, ridiculous innocent. It seemed he truly wanted to protect her. She wished she could get what she needed without selling him out. But sacrifices had to be made for the greater good. And in this case, the greater good was getting rid of Putin.

She climbed from the shower and dried off with a thick, white, luxurious towel. Wrapping it around herself, she exited the steamy bathroom. Flynn stood by the window in the light of a flickering fire, looking out at the sea beyond the bluffs. A waxing moon hovered over the water, illuminating the whitecaps.

"The shower's free if you want to take one."

Flynn glanced at her wrapped in the towel and smiled. "I can see that."

"Would you like to see more?"

"All in good time."

"*Vorfreude.*"

"Indeed."

Flynn pulled his navy mesh-knit polo shirt over his head and headed for the bathroom. Scars crisscrossed his muscular back. Knife wounds. Bullet wounds. The man had seen some action. Once he closed the bathroom door, she undid the chain and unlocked the front door to their room.

Now she would need to keep Flynn busy and distracted.

. . .

Flynn found the shower pressure disappointing but let the hot water drizzle away the day. As was his custom, he finished with a cold rinse. The icy dribble roused and revitalized him. Flynn felt some remorse over his decision to give Miranda Jacks their location. Harper would see that as a betrayal, and he needed her to trust him. He also knew Miranda would do her best to keep them safe and not let her superiors know what she was up to. Of course, once Harper gave them the intelligence, they'd likely give her to Putin. As much as he hated that likelihood, he also knew it was out of his hands.

Flynn dried off, wrapped a towel around his waist, and exited the bathroom to find Harper already in bed, the sheet pulled taut above the swell of her breasts, and the red ribbon from the lodge's complimentary bottle of champagne tied in a bow around her slender neck.

Flynn smiled. "Gift-wrapped and ready to go. I'm feeling a sense of déjà vu."

"Do women often gift wrap themselves for you?"

"It's been known to happen."

"Would you like to drop that towel and join me?"

Flynn sat on the edge of the bed. "What happened to the anticipation of pleasure is a pleasure in itself?"

"Aren't we done with the anticipation part and ready to move on to the main event?"

"Are we?"

Harper threw the covers back. "I am."

Rejecting her at this juncture might cause her to reject him, and everyone was depending on Flynn to acquire those files. He had sacrificed his virtue for king and country previously, but self-reproach had never entered the equation before. He and Caitlyn were far from married, yet they had an undeniable bond. He owed her his fidelity. By being unfaithful he was violating his unspoken commitment to her.

Harper patted the bed. "Well?"

"I'd like nothing more, but perhaps we *should* take things a little slower."

Her inviting smile widened into a grin. "How about we just snuggle then?"

"That might be a good place to start."

■ ■ ■

Kalishnik parked in the lot at the motel next door to the Whitecap Lodge. He avoided any security cameras that might capture the make and model of his vehicle. His Lebedev pistol rested in a holster that accommodated the suppressor. He wore black jeans, black gloves, black body armor, and a black leather jacket filled with multiple magazines. A combat knife nestled in a sheath lay flat against his thigh.

As he casually strolled next door, he contemplated the deep satisfaction of finally having his revenge. To be bested by that lunatic again and again diminished him in Ivanov's eyes. If it was up to Kalishnik, he would have hunted Flynn down immediately. But Ivanov wanted to do more than just eliminate Flynn. He wanted to point the finger of guilt at Putin and make the President of Russia even more of an outcast.

It was after midnight and no other guests wandered the grounds. Still, he kept to the shadows until he reached room 12. He glanced left and right to make sure he was alone, turned the knob, and slowly eased open the door.

No security chain stopped his progress.

■　■　■

Flynn, naked under the pristine white comforter, watched the light of the flickering flames of the fireplace illuminate Harper's beautiful face. Initially, they spooned, but the naked snuggling had a physical effect on him that was difficult to deny.

Harper turned around to face him, tenderly kissed him, and whispered, "Is this okay?"

"I thought we were just snuggling."

"I admire your restraint, but I'm beginning to believe you don't find me all that attractive."

Flynn smoothed her hair back and leaned in to kiss her when a chill suddenly filled the room. He turned and looked up to see a large man in a balaclava standing over the bed, pointing a gun at his head. The first thought that crossed Flynn's mind was that the FBI was obviously compromised. Even Miranda's most reliable colleagues couldn't be trusted.

"Goodbye, Mr. Flynn." The voice behind the balaclava sounded familiar, muffled as it was.

"Have we met before?"

"Many times. But this will be the last."

A distant buzzing grew to a thunderous thrumming. A helicopter. The roaring rotors of a helicopter distracted the assassin, and he turned slightly towards the window. Flynn kicked him in the chest, staggering him back. Silenced rounds ripped into the wall. Flynn sprang to his feet and threw the comforter over the attacker's head. The gun barked. Bullets tore through the cotton, barely missing Flynn. He shoved the intruder backward, driving him right through the large picture window. The hitman crashed through the glass onto the path below.

. . .

Kalishnik's head cracked against the cement. Jagged glass jabbed him in the back. He fought his way out from under the comforter, helped by the downdraft of a helicopter landing on the large front lawn of the Whitecap Lodge.

Commandos wearing FBI windbreakers jumped from the chopper. They saw Kalishnik with the gun in his hand, the balaclava on his face, and the white comforter puddled around his feet. They raised their weapons. Kalishnik fired on them. They scattered for cover while Kalishnik took to the shadows, running into the woods behind the motel. The FBI raced after him. He reloaded on the run, firing back at them to slow them down.

. . .

Flynn and Harper dressed in record time and peeked out the door. Miranda and her team pursued the assailant around the side of the lodge. When they disappeared from view, Flynn sprinted for the helicopter.

"Come on!" Flynn shouted.

Harper hurried after. "Did you tell the FBI where we are?"

"Of course not!"

"Then how did they find us?"

"I don't know!"

"They led Putin's assassins right to us!"

"Keep running!"

"Where? Where are we going?"

"To the helicopter."

"Why?"

"To commandeer it, of course."

The pilot recognized Flynn and urged him and Harper to jump in. They did and Flynn pulled out his hypno-spray and spritzed the pilot right in the face. "You are under my control! You will take to the air and fly us out of here!"

The pilot screamed and clawed at his eyes and tried to climb from the chopper and fell, hitting the ground hard. He got up and ran. Right into a tree.

Flynn watched this with disappointment. "This hypno-spray could use some improvements."

Harper climbed into the pilot's seat and started up the engine. "Sit down!"

Flynn did. He strapped himself in. "You know how to fly a helicopter?"

"I know how to do a lot of things."

. . .

Kalishnik evaded the FBI and doubled back towards the Whitecap Lodge. As he headed for his car in the parking lot next door, he noticed Flynn and Harper in the chopper.

"*Blyat!*"

An instant later, it lifted off. Kalishnik's FBI pursuers raced across the lawn towards the departing bird.

. . .

Flynn looked down at Miranda and her team. They grew smaller and smaller the higher the helicopter climbed. He shouted to

Harper over the roar of the rotors. "They must have used Stingray technology to trace my phone."

"The FBI cannot be trusted!"

"Miranda can, but I can't vouch for her superiors. Let's head north. San Jose has an international airport."

She nodded and banked the bird. Soon, they flew in a northerly direction. Flynn pulled out his phone to place a call.

Harper punched him in the arm. "Who are you calling now?"

"Someone I can trust!"

Caitlyn answered. "Hello?"

"It's me," Flynn shouted.

"I can barely hear you!"

"I'm in a helicopter, and I need your help."

"I'm about to board my flight to LA. I'll be there soon."

"You need to reroute to San Jose!"

"What? Why?"

"The FBI has been compromised!"

Caitlyn sighed. "What did you do?"

"We hijacked one of their helicopters and took to the air."

"Who the hell is flying it?"

"Harper Sinclair."

"She can pilot a helicopter?"

"Apparently so."

"Where's Dankworth?"

"The Russians have him. I believe MI6 has been compromised as well."

"Of course they have."

"You're the only one we can trust."

"*We?*"

"Find a flight to San Jose. Text me the details. We'll meet you there."

▪ ▪ ▪

Figuring the FBI would have the capability to track their own helicopter, Flynn directed Harper to find a place to land near

Santa Cruz. They located an empty high school football field and landed on the fifty-yard line. Hopping from the chopper, they made their way to the surrounding neighborhood. Flynn walked into an open garage, found the necessary tools, and hot-wired a late-model Dodge Caravan parked on the street a few houses down. This time he took the wheel, and they headed north.

Harper reclined in the passenger seat, clearly exhausted. "I hope you know where you're going."

"I will once you open Google Maps and guide me to the highway to San Jose."

Harper sighed, sat up, and did as requested.

Chapter Sixteen

The median household income in Menlo Park, California, is double the national average. The average home is worth over two million dollars. It's the fifth richest small city in America. Menlo Park is also the home of Meta Platforms; better known as Facebook. The campus occupies 250 acres and contains thirty buildings, housing ten thousand employees. The Frank Gehry-designed 435,000 square foot open-plan office is designed to encourage employees to perambulate widely and have chance encounters that will germinate "revolutionary" ideas. Though most employees would rather just have their own damn office with an actual door.

Far fewer flights from New York to San Jose meant Caitlyn had to wait all night to board a plane the next morning. She texted Flynn her arrival time and tried to get comfortable in a hard, plastic airport chair.

Fucking Flynn. He sounded happy as hell when she talked to him. He loved being on a mission. Loved dodging bullets and being in danger. He was deep in his delusion now, and all she could do was help him navigate his insanity. Sometimes, that crazy unpredictability was his only saving grace. His enemies could never anticipate his next move because it rarely made any sense.

Was the FBI compromised? Was MI6? Who the hell knew? Not Flynn. He was lost in his psychosis. Tormentors bullied and beat ten-year-old Jimmy Flynn mercilessly. To survive, he became the most powerful person he could imagine. A fearless, charming, indestructible superspy. At times, she caught glimpses of the timid, insecure, and awkward little boy who still lived inside of him. No wonder he worked so hard to bury that broken part of himself.

How much longer could she do this? Maybe she was just making him worse. Maybe he was better off in a mental hospital. At least there he had people who understood him. A community of crazies who didn't want to change him, but loved him for who he was. It devastated her to think she'd have to let him go, but this life they had was untenable.

She boarded her flight at 8:30 a.m. and finally caught some sleep on the leg to San Diego. After a three-hour layover, she boarded the flight to San Jose, arriving an hour and a half later. Flynn waited for her in baggage claim. He looked a little disheveled in his dark blue polo shirt and khakis, but somehow still brimmed with *joie de vivre*. He embraced her and held her close. She loved feeling his strong arms around her.

"I missed you," he whispered.

She wanted to resist, but instead whispered back. "I missed you too."

Her rolling suitcase finally appeared on the carousel, and she plucked it up. Flynn gallantly grabbed it and pointed towards the doors. "Here we go."

They walked outside, and he motioned to a white minivan with a *Baby on Board* sticker on the back window. Harper Sinclair sat in the driver's seat. Caitlyn suddenly felt dumpy in comparison. Harper didn't smile at Caitlyn. In fact, she wouldn't even look at her. She seemed angry. No surprise there. According to MI6, she had the hots for Flynn, and here he was picking up his girlfriend.

Flynn opened the rear door. Caitlyn climbed inside. Flynn didn't join her, but sat up front in the passenger seat next to Harper, who glared at her in the rear-view mirror.

"Harper Sinclair?" Caitlyn posed it as a question, even though she already knew the answer.

"Yep."

"Caitlyn Valentine."

"I know."

Harper wrenched the minivan into traffic. Caitlyn's head bumped against the passenger window. She tried to catch Harper's eyes again, but they were focused on the road ahead. Instead, Caitlyn turned her attention to Flynn. "Where are we going?"

"To the Rosewood Sand Hill Hotel in Menlo Park."

"Sounds fancy. How many stars?"

"Five," Flynn replied.

"How do you intend to pay for it? A place like that won't take cash, and you sure can't use a credit card."

"I was hoping you might take care of it."

"Me?"

"I'll reimburse you, of course."

Caitlyn sighed. "So, what's the plan?"

"Let's talk about that over dinner."

"You can give me the details over dinner, but right now I'd like to hear the broad strokes."

Flynn turned around to look at her directly. "Bettina O'Toole-Applebaum was arrested in Russia."

"No surprise there."

"She's being held in the same gulag as Oleg Ivanov."

"Polar Owl?"

"The Russians want to make a trade."

"Harper for Bettina?"

"And Duncan Dankworth. They grabbed him too."

"Jesus." Caitlyn shook her head. "What's the US government want to do?"

"Miranda says they haven't decided yet, but I believe they want to have their cake and eat it too. Take all the intelligence Harper has to offer and then trade her to Putin."

Harper spoke for the first time. "And there's no way in hell I'm letting that happen."

Caitlyn nodded. "That intelligence is your only bargaining chip."

Harper met Caitlyn's eyes with her own. "Which is why I can't give it up until they give me what *I* want. A signed contract promising their protection."

"I get that," Caitlyn said.

"Good," Flynn replied, "I knew you would. Which is why we need to go to Russia and liberate Bettina and Dankworth from Polar Owl."

Caitlyn laughed at that.

Flynn's smile disappeared. "I'm serious."

"I know you are."

"We do that, and Putin has no leverage."

"Yeah, no, I don't think so."

"Together, we can do anything."

Caitlyn shook her head. "Not that."

"Of course we can."

"It's a goddamn gulag in the Arctic Circle."

"I have a plan."

"I bet you do."

Harper reached over and touched Flynn's hand. "She doesn't believe in you. Not like I do."

Caitlyn wanted to give her a slap, but restrained herself and glowered instead. "Is she coming to Russia too?"

Flynn shook his head. "That wouldn't be wise. She's our ace in the hole."

Caitlyn nodded. "So, you're going to break Bettina out all by your lonesome?"

"Not if you're helping me."

. . .

The Rosewood Sand Hill resort sat on sixteen pristine acres surrounded by the foothills of the Santa Cruz Mountains. The contemporary architecture reeked of Silicon Valley elegance and sophistication. The low-rise buildings were designed to harmonize with the natural landscape. Serene and luxurious, it epitomized the laid-back California tech bro billionaire lifestyle.

Caitlyn hated it immediately.

The lobby was equally Zen and pretentious. Natural light streamed in floor-to-ceiling windows, offering a sweeping view of the surrounding hills. The sleek reception desk dominated the room with its exotic wood and inlaid tiles. Stunning California blondes manned the front desk. One male. One female. The male offered Caitlyn a warm smile and beckoned her closer.

Caitlyn blanched when she saw the room rates. A deluxe king was $1200.00 a night. A Rosewood Executive Suite was $2500.00 a night. Flynn had reserved one of each. Caitlyn wasn't sure if Flynn wanted to share the suite with her or Harper, so she booked a third room to keep things simple.

They were side by side by side on the same floor. Alone at last, Caitlyn wrestled with how to convince Flynn that breaking Bettina out of a Russian gulag was batshit crazy.

The wall of windows in Caitlyn's room offered a tranquil view of the surrounding hills. The phone next to the bed rang. She picked up. "Yeah?"

"Thank you." It was Flynn.

"For what?"

"For booking a third room. It saved me from having to make an awkward choice. Harper has bonded to me, and from the conversation in the car, it's clear she resents your presence."

"No shit."

"I thought that later tonight I might sneak into your room."

"Good. Because we need to settle this whole breaking Bettina out of prison thing."

"I thought we settled that."

"You thought wrong."

A pause on Flynn's end. "I made a 7 p.m. reservation at Madera."

"See you then." She clicked off before Flynn could say another word.

Caitlyn was tired of constantly having to save Flynn from himself. She drew a bath and took a soak in the deep tub. She followed that with a hot shower. Her muscles resisted relaxation at first, but eventually succumbed. As pretentious as the place was, she did enjoy that rainfall showerhead. The plush cotton towels were surprisingly soft, and after she dried off, she wrapped herself in one of the equally opulent robes, set her phone alarm, and took a two-hour nap.

■　■　■

Flynn put on the same outfit he put on two days earlier. He had no time to grab any clothes other than the ones on his back when they'd fled the Whitecap Lodge. He considered baths unhygienic and had no desire to soak in his own effluvium. So, he ignored the deep tub and took his usual hot shower, followed by an ice-cold one. He put on the white cotton terrycloth robe, lay in bed, and worked out various stratagems to convince Caitlyn that they needed to break Bettina out of Polar Owl prison.

At seven, he met Caitlyn and Harper in Madera for a cocktail. Caitlyn looked refreshed and dressed in a new outfit befitting the elegance of the room. Harper, like Flynn, wore the same dirty clothes from the last two days. She regarded Caitlyn with the same unfriendly irritation she exhibited on the drive up from the airport.

A stunning hostess seated them at a table next to a floor-to-ceiling window. The sun setting behind the hills painted the clouds in shades of orange and red. Flynn ordered a bottle of champagne for the table, hoping that it might lighten the mood as his two dinner companions continued to radiate waves of resentment.

Their waitperson, a trim woman in her forties with short blonde hair, returned with the bubbly, a Dom Perignon 2008, and poured a glass for each of them. Flynn ordered steak tartare and the pan-seared sole. Caitlyn went with the winter salad and the branzino with citrus salsa verde. Harper selected the oysters on the half shell and the truffle and winter mushroom risotto.

An uncomfortable silence dominated the table. Flynn tried to break the ice multiple times.

"I do believe this 2008 Dom Perignon rivals the 2004."

Neither one responded. Harper stared out the window. Caitlyn gave Flynn an irritated side-eye.

"These scallops are exceptional. Would either of you like to try one?"

Neither one even looked at Flynn, but focused on their plates as they quietly ate their appetizers.

"I understand the culinary director here was rated New York Magazine's best new chef of 2007."

Nothing.

"I sense a certain animosity between you two, and I believe if you got to know each other, you'd discover you have a lot in common."

"Yeah," Harper said, "*You.*"

Flynn set down his fork. "Look, we need to get our priorities straight. Let's put the hurt feelings aside for now and move on to more important matters."

Caitlyn pushed away her plate. "Like breaking Bettina out of a Russian Gulag?"

"Exactly."

"James, I know you feel responsible for Bettina being there, and I know you would do anything to break her out, but it's a suicide mission. Polar Owl is impregnable. No one's ever escaped from there. It's the northernmost prison in Russia. Above the Arctic Circle. Just getting there would be a major ordeal, let alone getting out. The average temperature in February is minus sixteen degrees. If we had any chance at all, I'd consider it. But we *don't*."

Harper looked up from her plate. "What if I told you there might be a way?"

"I'd say you're as crazy as he is."

Harper took a sip of wine. "A former oligarch with massive resources has hired a small army to break him out of Polar Owl in a week's time. If you took advantage of the chaos, you might be able to free your friend."

Flynn raised an eyebrow. "Are you talking about Oleg Ivanov?"

Caitlyn raised her hand. "How would you even know about a plan like that?"

"Because I'm working with him to bring down Putin. He's paying me ten million dollars to turn those files over to the FBI."

Flynn put down his fork. "So, this isn't about your brother?"

"It's *always* been about my brother. The ten million dollars is just a bonus."

"How did he even find you?"

"I found *him*. I hoped he would be receptive, and he was. He wants to destroy Putin as much as I do."

Flynn thought Caitlyn might leap across the table and choke Harper out. "Ivanov doesn't just want Putin," Caitlyn snapped. "He also wants Flynn."

"Yes, he does, but *I did not give him up*."

"Then who keeps trying to kill him?"

"It's the GRU, and they're not trying to kill him, they're trying to kill *me*. Once Flynn got in their way, he became a target too."

"So now you're trying to *protect* Flynn? Do you really expect us to believe that?"

"I don't care what you believe."

Caitlyn turned to Flynn. *"Did you sleep with her?"*

Flynn opened his mouth, but nothing came out.

Harper answered for him. "We shared a bed, but were interrupted by a GRU hitman. Then the FBI landed."

Caitlyn grabbed Flynn by the chin. *"You slept with her?"*

"We didn't actually do the deed."

"Then why does she suddenly want to help you?"

Harper smiled. "It's not like James has magic jizz that turns enemy agents into allies. If Flynn can free Bettina, then the US government has no reason to trade me to the Russians. If I give them the files, they give me witness protection, and Ivanov gives me ten million dollars. It's a win-win-win. Besides…" Harper offered Flynn a provocative grin. "I happen to like him. And I think he likes me."

Caitlyn sat back and glared. "Is that true?"

Flynn touched her hand. "You're missing the point here. Harper just told you we have a way to free Bettina."

"I don't trust her."

"I do."

Caitlyn sighed. *"Jesus Christ."*

"Look, I understand if you don't want to come to Russia. But if you're going to stay here, can you at least keep an eye on her?"

"Who?"

"Harper."

"Are you kidding me?"

"So that's a no?"

"No fucking way."

"Okay, then." Flynn shrugged and made eye contact with Harper. "I have a friend in L.A. She lives in a gated community in Malibu. A place no one would ever look for you. I'll give her a call and see if you can stay with her."

Caitlyn punched Flynn in the shoulder. "You'd put Alessandra in that kind of danger?"

"No one will have any idea Harper's there."

"You have no good reason to trust her. You know that, right?"

"By telling us about Ivanov, she just gave me a reason."

Chapter Seventeen

Alessandra Bianchi had her right knee replaced the previous year. Now her left knee needed replacing, but she was in no rush to get it done. It took her six months to recover last time, and she still walked with a limp. Alessandra did her physical therapy exercises and stretches every morning along with the rest of her daily exercise routine. *Move it or lose it.* That's what her late husband used to tell her. Philip was a billionaire and much kinder than her first four husbands.

She loved walking Peanut on Malibu Beach every morning. It was harder than it used to be, but what wasn't? As long as she could walk, it didn't matter how quickly. Plus, it kept her somewhat firm and fit. At eighty years of age, she still took some pride in her appearance. She didn't look like she did in the 1960s, but neither did Jane Fonda.

Seeing herself in the mirror sometimes startled her. Most of the time, she didn't feel like an octogenarian. She didn't bother with plastic surgery or fillers, so her face had a few wrinkles, but not many. She never smoked, rarely drank, and always stayed out of the sun, unlike some of her contemporaries who didn't always take care of themselves. The ones still around were an inspiration. Ann-Margret. Catherine Deneuve. Sophia Loren. Jane would sometimes stay with her at the beach. Poor Raquel passed a few years back. In their prime, they were all so competitive. Except for Raquel. Raquel helped Alessandra navigate her early days in Hollywood and introduced her to her last husband, the late Mr. Zimmel. For that, she'd be eternally grateful.

As she finished her evening beauty regimen, she still caught traces of the bombshell she used to be. Her mouth and famous blue eyes were surrounded by laugh lines. Her shoulder-length silver hair framed her equally famous cheekbones. She wasn't as tall as she once was, but tried to maintain the posture she developed as a young dancer. Alessandra watched what she ate and exercised every day. Not because she expected to be cast as the femme fatale in some spy thriller, but to stay healthy, mobile and strong.

She dried her face and headed into her bedroom. Peanut was already fast asleep on top of the comforter. Alessandra wore a pair of tiny Resound hearing aids. A quick beep indicated an incoming call. Her iPhone vibrated on the nightstand. She didn't recognize the number and nearly let it go to voicemail, but her intuition told her to answer.

"Hello?"

"Alessandra! It's so wonderful to hear your voice."

"James?" Traces of her native Italy could still be heard in her accent.

"I hope you're well."

"I'm very well. How are you?"

"Great."

"And Caitlyn?"

She heard a brief hesitation before he answered. "Good."

"I do hope to head to Switzerland again. It's been far too long since I've seen you two."

"I'm actually not in Switzerland at the moment."

"Where are you?"

"Northern California. And I have a favor to ask."

"Of course."

"There's a young woman who needs my help, and I'm hoping you might be able to help her as well."

"What can I do?"

"I'd like her to stay with you for a short while."

"Is she in danger?"

"She is, but I think she'd be safe with you. If you'd rather not put yourself in that position, I completely understand and will find alternate arrangements for her."

"Don't be ridiculous. I'm glad to help any way I can."

"Are you sure?"

"Of course I'm sure. What's her name?"

"Harper Sinclair. I'd tell you more about her situation, but the less you know, the better."

"Have you given her my address?"

"Not yet, but I will once I get your permission."

"You have it. I'm always glad to do my part. You know that."

"You are beautiful and brave, and I am grateful for you and everything you do."

"When can I expect her, James?"

"Sometime later today."

"I'll make up a guest room for her then."

"Thank you, Alessandra."

"No need to thank me. I could use a little more excitement in my life. I hope to see you soon."

"I hope so too. Though I do have one more favor to ask. Could you please wire fifty thousand dollars to Halyk Bank in Astana, Kazakhstan? Of course, I'll reimburse you. I'd just rather not leave an obvious paper trail."

"Kazakhstan?"

"I'll tell you all about it when I return."

"Be safe."

"Always."

And with that, Flynn clicked off. Alessandra felt a little thrill. She loved her life, but it could get so predictable, and she adored the occasional break in her routine. Especially if it had to do with James Flynn. If she were forty years younger and he wasn't with

Caitlyn, she would have pursued him. Aggressively. She loved the man's *viva la vita*. The rest of him wasn't too bad either.

■ ■ ■

Caitlyn considered having Flynn committed against his will for a seventy-two-hour hold. But not being an official member of his family, she didn't have the legal authority. And even if she could pull it off, he'd probably be sent to Hornitos State Hospital. That was where they met. The infamous forensic psychiatric facility housed those considered not guilty by reason of insanity. Mass murderers. Serial killers. Not the safest place to be. She and Flynn barely escaped with their lives, and she wouldn't want to put him in that kind of danger again. Plus, that would also put him in the crosshairs of Kalishnik and the GRU. Sadly, she realized there was no saving him from his delusion. Though she hoped she could at least get him to see some modicum of reason.

To that end, just after midnight, she fixed her hair and makeup and put on the sexiest sleepwear she had. A silky charmeuse and lace chemise with a matching thong. She usually wasn't one for sexy lingerie. Comfort was more her thing. She bought something similar back when she was trying to entice a Russian oligarch to tell her his secrets. It worked on him. Perhaps it would work on Flynn. She covered herself with the complimentary terrycloth robe, stepped into the hallway, and quietly knocked on Flynn's door one room over.

No answer.

She knocked again. This time, a little louder. After a moment, she heard rustling and then Flynn on the other side. "Harper?"

That pissed her off, but she did her best to not let her possessiveness get the best of her. "No. Sorry to disappoint."

"Caitlyn?"

"Yeah," she said dryly.

Flynn undid the chain, opened the door, and Caitlyn ducked inside.

He too wore a white terrycloth robe. She slid her hand beneath, held it against his chest, and whispered in his ear. "I'm sorry I was such a bitch at dinner."

"That's okay. Your bitchiness was just proof you still have strong feelings for me."

"Feelings, maybe. I don't know how strong."

"Strong enough. Otherwise, you wouldn't have knocked me up just now."

"Let's not get ahead of ourselves." She removed her robe to reveal her slinky lingerie.

Flynn smiled with surprise. "What's the occasion?"

"You."

Flynn's smile widened. "There's a split of Moët & Chandon in the minibar. Unless there's something else you'd like?"

"I could do with a glass of champagne."

Flynn opened the bottle and poured them each a glass. "I'm guessing you're not here just for the bubbly."

She took Flynn's hand and led him to the bed. "I'm not."

Flynn sat beside her and kissed her hand. "Somehow, I think there's something you want beyond the obvious."

"There is."

"You don't want me to go to Russia." Not a query. A declaration.

"Bettina is a good friend, and I understand why you want to help her escape, but I'm worried you're rushing this."

"If Kalishnik is indeed busting Ivanov out, there couldn't be a better time."

"If that's what's happening."

"You think Harper is spinning a tale?"

"I don't know what to believe, and you shouldn't either. Not until we know Harper's true intent."

"Sometimes you have to go with your gut. This is one of those times."

Since gentle prodding wasn't working, Caitlyn moved on to Plan B. Beguile him. Relax him. Make him more suggestible to her suggestions. She took his hand and rested it against her chest and leaned in close to kiss him on the neck, his cheek, and finally his lips. Then she slowly pushed him back until he was lying flat on the bed. A gentle knock at the door broke the mood.

Flynn looked irritated. "Who could that be?"

"Maybe if we ignore them, they'll go away."

Another gentle knock, followed by a breathy voice tinged with a syrupy Southern accent. "Flynn?"

Caitlyn huffed a disappointed sigh. "You gotta be fricking kidding me."

Flynn sat up on the edge of the bed. The gentle knocking grew more insistent. "I better get that."

Caitlyn knew he was right. Harper might knock all night if Flynn didn't answer. He pulled his robe together and called to her through the door. "Are you all right?"

"We need to talk."

"I'm about in bed."

"I'll join you then."

Flynn glanced back at Caitlyn and pointed under the bed while mouthing the words *get under*.

She glared and mouthed, "*Are you fricking kidding me?*"

He pointed again, sharper this time, and she sighed, shook her head, and dropped to the floor. After she slid under the bed, she pulled the comforter down like a curtain.

She peeked through a tiny gap and watched as Flynn hid her champagne glass behind a lamp. When he opened the door, Harper hurried inside, quickly closing it behind herself. Before Flynn could say a word, she grabbed him by the wrist and dragged him towards the bed. Caitlyn could only see their legs as they sat down on the edge.

She heard kissing sounds.

"Can I say something?" Flynn said.

"I'd rather you didn't," Harper replied.

"As attracted as I am to you, I'd rather we wait until we're both ready."

"I'm ready."

"I can see that. I, however, need a little more time."

"More time for what?"

"More time to get to know you."

A mirthless laugh. "It's Caitlyn, isn't it?"

"What?"

"That's why you're reluctant to take this to the next level."

"I don't think that's it."

"Sure it is. You feel guilty because she's sleeping in the next room. And I respect that. You have a moral compass. It's one of the reasons I'm so attracted to you."

"I have to admit. She *is* on my mind."

"If you gave me half a chance, I could show you how serious I am, and by the time I'm done, she'd be the last thing you'd be thinking about."

"I don't doubt our run is about done, but right now I'm not sure I could give you my all, and I wouldn't want to make our first time less than…exceptional."

"So, y'all still feel the same way about me? Your feelings haven't changed?"

"Of course not."

"Good, because if you want to get what *you* want, I need to get what *I* want. And if that happens, I am confident that you'll never want for anything else again."

"What are you doing with your hand?"

"What does it feel like I'm doing?"

Caitlyn heard a soft sigh from Flynn and wanted to jump out from under the bed and smack Harper upside the head.

"Can we not—can we just—please!" The bed squeaked as Flynn jumped to his feet. "I called my friend Alessandra, and she's agreed to put you up. After you drop us off at the airport, you can drive straight down to Malibu. I'll give you her address, and you can plug it into Google Maps."

Caitlyn heard the smile in her voice as she took Flynn by the hand. "You don't want me to stay the night?"

"Not tonight."

"Caitlyn doesn't believe in you. Not like I do. She is done with you. She just doesn't know how to tell you."

"I'm not sure that's true."

The bed squeaked as Harper stood. "You're in denial, darling." She moved for the door. "Sweet dreams."

"You too," Flynn said.

She walked back and planted a kiss on Flynn before finally leaving the room. Flynn shut the door and locked it as Caitlyn slid out from under the bed. *"Our run is about done?"*

"You heard what she said. She needs to believe she has a future with me."

Flynn retrieved Caitlyn's champagne and handed it to her. "Now where were we?"

"Wherever we were, we are no longer there." She drained the rest of the champagne and set down the empty glass. "I'm heading back to my own bed. We have a big day tomorrow."

"Darling, I'm just doing what I need to do."

"And *I'm* just doing what *I* need to do."

. . .

The ride to San Jose International Airport took thirty awkward and interminable minutes. Caitlyn drove, glaring at the road. Flynn rode shotgun, and Harper sat in the back, jaw set, glowering at the passing scenery. Flynn kept trying to lighten the mood.

"I hope everyone slept well."

Silence.

"I slept very well. The mattress was wonderfully comfortable, and the thread count on those Egyptian cotton sheets has to be four hundred at least."

Silence.

Flynn turned to glance back at Harper. "By the way, before I retired for the night, I changed the license plates on the minivan. Swapped them out with those on another vehicle in the car park. By the time the owners of that other vehicle realize they have new license plates, you'll be halfway to Malibu."

Silence.

Caitlyn glanced at Flynn and decided he had suffered enough. "I was hoping you might see things differently in the morning and finally come to your senses. So, I bought you a ticket to Zurich."

Harper harrumphed. "I think he knows what he's doing."

"I'm not saying he doesn't," Caitlyn countered. "I'm just giving him a less suicidal option."

"You are so manipulative."

"I just don't want him to do something he might regret."

"Living with a schemer like you, I think he's already full of regrets."

"Now, now, ladies, let's keep this civil. Caitlyn, I appreciate your concern, but I already have my itinerary. I'm flying to Astana, Kazakhstan. Twenty hours in the air with layovers in Los Angeles and Istanbul."

Caitlyn let go with a despairing sigh and took the airport road exit.

She parked at the curb by departures, and everyone climbed from the minivan. Flynn and Caitlyn unloaded their luggage.

Harper stepped right up to Flynn and took his hand. "Thank you for doing this."

"No need to thank me."

"I know the risks. And Caitlyn isn't wrong. You're putting yourself in harm's way, and I just want you to know that I appreciate all you're doing for me."

Caitlyn couldn't stand her sexy, breathy, phony southern accent, but held her tongue. She was done arguing with the woman.

"We should probably get going." Flynn tried to extricate his hand, but she held tight.

"And thank you for arranging for a safe place for me to stay."

"Of course. I'll call when I reach Russia. In the meantime, call Kalishnik and see if you can find out exactly when that escape plan is happening."

"Leave it to me."

She gave him a peck on the cheek, and when he didn't pull back, she grabbed him firmly by his right butt cheek and kissed him passionately. Flynn didn't flinch or pull back. He just let her have her way with him. Then she worked up some phony tears, caressed his face, climbed behind the wheel of the van, and took off.

"You're enjoying this," Caitlyn said.

"Don't be ridiculous. You don't think that gave me any pleasure, do you? What I do I do for king and country."

"You can fool yourself, but you can't fool me."

"If after all this time you still don't trust me, I don't know what to tell you."

"You don't have to tell me anything. Actions always speak louder than words." Caitlyn dramatically walked away from Flynn to check in for the first leg of her journey. She waited in line at the Alaska Airlines desk and turned around to find Flynn right behind her. "I think we said all we need to say."

"This is my airline."

"You're flying on Alaska to Los Angeles?" Caitlyn couldn't believe it. "What's the flight number?"

"3485."

"Jesus Christ."

On the way to LA, Flynn sat one row behind her. Upon arrival they silently rode the tram to the international terminal, and that's where they finally split up. She could tell Flynn wanted to say something before they parted, but she left before he could.

Chapter Eighteen

Kazakhstan is the world's largest landlocked country, occupying nearly three million square kilometers. It sits between China and Uzbekistan, and its border with Russia is the longest continuous land border in the world. The Baikonur Cosmodrome in southern Kazakhstan is the largest and oldest space launch facility in existence. Built by the Soviets in the 1950s, it was the launch site for Sputnik 1. As a former satellite of the Soviet Union, Kazakhstan and Russia have a complex relationship. The country is an important source of parallel imports: goods that violate sanctions imposed on Russia by the international community. On paper, trucks claim to be transporting women's wigs or canned meat, but in reality they're loaded with drones, armaments, and microchips.

After thirty hours of air travel and layovers, an exhausted Flynn arrived at Nursultan Nazarbayev International Airport in Kazakhstan's capital city of Astana. Most locals spoke either Kazakh or Russian. Flynn understood a smattering of Russian, but Kazakh was like nothing he had ever heard. Some have described it as the sound a diesel engine makes when you try to start it on a cold morning. Many of the locals looked vaguely Asian or very Asian. Not surprising, as Kazakhstan shares a border with China, and some historians believe Genghis Khan was Kazakh.

Flynn went through passport control and, after getting his stamp, picked up his single suitcase and trekked through immigration and customs. Uber didn't operate in Kazakhstan, so Flynn downloaded a Russian rideshare app called *Yandex Go*.

He found his driver waiting for him at the curb. Flynn had encountered assassins masquerading as taxi drivers in previous missions and sized up the driver carefully. He was about as wide as he was tall, with massive shoulders encased in a burgundy tracksuit. Except for a big, black, bushy unibrow, he had no hair anywhere on his perfectly round head. His joyful grin revealed several missing teeth. He poked his finger into his chest and said, "Takhir!"

Flynn pointed to himself. "Flynn."

"English?"

"Yes. Do *you* speak English?"

"I talk okay English." He pinched his index finger and thumb together and held them up. "Little bit."

"Excellent." When Takhir raised a quizzical unibrow, Flynn followed up with, "Good."

"Good!"

"You drive me?"

"Yes. Where you go?"

"The Rixos President Hotel."

"Ohhhhh." Takhir, obviously impressed, grinned and rubbed his fingers and thumbs together in the universal symbol for money.

"Shall we go?"

Takhir nodded, grabbed Flynn's lone piece of luggage, and loaded it into the trunk of his Lada Priora, a compact car manufactured by Russian automaker AvtoVAZ. He opened the rear passenger door and gestured for Flynn to get in. Though tidy, the intense stench of stale cigarette smoke caused Flynn's eyes to water.

The ride to the Rixos took Flynn past a truly impressive sight. An enormous structure with multiple massive domes and towering minarets. Takhir caught Flynn's eye and pointed. "Grand Central Mosque."

The route continued past the Medical Centre Hospital of the Administration of Presidential Affairs and the Nur Alem Museum of Future Energy. As they approached the Rixos, they passed another grand structure: the Ak Orda Presidential Palace. A striking combination of classical and contemporary design, clad in pristine white marble, and topped with a gold and azure dome. Beyond the Presidential Palace, the gleaming silver pyramid known as the Palace of Peace and Reconciliation rose in the distance.

The Ishim River divided Astana between the old and the new. The old half resembled many cities formerly under Soviet control, with dozens of blocky concrete apartment houses, a Soviet-era train station, a statue of Lenin, and other symbols of the former USSR. The newer half of town looked shockingly modern. Wide boulevards with towering futuristic skyscrapers, sleek high-rise apartment buildings, and large modern green spaces with lush gardens.

Kazakhstan wasn't the primitive backwater Flynn had expected. There were no muddy streets or ragged beggars or angry goats or toothless crones. In fact, the Rixos President Hotel was one of six five-star hotels in Astana's city center. Hotels like the St. Regis and the Ritz-Carlton.

Flynn requested Takhir stop by a Halyk bank branch to collect eleven million *tenge*, the equivalent of twenty-five thousand US dollars. Because of Alessandra's help, Flynn withdrew not just Kazakhstani currency, but also twenty-five thousand dollars in *rubles*.

Takhir then took Flynn to the Rixos and unloaded his bags. Flynn generously tipped him. Takhir grinned and vigorously shook Flynn's hand before slipping him a business card with his phone number. He placed his palm over his heart to show how grateful he was.

The lavish lobby of the Rixos President Hotel exuded luxury. Opulent oriental rugs covered the white and black marble floors. Sitting areas furnished with elegant mauve and dark purple upholstered couches and chairs beckoned to every bottom in the place. Massive crystal chandeliers dangled high above. A cobalt blue marble arch framed the front desk. Three desk clerks stood waiting at computer consoles. The clerk he approached, a slender man in his thirties, smiled and nodded when Flynn told him he wanted to check in. The male clerk pointed toward an attractive female with long dark hair one station over and said, "English."

Flynn didn't want to flag his location by using a credit card. Luckily, they were more than happy to take his *tenge*.

A well-appointed deluxe room awaited him. Flynn took a shower and then rang up room service. He ordered from the traditional Kazakh menu, choosing *beshbarmak*, a hearty dish of boiled horsemeat on a bed of flat noodles. This was served with a fried bread called *shelpek*.

Flynn had slept little on the plane so he could adjust to the time change faster. Having been up for more than thirty hours straight, he quickly fell asleep and awakened six hours later, still feeling groggy.

His room service breakfast consisted of toast, marmalade, and two boiled eggs. Flynn detested tea, and ordered a small pot of coffee. The caffeine didn't alleviate his grogginess, but left him feeling jittery and spacey. A vigorous workout in the gym at the Rixos finally got his blood moving. After showering and dressing, he used the phone in his hotel room to call the number on Takhir's business card.

"Takhir!"

"Hello, Takhir. It's Mr. Flynn."

"Mr. Flynn!"

"I could use your services."

"When?"

"Now."

Takhir barked something joyful in Kazakh and immediately clicked off. Flynn hoped that meant that Takhir would soon arrive to pick him up. He checked out and waited in the lobby. He wouldn't be going to the Russian embassy for a visa. Instead, he'd have to find another way to cross the border into Russia, and hoped Takhir might help him with that.

Takhir's blue Lada Priora rolled up in front of the hotel. He hopped out, loaded Flynn's suitcase into the trunk, and jumped back behind the wheel. Flynn kept his leather messenger bag as he climbed inside.

Takhir offered him a bottle of water. "Turan water. Very good. From fifteen-thousand-year-old glacier."

"Thank you." Flynn unscrewed the cap and took a sip.

"Where I take you? You want tour? I born here. I can show you everywhere."

"Actually, I was hoping to go to Petropavl."

Takhir's eyes went wide. "Petropavl? That very far. Five hours driving. Too far. I take you to Byterek Tower. Very tall. Ride to top. See everything. All of Astana! Okay?"

"Not okay. I need to go to Petropavl."

"Nothing there. Astana much better. More things to see. Not so boring."

"I'll pay you to take me there, and I'll pay for your drive back. Plus, I'll give you a very large tip for your trouble. Would two hundred thousand *tenge* do it?"

"That is *much* money!"

"I know a train would be cheaper, but it'll also take me almost twice as long to get there."

"No, no, no! I drive. No problem."

"Here's the thing, Takhir. That's just the first part of my journey. Once I'm there, I'd like to cross the border into Russia. But I don't have a visa, and I don't want to get one."

"You want to sneak in?"

"I do. But I don't want to get you into trouble."

"No trouble. I call my cousin Zangar. He drive truck. Into Russia. Back from Russia. He go all the time."

"He doesn't go through border control?"

"Yeah, but there is free trade between Russia and Kazakhstan. No…how you say…looking inside truck to see what Zangar carry. They wave him through."

"How soon can he do this?"

"I call. We see." Takhir called his cousin. They had a long conversation in Kazakh. After ten minutes of talking, Takhir turned to Flynn. "He can do, but it cost you five hundred thousand *tenge*. Too much?"

"No, tell him we have a deal. Can he take me to Omsk?"

"Omsk? I ask." It took Takhir five minutes to ask. Flynn only understood one word. *Omsk.* Finally, Takhir held the phone to his chest and said, "Yes."

"When can we meet?"

"Today if you want."

"Okay."

Takhir offered Flynn a big, gap-toothed grin. "Okay!" He barked more Kazakh into the phone before clicking off. He glanced at Flynn in the rearview mirror. "We go?"

"I have one more question."

"Tell me."

"I'd like to buy a gun."

Takhir narrowed his eyes. "Why you need gun?"

"For protection. It's a dangerous world."

"What kind of gun you want? Shotgun? Hunting rifle?"

"A pistol. Is that possible?"

"Possible. But not from store."

"From where then?"

He tapped his chest. "Me."

Takhir popped open his glove compartment to reveal a pistol. He held up a Makarov PM, a Soviet-made automatic pistol first manufactured in 1951. This particular one had to be at least thirty years old, as the USSR stopped manufacturing them in the 1990s.

He handed it to Flynn, who checked the magazine to see that it was loaded. "Do you have more ammo for it?"

"In trunk."

"How much for the gun?"

"Two hundred thousand *tenge*."

"Deal."

Takhir grinned and handed Flynn the gun. "Now we go?"

"Now we go to a clothing store. I need to buy some winter clothing."

Takhir nodded. "Okay."

At *Zara*, a fashion-forward clothing store in Astana, Flynn purchased a long black quilted coat with huge pockets and a hood, a navy wool sweater, and a black stocking cap. Flynn wore the clothing out of the store, and once back in Takhir's car, they hit the road.

Just outside of Astana, the horizon became a vast, treeless, endless prairie. Flat open grasslands as far as the eye could see. The vegetation was sparse, and so were the infrequent towns and villages. Hundreds of years ago, tribes of horse-riding nomads ranged across this harsh and rugged landscape. Freezing in the winter, blazing in the summer.

Takhir held off smoking for a full thirty minutes before he asked Flynn's permission. He lit up before Flynn could answer. He cracked the window to let out the fumes, and Flynn opened his own window to get a bit of fresh air. Takhir's late-model Lada Priora struggled to keep up with the speed limit of 140 kilometers per hour. Cars and trucks roared past them, even as Takhir's car vibrated like a washing machine with an uneven load. Flynn lost cell service almost immediately. With nothing else to do, he stared out the window at the endless, monotonous scenery.

Grassland and sheep.

Lots of sheep.

They drove past the town of Shchuchinsk, and as they headed farther north, vast farms with fields of wheat replaced the grassland. Amber waves of grain blowing in the wind.

They stopped twice for bathroom breaks, drinks, and snacks. Chaga tea was brewed with wild Siberian mushrooms. Tarragon soda tasted like black licorice. *Qurt* were small, white, hard, fermented cheese balls made from soured mare's milk left to harden in the sun. Flynn found them incredibly salty and cut the taste with a Snickers bar made with sunflower seeds instead of peanuts.

A little over five hours after leaving Astana, Takhir pulled into the *Stoyanka Gruzovikov Al'tira*. The large truck stop boasted a café, a bathhouse, and a small hotel. Takhir's Lada Priora looked tiny amidst all the massive semis and panel trucks. Flynn followed Takhir into the packed café. The loud, hot, humid, sweaty crush of humanity shouted and laughed and stuffed their faces. A cloud of acrid cigarette smoke hung halfway between the floor and the ceiling. A man who could have been Takhir's twin beckoned them over.

Zangar had the same unibrow and was just as bald and stout, but had a few less teeth. Before making introductions or even commencing business, Takhir insisted they order dinner. "Order food first. Zangar says service slow here."

With the menu completely in Kazakh, Takhir playfully punched Flynn in the shoulder and told him he'd order for him. A sour-looking middle-aged waitress approached the table. Flynn offered her a smile, but she seemed immune to his charms. Takhir ordered a long list of dishes in Kazakh. Zangar piped in occasionally. The waitress wrote nothing down. She just stared at them like she wanted to stab them both.

After she slowly shuffled off, Takhir pointed at Zangar. "My cousin Zangar. This is Mr. Flynn."

Zangar put out his hand for Flynn to shake. Zangar put his hand over his heart the same way Takhir did. "Good to meet you."

"You speak English?"

"I do. But not so much. Not like Takhir."

Zangar addressed Takhir directly with a long spiel in Kazakh. The waitress returned with their drinks. Three bottles of Kruzhka Svezhego beer. Flynn found it crisp and malty, much like a pilsner.

After a few sips, Zangar stopped talking and started drinking, and Takhir stopped drinking and started talking. "Zangar say you ride in back of truck. You stay hid, and he take you to Omsk."

"That's all he said? He went on for quite a while."

"That the important part. Other had to do with aunt and uncle and sister who I almost marry."

"You almost married his sister? Isn't she your cousin?"

"Second cousin. Very pretty, but..." He pointed at his temple and twirled his finger. Zangar laughed and choked on his beer. "Kazakh women are known for great beauty. Many become supermodels."

Takhir found a picture on his phone and showed it to Flynn. A selfie of Takhir and Zangar standing on either side of a female version of themselves. Zulfiya was just as squat and wide, but wore lipstick, a scarf on her head, and had two gleaming gold teeth.

"Stupid sexy, but loony as bedbug." Takhir repeated that in Kazakh and Zangar laughed mid-sip, shooting beer out of his nose.

It took an hour before the slow-moving waitress brought their food and dropped the dishes randomly on the table. She then plopped an empty plate in front of each of them. Flynn offered her a thank you in Kazakh. She glared at him and walked away.

Takhir then went on to explain the various dishes on the table. "*Sorpa.* Soup made from lamb. *Qazy.* Sausage made from horse intestine and meat from rib. *Lagman.* Round noodle with goat. And *manti.* Big soup dumpling filled with lamb fat and onion. Enjoy!"

None of it sounded especially appetizing to Flynn, but much to his surprise, he enjoyed each dish immensely. Takhir ordered another round of beer, and by the time they had finished their meal, Flynn felt himself slipping into a food coma.

Flynn looked at Zangar. "When do we leave?"

Zangar grunted and replied, "Tomorrow morning. Tonight, we stay in hotel." Then Takhir beckoned their irritated waitress over and ordered dessert. They each drank another beer before the sweets finally arrived. The balkaymak, a kind of pudding made from boiled cream and honey and kustil, looked like miniature branches fallen from a tiny tree.

It unnerved Flynn that the waitress couldn't stand him. Women usually found him charming. Some found him extremely charming. He left her a large tip, and that just seemed to make her angrier. She glowered at Flynn, cursing under her breath as she walked away with the money.

Flynn whispered to Takhir. "I don't think she likes me."

"Did you give tip?"

"A big one."

"How big?"

"Stupidly big."

"Ah, okay. She think you trying to buy her. Like she is whore."

"What?"

"Maybe we go before she get boyfriend."

"*What?*"

"Igor. Big bouncer guy in bar."

They scurried out of there and retired to their rooms.

Flynn's space in the old hotel was rudimentary at best, but at least he had it to himself. Zangar and Takhir bunked together in the room next door. They laughed and then snored late into the night. Luckily, all that Kazakh food and beer knocked Flynn out like a cricket bat to the back of the head.

■ ■ ■

A heavy fist pounded on his door at dawn. Flynn awakened with a start.

"Flynn!" Takhir shouted. "Zangar need to go!"

Flynn, a bit hungover from the night before, dressed for a day of hiding in the back of a truck. A long-sleeve polo shirt, navy chinos, gray Nikes, and a midnight blue Harrington jacket. He joined the cousins for a quick bowl of porridge in the café. They drank tea, and Flynn made do with instant coffee. Nescafe.

Flynn then followed Zangar to his truck. A Chinese-made Shacman X300 cab hauling an enclosed 48-foot-long trailer. Zangar opened the roll-up door to reveal the back packed with stacks of wooden crates labeled in Kazakh.

Flynn pointed to the label. "What's that say?"

"Canned meat. Spem," Zangar replied.

"Spam?"

"Spem."

"Is it really Spam?"

Zangar shrugged and held his hands palm up with a sheepish grin. Flynn assumed he was transporting something else. Something he shouldn't be because of the international economic sanctions on Russia. Zangar pointed into the truck. "Time to go. Get in back. I have mattress, blanket, water, snacks."

"How long will the drive be?"

"From here to Omsk? Four hour."

Zangar handed Flynn a flashlight and pointed again. Flynn put his rolling suitcase and messenger bag inside and climbed in with a boost from Takhir. He saluted his new friends.

Takhir saluted back with a grin. "Safe travels, my friend."

Zangar pulled the door shut, plunging Flynn into total darkness.

Chapter Nineteen

Harper stayed on US 101 for most of the drive south. She drove through Gilroy, whose billboards billed it as the garlic capital of the world, through Soledad, known for its vineyards and infamous state prison, and through San Luis Obispo. From there, the drive grew familiar as it was the same route she and Flynn took from Solvang. US 101 stayed closer to the coast from Pismo Beach on. She considered stopping by her apartment in Lompoc to pick up some additional clothes, but was worried her enemies might be staking it out.

With a stop for gas in Santa Barbara, she continued on through Ventura, and exited at Lost Hills per the directions on her burner phone's map app. She found the ride over the Santa Monica Mountains a bit more fun with its hairpin turns and sheer cliffs, but since the minivan didn't exactly hug the road, Harper eased off the gas and practiced patience. No point in dying in a fiery crash for no good reason. The sight of Pepperdine University let her know she'd arrived at California Highway One.

The Pacific Ocean filled her field of vision. An orange sun hovered over the horizon. She made a right on Webb Way, a left on Malibu Road, and one more left on Malibu Colony Road.

Her chest tightened at the sight of the entry gate and the security officer in the kiosk. She pulled to a stop and offered the large African-American guard a sunny smile. "Hey there."

"Welcome to the Malibu Colony. Can I please have your name?"

She laid the Southern accent on thick. "Harper Sinclair."

The man was used to dealing with supermodels and movie stars, so Harper figured her charms probably paled in comparison and wouldn't sway the man one way or another. He checked a computer screen in the guard kiosk and tapped the screen, nodding. "Found ya!" He immediately opened the gate. "Have a beautiful day."

"I plan to. Thank you."

The map app led Harper directly to the address Flynn provided her with. The house looked nice, but hardly grandiose. Some of the houses she passed were positively palatial. This slightly more modest beach cottage had a steep slate roof and whitewashed shingle siding.

She killed the minivan's engine, reached for the door handle, and hesitated. Should she call Kalishnik first? The more time she spent with Flynn, the guiltier she felt sending him to his doom. And that surprised her.

After her relentless indoctrination as a youngster and her brutal GRU training, she didn't think she had a guilty bone left in her body. She never thought she'd turn against the motherland. But that steadfast patriotism disappeared soon after her brother did. Now all she thought about was getting revenge on Putin. To do that, she'd have to avoid his hit squads. Specifically, Unit 29155. She needed to disappear, and that would require witness protection *and* Ivanov's money. Flynn landed in the category of collateral damage. But was that such a terrible thing? His entire life was an embarrassing lie. A sad and pathetic delusion. Perhaps killing him was a kindness.

Harper did her best to rationalize her decision, but some ghostly scruple still nagged at her.

And that pissed her off.

The anger motivated her to place a call to Kalishnik. It was ten hours ahead in Kharp. He might already be awake. He wasn't. The phone rang five times before he picked up. "*Chto?*"

Harper replied in English. "It's me."

Kalishnik asked her where she was. In Russian.

"Where I am isn't important."

Kalishnik barked at her to speak the mother tongue.

She replied in English with that sugary southern accent. "Sorry, darlin', but I can't risk being seen or heard speaking Russian. Not to anybody."

Harper caught the fury in his voice. "Where? Are? You?"

"Doesn't matter, sugar pie. What does matter is where Flynn is. Or am I wrong about that?"

"Where is *he*?"

"On his way to you. I sent him to Kharp, and he should be there soon. He won't be hard to miss in that toilet of a town. He's planning to tag along on your prison break and take advantage of the chaos to break out two friends of his."

"Flynn's coming here?"

"Didn't I just say that? I figure in all the craziness of the prison break, no one will ever know who put a bullet in him, but most will believe it was someone in the employ of Putin."

"So, you no longer have feelings for him?"

"He's cute. Like a puppy. But I need my money."

"When does he arrive?"

"In the next day or two. Knowing him, he'll probably check in under his own name. There can't be all that many hotels in a hellhole like Kharp."

"There's one hotel in this *pizdets* town, so that should be no problem."

"He wants me to find out the day and time you're planning to break Ivanov out."

"Tuesday. 3:00 a.m."

A fist banged on her window. Harper jumped. The smiling face of a strikingly beautiful older woman smiled at her through the glass. "Harper?"

"Gotta go. Got company. Catch you on the flip-flop, cupcake." Harper lowered the window. "Sorry, I was just getting off a call."

"You are Harper, aren't you? Flynn's friend?"

"Yes, ma'am."

"I'm Alessandra. Let's get you inside."

Harper grabbed her one flimsy piece of luggage, a kid's backpack she found in the minivan, and followed Alessandra up the walk and inside the house. The woman seemed vaguely familiar, but Harper couldn't quite remember where she had seen her before. She had a slight European accent. *Italian?*

The inside was a bit fancier than the outside, but not by much. The relaxed décor echoed the laid-back feel of the exterior. White beamed ceilings, white walls, and vintage furniture. Off-white textured rugs covered the hardwood floors. Beautiful plein air paintings decorated the walls. All very cozy and genteel. A tiny Pomeranian came bouncing up, yipping and nipping at Harper's ankles. Alessandra scooped her up. "This is Peanut. She's very protective."

"What a cutie." Harper scratched her under the chin. Peanut leaned into it.

"She likes you."

"She's adorable."

"Would you like me to give you the grand tour?"

"Lead the way, darlin'."

"My friends call me Alessa."

"Are we already friends?"

"Any friend of James' is a friend of mine."

"I can't tell you how grateful I am for your kindness, Alessa."

She offered Harper a warm smile and led her into the kitchen. "You're welcome to anything in the fridge or the pantry. Take whatever you want. Make whatever you want." She pointed out each room as they passed by it or through it. "The dining room.

The living room. My study is in there. That's my sitting room. This is your guest bedroom with your own private bath."

The four-poster bed had a fluffy white goose down comforter in the European fashion. A large multi-paned window offered a magnificent view of the Pacific. Something felt off about this whole situation. The old woman seemed awfully accommodating. Had Flynn sent her into a trap? Harper set her small backpack down on a dresser.

"You didn't bring much to wear, did you?"

Harper shook her head. "We had to hit the road in a hurry, so I didn't really have time to pack."

Alessandra looked her up and down. "I think we might wear the same size. Let me loan you some clothes."

"I couldn't."

"Nonsense. My late husband loved to buy me clothes, so I have more than I'll ever wear in this lifetime. Let me sort through what I have and bring you something appropriate."

"You are too kind."

"Would you like to take a shower?"

"I would love a shower."

"There are towels in the bathroom and a robe in the closet. In the meantime, I'll make us some lunch. Is there anything you don't eat?"

Harper smiled. "I eat pretty much everything."

"How does a frittata and a salad sound?"

"Scrumptious."

Alessandra bustled off, and Harper shut the door. She'd been wearing the same clothes for days and couldn't wait to get out of them. The large stall had three showerheads. Hot water hit her from top to bottom. Steam filled the stall, fogging the glass door. Sunlight streamed down from the skylight above, and Harper tilted her head back to see a clear blue Southern California sky.

For the first time in days, she let herself relax. She desperately needed a break from the constant tension and danger. The *Caudalie Thé des Vignes* shower gel relaxed her with the aroma of orange blossoms and white musk. The *Kérastase* hydrating shampoo worked up a thick lather. She let the hot water pummel every part of her, washing away her agitation and dread. After she completely rinsed, she let the hot water cascade off her for another ten minutes before finally shutting it down. She wasn't about to let her guard down completely, but she needed to let go. At least a little.

Harper rubbed herself dry with a white Turkish towel, wrapped another towel around her hair, slipped on the soft terrycloth bathrobe, and headed out to find Alessandra. She passed by the room Alessandra referred to as her study. An old movie poster caught her eye. She poked her head in to look around. Several vintage movie posters covered the walls. Many featured what looked like a much younger version of Alessandra. In that moment, Harper finally realized who was hosting her.

Alessandra Bianchi.

As a child in Russia, she watched many of her films on her parents' old black-and-white TV. Most were made in the 1960s and 70s. She even watched the TV series from the 1980s, where she played a Russian spy who had a rivalry and romance with an American CIA agent played by Bill Bixby. The posters decorating the walls were from many of Harper's favorite films.

Alessandra always played sexy, but never the dumb blonde. Her characters were strong and smart and not the least bit subservient. *Fun in Acapulco* with Elvis Presley. The Hammer horror film, *Revenge of the Vampire Killers. The Wrecking Crew* with Dean Martin. *Sodom and Gomorrah. In Like Flint.* A huge collection of books packed floor-to-ceiling bookshelves. A tarnished Golden Globe for Most Promising Newcomer sat on a shelf as a bookend. The name engraved in gold — *Alessandra Bianchi.*

"Are you ready for your frittata?"

Harper turned to see Alessa framed in the doorway. "Alessandra Bianchi! *You're Alessandra Bianchi!*"

"Alessandra Zimmel now. My days as a sex goddess are long gone. I'm now a mere mortal closing in on the ripe old age of eighty-one."

"You still look amazing."

"No, I don't, but thank you for saying so. Not that that should matter at my age. I have far more important concerns now."

"How do you know James?"

"It's a very long story, but suffice it to say, he saved me in more ways than one."

"Me too."

"He does love to rescue people. Especially fair damsels in distress."

"Did he tell you much about my situation?"

"Not a thing."

"Yet, you agreed to help him anyway."

"I trust him. And if he trusts you, I trust you too."

Harper's face heated up. She smiled to hide her shame. "You must think a lot of him."

"He's the best man I know. The best man I've ever known. Brave. Selfless. Gallant. Intrepid. I appeared in movies with many men who pretended to be heroes. James Flynn isn't pretending. He lives by a code and will do whatever it takes to protect those who cannot protect themselves. I know some claim he's delusional, but then who isn't? We all experience reality in our own way. I just happen to prefer Mr. Flynn's version."

Chapter Twenty

Yaroslav Yuryevich Dronov's big break came on Faktor, *the Russian version of* The X Factor. *He took the stage name Shaman and released the song that would be his first big hit. "Rise Up" celebrated a soldier who died defending Russia from its enemies. It dropped on the eve of the invasion of Ukraine. The single amassed forty-six million views on YouTube and was dedicated to the war heroes who perished in the Great Patriotic War. In 2022 he released* Ya Russky! (I am Russian!), *which featured a video of Shaman wearing a puffy white shirt and blond dreadlocks, walking through fields of wheat. He campaigned for Putin in 2023 and has been criticized in the West for being part of the Kremlin's propaganda machine. Russian artists who oppose the war have been blacklisted, prosecuted, or forced into exile. When Putin celebrated the annexation of four Ukrainian regions, Shaman shared the stage with him and sang the Russian national anthem.*

Bettina's windowless eight-by-eight-foot cell had a cold cement floor, a thin mattress on a rusty metal bunk, and a hole in the floor for peeing and pooping. From her research, she knew the FSB kept foreigners, political prisoners, and the mentally ill isolated in solitary. Her only roommates were cockroaches and lice. The guards brought her food three times a day. Some kind of bitter gruel for breakfast, thin potato soup for lunch, and a putrid meat sandwich made with moldy bread for dinner.

The guards turned on the flickering fluorescent light at 5 a.m. every morning as they banged their truncheons against the bars and shouted in Russian for the prisoners to wake up. *"Proznut'sya! Proznut'sya!"*

Next, they blasted the Russian national anthem just in case the screaming and banging didn't do the job. That was followed by a song from Putin's favorite pop star. Shaman. *Ya Russky!* 8 p.m. was lights out, and for the next nine hours she would lie in the dark, listening to the scuffling of cockroaches and the occasional rat that climbed out from the hole in the floor.

The 5 a.m. lights at least scared the roaches and rats back into the stinking hole. She could hear the prisoners in the other cells. One man constantly ranted and raved in Russian. Sometimes he'd scream day and night. Another prisoner had a horrible hacking cough. It sounded like he was dying, and maybe he was. They never let her out to exercise. Perhaps because she was female. Or a foreigner. They told her they'd be transferring her to a women's penal colony soon. The dreaded IK-14 prison for women in Mordovia. But since then, she hadn't heard another word about it.

Two weeks into her captivity, guards dragged a new prisoner inside and tossed them into the cell next to hers.

"Bloody hell! You're breaking my bloody arm! Get off me, you wanker!" The cell door clanged shut. He shouted at the guards through the food slot. "You can't do this! I need to talk to my embassy! You hear me? Hey!"

Bettina knelt next to the food slot and called out into the hall. "Are you a Brit?"

"Who are you?"

"I'm a reporter for *Rolling Stone*. Bettina O'Toole-Applebaum."

"American?"

"Yep."

"What are they accusing you of?"

"Spying. What about you?"

"They haven't told me a damn thing. They just grabbed me up off the street and pumped me up with some kind of sedative. The next thing I know, I'm in Russia."

"Where'd they snatch you up?"

"Solvang, California."

"Jesus."

"Right? I'm guessing we're somewhere in Siberia."

"Polar Owl Prison."

"*Polar Owl?*"

"I came here to interview Oleg Ivanov."

"Did you get the interview?"

"I did. And now I'm being charged under Article 276 of the Russian Criminal Code for espionage."

"Bastards."

"So, what's your name?"

"Duncan Dankworth."

■ ■ ■

Even with his heavy woolen peacoat, lambswool scarf, stocking cap, and fur-lined gloves, Kalishnik continued to freeze his balls off. He hated the cold. Especially damp cold. All his joints ached. Even his bones hurt. Standing in line to enter Polar Owl was torture. The frigid wind made his eyes water and his teeth hurt. He stamped his feet to stay warm, but that didn't do dick.

Luckily, he was here to see Ivanov and, once past the front gate, a young guard led him directly to Ivanov's cell block. The smell of piss and shit and sweat and fear began to fade, overtaken by the sweet aroma of some kind of delicious stew and freshly baked bread. Upon seeing Kalishnik, the massive prisoner guarding the large steel door at the end of the hall knocked three times. Instantly, the door opened.

Kalishnik entered to find Oleg Ivanov sitting at a butcher-block table, wearing a Fila tracksuit, and enjoying his midday meal. He insisted on speaking English. Partly to stay in practice. Partly to irritate Kalishnik. "You want some Irish stew?"

Kalishnik grunted and nodded. Another prisoner brought a bowl to the table.

Ivanov pointed at a copper mug. "Moscow Mule?"

Kalishnik grunted and nodded again, and a Moscow Mule materialized in front of him. Kalishnik took a big sip, let out a little burp, and then dug into the stew.

When both bowls were empty, cigars were lit and cognac poured. Ivanov pointed his stogie at Kalishnik. "So?"

"Has room been swept?"

"Three times a day. I told you before."

"So I can talk?"

"In English? Not very well, but that's okay. Just say what you came to say."

Kalishnik endured the crack and continued. "All arranged."

"When?"

"Two days."

"Time?"

Kalishnik wrote the number three in Cyrillic in the condensation on his Moscow Mule mug.

"I'll let those on the inside know."

"You'll take care of them?"

"It's already done."

Kalishnik stood. "When it happens, I find you. Keep you safe."

"I should hope so. That is what I pay you for, after all."

Chapter Twenty-One

Flynn sat in the dark and bounced around the back of Zangar's truck as they breezed past the border without an inspection. The boxes rattled and shifted ominously. Flynn flicked on the flashlight to make sure they weren't about to come down on him. He drank the bottled water and peed in the plastic urinal. The snacks consisted of *qurt*, the tiny, intensely salty dried cheese balls made from mare's milk, and *baursak*, the small, puffy pieces of fried Kazakh bread. A little over four hours after they left Petropavl, they came to a stop. Presumably in Omsk.

Muffled voices bickered outside the trailer. The plastic urinal was full and Flynn had to pee. He considered banging on the trailer wall, but hesitated since he didn't know who Zangar was quarreling with.

Finally, the roll-up door opened and light flooded the back of the trailer. Flynn squinted into the brightness.

Zangar clapped twice. "Come!"

Flynn grabbed his messenger bag and rolling suitcase and stumbled forward, maneuvering around the boxes, blinded by the light. Zangar took his luggage. Flynn took Zangar's arm. The Kazakh helped him down. Flynn kept his eyes shut tight as he slowly adjusted to the light. Eventually, Zangar came into focus along with two other guys twice Zangar's height. One had a shotgun. The other held a crowbar. The one with the shotgun did the talking. "All your money. Now."

The Makarov PM sat out of reach at the bottom of Flynn's messenger bag. He glanced at Zangar. "Are you renegotiating our agreed upon price?"

The Russian with the crowbar took Flynn's rolling suitcase and messenger bag as his comrade kept his shotgun trained on Flynn's face.

Flynn shook his head. "Takhir will be disappointed in you."

Zangar shrugged. "Not first time."

The shotgunner pointed the barrel at Flynn's wrist. "Watch. Wallet. All your money. Everything."

Flynn stood firm. "Do you have any idea who you're dealing with?"

"Stupid tourist," Zangar said.

"I'm an agent in His Majesty's Secret Service and I have a license to kill. If you continue on this foolish path, I will have no choice but to take your lives without compunction."

"Without what?"

"Compunction."

Zangar shook his head. "I don't know that word."

"It's like regret. Remorse. You know?"

"No."

"The point is this will end badly for you."

Zangar looked at the shotgunner and pointed at Flynn. "Shoot him."

Flynn held up his hands. "Wait, hold on. There's no reason this has to get ugly." Flynn slipped off his vintage Rolex and handed it to Zangar. "Now I'm reaching for my money belt." Flynn undid his money belt, held it out, and dropped it. As all three pairs of eyes looked down, Flynn pulled out Q's hypno-spray. He spritzed the Russian with the shotgun directly in the face. The guy screamed in pain and raised his gun. Flynn dove to the side, shouting, *"You are now under my control!"*

The shotgunner blasted the crates in the back of the trailer. Zangar cursed and pushed the shotgun down. Flynn rolled to his feet and spritzed the man with the crowbar. He too screamed as Flynn yelled, "*You now work for me!*"

Blinded, the Russian advanced on Flynn, angrily swinging his crowbar, missing by a good foot, and cracking the shotgunner's skull on the backswing. Flynn dove and rolled again. When he came up, he had the shotgun. Blind and furious, the crowbar guy swung and missed. Flynn cracked him in the bonce with the butt of the shotgun, knocking him flat. Out cold.

Zangar looked down at his two unconscious accomplices and then at Flynn, who now held the shotgun. Zangar thrust both his hands into the air. "Sorry."

"It's a little late for sorry, I would say."

"Please don't shoot me."

"I should, you know. And as I mentioned, I have a license to do so. But with great power comes great responsibility. I'm hopeful you learned a lesson today."

"I did. Very good lesson. Thank you!"

The truck sat parked in a secluded wooded area. A late-model LADA 4x4 Bronto squatted close by. Flynn pointed at the car. "Keys, please."

Zangar went through the pockets of his unconscious confederates and found a key ring. He tossed it to Flynn.

"Wallets too."

Zangar scrunched up his face. "Wallet?"

Flynn pulled out his own wallet and held it up as an example. "Wallet."

Zangar sighed and fished the wallets from his fallen comrades. He tossed them to Flynn, who pocketed both of them. Zangar didn't offer his own wallet and Flynn didn't push the issue. Instead, he turned and blasted out the sidewalls on three of the trailer tires. Zangar winced with each shot. The trailer immediately listed to one side.

Zangar shouted, "Why? Why you do? I already learn lesson!"

"I certainly hope so."

Flynn opened the back of the Lada 4x4 and instructed Zangar to load his luggage. Once he did, Flynn asked him one last question. "How far are we from Omsk?"

"Not far." He pointed to the gravel road behind them. "Take this to P-254. From there straight shot to *aeroport*."

"So, Zangar, tell me, what did you learn today?"

"Don't fuck with Mr. Flynn."

■ ■ ■

Flynn found P-254 and followed the signs to the airport. He couldn't make heads or tails of the Cyrillic, but the silhouette of an airplane was a dead giveaway. He left the Lada 4x4 in the tiny airport's outdoor lot and bought a ticket to Salekhard on Yamal Airlines. The plane, a Russian-made Sukhoi Superjet 100, had a troubling history of fiery crashes. But, considering the circumstances, Flynn considered the flight an acceptable risk.

The plane accommodated seventy-five passengers, but just barely. Leg room was nonexistent and everyone sat elbow to elbow. Flynn could find no charging outlet or in-flight entertainment other than a two-year-old Russian magazine. The huge man next to Flynn smelled of boiled cabbage and body odor. That combined with the overall aroma of diesel fuel and cigarettes created a distinctly disgusting olfactory ambiance. Dinner, on the other hand, was surprisingly edible. Some kind of meat with pasta and two pieces of rye bread.

On the way, they flew through a storm that tossed the plane to and fro. The turbulence inspired the large man next to Flynn to spew into his airsickness bag. Lightning flashed outside the aircraft as it dipped and bobbed and dropped alarmingly. The nauseous man next to Flynn grabbed him by the wrist on a downdraft and continued to hold on tight.

Flynn had the window seat. Below, endless snow-covered vast expanses of nothingness. No towns. No roads. No cars. Just frozen rivers, icy lakes, and snow-topped trees. If they had to make an emergency landing, they'd all freeze to death in a matter of minutes.

One hour later, they landed in Salekhard. Flynn still felt queasy, but was grateful to have avoided either dying in a fiery crash or freezing to death.

Salekhard Airport was barebones, but reasonably modern, and even smaller than the airport in Omsk. It took almost half an hour for the checked luggage to arrive.

No one stood at the rental car counter. Flynn walked up to various airport employees and pointed to the empty rental car kiosk, but they either ignored him or shook their heads in disgust. After waiting for over an hour, a sour young woman finally arrived behind the counter.

Flynn bolted to his feet and accosted her before she could leave again. "I'd like to rent a car!"

She stared at him. Confused.

"Car. I'd like to rent one."

More staring. No answering. "Do you speak English?"

"English?"

"Yes!"

She shook her head. "No English."

Flynn mimed driving a car. Finally, the pantomime connected and she pushed a bunch of paperwork in Russian Cyrillic to Flynn. She pointed at various lines in the contract and, even though he couldn't read a damn thing, signed or initialed every line. He had no idea what the car might be or cost, but didn't really care at this point. She laid a map on the counter and a set of car keys before holding up a credit card reader. Flynn pulled out a wallet belonging to one of the fallen Russians, found an *МИР* credit card, and handed it over. She swiped the card without even asking for ID, handed it back, and pointed to the door.

"What are you trying to tell me?"

She picked the keys off the counter, thrust them in Flynn's direction, and pointed at the door again.

He nodded, grabbed the keys, map and his luggage, and headed for the door. A sign with a logo similar to the rental car company identified the correct car park. The key didn't come with a fob, so Flynn had to try every door lock in the lot before he found his rental, a Lada Granta. Flynn referred to the rental car company map, but that too was in Cyrillic and he couldn't make heads or tails of it. Google Translate solved that problem, but to make his drive a little easier he opened Google Maps and typed in *Kharp*.

Chapter Twenty-Two

"Unbelievably horrible place. Awful place. Awful weather, buildings, scenery, food, roads, and ambience. Nothing to see or do. One awful café. Crummy old church. Terrible."
– Actual review on TripAdvisor for the Sob Hotel in Kharp.

The one-hour drive took over two hours as ice and snow covered the road to Kharp. Flynn didn't pass a single car, but spotted an abandoned snowplow stranded in a ditch by the side of the road. He pined for a Subaru with all-wheel drive and studded snow tires. His rented Lada Granta constantly fishtailed on the ice. He passed the tiny town of Labytnangi, home to the Arctic Ecological Research Station. This time of year, the sun never rose above the horizon and even then only appeared for four hours. Once it set, absolute darkness swallowed everything.

His car's headlights lit the two-lane highway ahead and the mounds of snow plowed to either side of the road. An endless tunnel through the icy dark. The heater in his rented vehicle barely kept out the cold. If Flynn were to break down or run out of gas, he'd freeze to death before help would arrive. Gloom and foreboding rode with him all the way to Kharp, a tiny town on the far edge of the far north, even gloomier and more depressing than the endless frozen tundra surrounding it.

Reviews on TripAdvisor weren't uniformly horrible. People who visited in the spring and summer commented on the natural beauty of the area. The surrounding mountains. The flora and fauna. Rafters loved running the River Sob, the Mississippi of Siberia.

But on this day in January, the ramshackle town, covered in ice and dirty snow, projected an air of desperation and melancholy. The crumbling and decrepit buildings, constructed from whatever leftover materials the builders could scrounge, appeared close to collapse. He knew much of the labor came from the prisoners in the nearby gulags.

The fading sign of a shuttered grocery store blew and creaked in the icy wind. The blocks of decaying apartment buildings likely housed the prison guards. Citizens bundled in heavy winter coats trudged the dark, snowy sidewalks. A sprawling, whitewashed Russian Orthodox church with a golden onion dome stood in stark, opulent contrast to the rest of the rundown town.

Flynn quickly found Hotel Kharp. Named after the town and not the complaints most guests made when they first saw the hotel. The long square rectangle with rusty metal siding had a blue metal roof covered in snow. A tiny white fence in front sheltered a bed of dead weeds. The place looked more like a bunkhouse or a barracks than a tourist hotel. Flynn found an open spot in the gravel parking lot, unloaded his luggage, and lugged his rolling suitcase up the pitted stairs and through the door into the minuscule lobby area.

The sullen, middle-aged desk clerk sat in a tiny kiosk watching an ancient and equally tiny black-and-white TV. He sighed at the interruption and leveled his gaze at Flynn.

Flynn smiled. "Do you speak English?"

He shrugged and wobbled his hand. "Not too much."

Flynn forged ahead anyway. "I'd like a room."

"No."

"No what?"

"No rooms."

"You're all booked up?"

"Fifteen rooms. All full."

"Can you recommend another hotel in town?"

"No."

"Can you point me to one you don't recommend?"

"No."

"There are other hotels in town, though, right?"

"No."

"So, this is the only hotel in all of Kharp?"

"Da."

"Well, this is awkward," Flynn said with a smile. The man went back to looking at his TV. Flynn pressed on. "Can you recommend the closest hotel in the vicinity?"

"Hotel Arktika in Labytnangi."

"I just came from Labytnangi."

"So you know way."

"I'd rather stay here."

"No room here."

Flynn opened his money belt, counted out ten thousand rubles, and laid them on the counter. "What if I were to give you 10,000 rubles?"

"I would like that."

"Would I have a room?"

"No."

"Well, I can't very well sleep outside."

"No."

"What do you suggest I do, then?"

The man pointed at the door. "Go."

Flynn would have to drive all the way back to Labytnangi. Maybe that was for the best. He turned around to find a squat, buxom woman in late middle age. She had dyed bright blonde hair and grinned at him with an almost full set of teeth. The few that were missing did not dim her enthusiastic smile.

"You American?"

With the current hard feelings between the Kremlin and Washington, Flynn opted to say he was from somewhere else. "Canadian."

"Like William Shatner?"

"Exactly."

"You need room?"

"I do indeed."

"Sleep with me."

"That's very kind of you, and I do appreciate the offer, but I couldn't impose on you like that."

"For ten thousand rubles?"

Flynn was taken aback. "You'll pay me ten thousand rubles?"

"No, you'll pay *me* ten thousand rubles."

"Ah, I see."

"You drive back to Labytnangi, might not be room."

"That's a possibility."

"I have reservation. Two beds. I sleep. You sleep. No hanky-panky."

"So I would have my own bed?"

"I'm married woman. Here to visit husband in prison."

"What's your name?"

"Polina. You?"

"James."

She put out her hand. Flynn went to shake, and she said, "Ten thousand rubles."

Flynn paid her, and she took her sweet time counting the money before tucking it inside her cavernous cleavage. She then stood belly up to the counter and slapped her hand on it, startling the desk clerk. She said something to him in Russian and he shook his head. She said it again, only much louder and he sighed and handed her an extra key, which she gave to Flynn. "Follow me," she said.

Flynn rolled his suitcase down the narrow hallway to Polina's room. The two twin beds were topped with thin gray bedspreads and small mismatched pillows. A square wooden armoire stood against one wall. On the opposite wall, a flatscreen TV hung crookedly. A mass of wires snaked down the wall and disappeared behind a cheap wooden desk.

Polina pointed at the bed closest to the window. "You take?"

"Okay."

"You hungry?"

"I could eat. Is there a restaurant here at the hotel?"

"No. Outside. Come. You pay."

Polina moved quickly for someone her size. Flynn followed, trudging after her through the snow. They arrived at a plain brick building. IPonka Sushi served Russian-style sushi, pizza, Chinese food, and a few traditional Russian specialties. The place was surprisingly busy and loud and humid and warm with all the body heat. Flynn took off his heavy jacket. Polina ordered for both of them. Cheese and sausage pizza, chicken rolls, piroshki, boiled beef, and borscht topped with a dollop of sour cream.

They washed it down with *Baltika* beer and shots of *Russkaya* pepper vodka. Polina drank three beers and three shots for each one Flynn pounded down, and what Flynn didn't eat, Polina did. He never saw a woman eat with such energy and relish. Flynn was stuffed, but figured he'd need the fuel to power him forward in this harsh climate. For all she drank, Polina didn't seem drunk. At least, not at first. When it finally hit her, it hit her all at once. She grinned crookedly, her eyes blurry and squinty, mumbling in Russian and then laughing uproariously. She grew louder and louder and then instantly quieter as she laid her head on the last piece of pizza and began to snore.

The waitress brought the check. Flynn paid. It took some time to rouse Polina, but once awake, drunk as she was, standing or walking proved to be a near impossibility. Flynn helped her up and out of the restaurant and down the short flight of stairs. When she lost her balance and Flynn couldn't hold on to her, she hit the ground face down. Luckily, she landed in some snow, so she didn't break her nose. Flynn struggled to get her up and walking again. It took some effort to get her back to the hotel.

She staggered to her bed and landed half in, half out. Flynn didn't undress her, but wrapped the bedspread around her the best he could. Then Flynn readied himself for bed and took a tepid shower. Polina's snores reverberated through the bathroom door, like the rhythmic rumbling of a freight train punctuated by the occasional sharp, grinding roar of a chainsaw tearing into a log.

Flynn climbed into bed and held the pillow over his head to drown Polina out. He eventually drifted off to sleep, but awakened sometime later in the night to find Polina pressed up against his back, her stubby arms encircling his torso as she aggressively spooned with him. Still snoring, the cacophonous rumbling was now inches from his ear. He tried to extricate himself, but her hold on him was like a vise grip. He reached back and pinched her nose shut until she finally awakened with a start. Flynn used the distraction to slip out of his bed and into hers. When he finally awoke three hours later, she was back in her own bed, squished against Flynn, snoring to beat the band, her stubby arms wrapped around him once again.

He plucked up one of her pinky fingers and twisted it back until she finally grunted and released him. He rolled out of bed and looked back to see if she was angry and awake. She wasn't. In fact, within seconds, the freight started rolling and the chainsaw started sawing.

Flynn wasn't hungry after the eclectic feast the previous night, but he desperately needed caffeine. He quickly dressed and made his way to the hotel breakfast room. The buffet had already been taken away and there was no coffee. Only tea. Flynn despised tea, but made the sacrifice for a piddling jolt of caffeine. He sat at the table closest to the window and used a burner he bought at Astana Airport to call Alessandra Bianchi. 10:00 a.m. in Kazakhstan was 10:00 p.m. in Los Angeles.

Alessandra answered on the second ring. "Hello?"

"Alessa?"

She replied with a smile in her voice. "James?"

"Hello, beautiful."

"I was hoping you might call."

"Did Harper get there okay?"

"She did indeed. We just had dinner, and she's out on the patio, enjoying a cocktail."

"Thank you so much for taking her in."

"It's my pleasure."

"Would it be all right if I had a word with her?"

"Only if you promise me something."

"Anything."

"Promise me you'll make it back here."

"Isn't that a given?"

"I need to see you here in person so I can make you your favorite."

"Spaghetti Carbonara à la Bianchi?"

"That's right. I'm going to Gelson's today to buy the ingredients, so don't disappoint me."

"I promise I will be there as soon as I can."

"I'm going to hold you to that."

He heard Alessandra open her French doors and step out onto her patio. Ocean waves crashed in the distance.

"James is calling."

Some bumping noises as Alessa handed the phone over to Harper. "James?"

"I just wanted to make sure you got there safely."

"Why didn't you tell me I'd be staying with a movie star? How the hell do you know Alessandra Bianchi?"

"It's a long story, and I'll tell you the tale over a leisurely dinner when I get there."

"Are you in Kharp?"

"I am. Do you have a date and time?"

"Tonight. 3:00 a.m."

"Good." He peered through the frosted window. "The less time I have to spend in this unpleasant place, the better."

"You be careful."

"Always. Enjoy Malibu. Hopefully, I'll see you there soon."

"Not hopefully. Definitely. You are an amazing human being and I am looking forward to getting to know you much, much better."

"Good night, Harper."

"Good night, James."

Flynn clicked off. He felt a glimmer of guilt. Though at this point he wasn't sure if he was lying more to himself than to her.

He took a sip of that miserable tea and glanced up at a terrifying sight.

Kalishnik.

He passed by the door to the guest kitchen without bothering to look in. Flynn's heart stopped for a moment. He crept to the door and peeked outside. Kalishnik clomped towards the front desk. Flynn silently berated himself. *Of course, Kalishnik's staying here. It's the only bloody hotel in town.* He should have been more careful.

Kalishnik's heavy footsteps returned from the lobby. Flynn could duck back into the kitchen, but what if that was where Kalishnik was headed? He turned to walk the other way as two incredibly massive individuals exited a room three doors up. *Are they part of Kalishnik's crew?* No wonder the hotel was completely booked. The place was probably crawling with ex-Spetsnaz commandos. Flynn had no weapon. His Makarov still sat in his messenger bag. He'd have to stand and fight, and the last time he went one-on-one with Kalishnik, the former Olympic boxer kicked his arse.

A door opened nearby and a hand grabbed Flynn by the collar. Before he knew what was happening, he was wrenched inside. *Another commando?* He turned to fight. His assailant flipped him into the air. Flynn landed hard on the wooden floor as his attacker quietly shut the door. He tried to get up, but his attacker shoved him back down with a foot on his chest.

Caitlyn Valentine loomed over him and held her finger to her lips.

Flynn was dumbfounded. "Caitlyn?"

Chapter Twenty-Three

Caitlyn peered through the peephole. Kalishnik clomped past, shouting something in Russian to his burly cohorts. She glanced back to Flynn pulling himself to his feet, painfully rubbing the back of his head. "Sorry if I was a little rough."

"No apologies necessary. Kalishnik would have been a lot rougher."

"No doubt."

"Did you have a change of heart? Are you here to help me free Bettina?"

"I'm here to bring you home."

"Not until I free Bettina. Kalishnik and his team are breaking Ivanov out tonight. At 3 a.m. Though, technically, I guess that's actually tomorrow."

"But you don't know *how* he's breaking Ivanov out."

"We know Ivanov started as a software engineer. Some believe his team created *Stuxnet,* that cyberworm used by ransomware gangs to take over and control everything from electrical grids to nuclear power plants. I'm sure he's still in contact with his network of digital extortionists. I have no doubt the software is even more sophisticated now. I'm guessing he plans to take control of the prison. Shut down the security cameras, turn off the lights, and unlock all the doors. Anything and everything to create chaos."

"But he still has to breach the facility," Caitlyn pointed out.

"That's what Kalishnik and his team are for."

"But how? Where?"

"That's what we need to figure out."

"What *we*? There's no *we*!"

"No *we*? Why come all this way if you don't intend to help me?"

"I do want to help you. I want to save you from getting your head blown off. Penal Colony 18 is a supermax. There are hundreds of elite FSIN guards armed with assault rifles, combat shotguns, and sniper rifles. Unless Kalishnik is bringing an army, this is going to be a very one-sided fight."

"He doesn't have to bring an army. He just has to set one free."

"We can't wade into the middle of a prison riot. If we try to pull Bettina out, all we'll do is put her in harm's way. She's safer staying put."

"Is she really?"

"I can't let you do this."

"And I can't let you stop me."

Caitlyn put her arms around Flynn and pulled him close. "I'm sorry."

"For what?"

Caitlyn slipped heavy-duty zip tie handcuffs around his wrists and pushed him back on the bed. He fell hard and banged his head on the wall. She quickly fastened zip tie restraints around his ankles as well, binding his legs together.

Flynn wriggled and struggled. "What did you do? What are you doing?"

"I'm sorry."

He fought to get himself to his feet and teetered for a second before toppling over and slamming into the floor. "You have to let me go!"

"I will. Tomorrow morning."

"Caitlyn! CAITLYN!"

She ripped off a length of gaffer tape and covered Flynn's mouth with it. He continued to shout, but the muffled words were unintelligible. Flynn bucked and wriggled and struggled to free himself. He stared with hurt and angry eyes.

Caitlyn knelt next to him and stroked his forehead. "I'm so sorry."

. . .

Flynn knew this was no spur-of-the-moment decision. Caitlyn traveled to Kharp fully intending to truss him up and hold him prisoner until after the escape attempt. He knew she only wanted to protect him, but that didn't lessen his fury.

Caitlyn hauled him up onto her bed and lay him sideways, facing the wall. She obviously didn't want to deal with his angry glare. When did she lose faith in him? She used to trust him. Used to believe in him. At least, he always assumed she did. She hadn't been the same since Kalishnik shot her in the head. She seemed fearful now. More fragile. More vulnerable. Maybe that same vulnerability carried over to Flynn. She worried more about him now than she ever had. She obviously cared, but this constant worry and anxiety did more harm than good.

Flynn rolled over to face her. "Ah bib ba bib bib."

By the blank look on her face, it was clear she couldn't understand him. Not with the gaffer tape firmly affixed to his mouth. He said it again more insistently, and she reached down and ripped the tape off, taking some of the skin with it.

"Ow."

"What?"

"I need to piddle."

"Bullshit."

"Do you want me to wet the bed?"

She sighed and unhooked the zip ties holding Flynn's ankles. She pulled him to his feet and led him into the bathroom. Standing over the toilet, he looked over his shoulder. "Can you undo my hands too?"

"No way." She unzipped him, fished around his pants for his John Thomas and aimed it at the toilet. Flynn found the entire episode both humiliating and somewhat titillating. After stuffing his willy back into his trousers, she re-fastened his fly, led him back to the bed, zip tied his ankles, and sat him on the edge.

"Knowing we might be here awhile, I picked up some food in the weird little market. You want a sandwich?"

"Sure."

She fed Flynn a salami sandwich on black bread and offered him sips from a bottle of *Buratino* lemonade.

Flynn swallowed a bite of food. "Can I ask you a question?"

She lowered the sandwich. "Of course."

"If we aren't going to free Bettina, perhaps we should warn the Russian authorities that Ivanov is planning a prison break. If that sociopath gets free, he could create all kinds of mayhem and havoc."

"They'll ask me for the source of the intel. If I tell them it's you, they'll think I'm crazy. No one's ever escaped from a Russian supermax."

"As far as we know."

She wiped his face with a napkin. "Are you done with lunch?"

Flynn motioned to the lemonade with his head. She held the straw up to his lips. After Flynn drained the last of the beverage, Caitlyn ripped off another piece of gaffer tape and slapped it on his gob.

Hours dragged by. Caitlyn read and tried to ignore him. After a few more bathroom breaks and another two sandwiches, Caitlyn readied herself for bed. Flynn knew he just needed to bide his time. He had watched countless YouTube videos on how to escape from handcuffs, gaffer tape, and zip ties. Some proved to be complete bollocks, but others he had tried in the field, and a few of them even worked. He had a technique he wanted to try, but he had to wait for Caitlyn to fall asleep.

More hours passed, and Caitlyn finally flicked off the light. She crept closer to him and whispered in his ear. "Tomorrow this will all be over and we can go home."

"Please don't do this."

She kissed him on the cheek. "Get some sleep, okay?"

Fifteen minutes later, Caitlyn's breathing pattern changed, indicating she had finally fallen asleep. Flynn waited for her breathing to get quicker and more erratic. An indicator of REM sleep. Still lying on his side, he pulled up his knees and reached for his shoes. He undid one shoelace, reached back between his legs, and threaded it over the zip tie securing his arms. He held on to one end and quietly pumped his legs, pulling the shoelace back and forth to create friction. The bed had a tiny squeak. He worried he'd wake her, but kept the zip tie taut and sawed away.

Finally, it broke apart. He eased himself up on the edge of the bed, undid the zip tie that held his ankles together, and crept across the room to her duffel bag. He found the additional zip ties, but rooting through the bag awakened her.

"Flynn?"

He flipped her over and quickly zip tied her wrists and ankles. She bucked and struggled and Flynn wrapped gaffer tape over the zip ties to hold her even more securely.

"What the hell are you-"

He taped her mouth shut before taping her to the bed so she couldn't move at all. He then flicked on the overhead light, blinding her as she fought to escape.

Tears filled Caitlyn's eyes. Flynn felt terrible about leaving her like this, but he had to save Bettina from that awful place.

Flynn kissed her on the cheek. "I do apologize, but I'll be back before you know it."

He returned to his room to find Polina sawing logs. He put on his snow boots, heavy black winter jacket, gloves, and scarf, and dropped the Makarov into his pocket. Flynn checked his Rolex. It was 2:17 a.m.

Chapter Twenty-Four

"Everything is on such a vast scale that it makes one feel small, insignificant. The weather is cold and dry, with frost like needles of steel; the trees are small and scattered, the earth is stony, and one is inclined to wonder if it is the same sun that shines on Siberia as on the rest of the world." —From Notes of the House of the Dead by Dostoevsky

The intense cold hit Flynn like a frozen sledgehammer. It had to be twenty degrees below zero. Even with his heavy jacket, the biting chill penetrated to his bones. A wool scarf covered most of his face, but any exposed skin burned and stung. His eyes watered, his tears froze to his face, and he had a hard time catching his breath. How long could someone survive in these temperatures? If most of the liberated prisoners tried to flee, how far would they get before they froze to death?

The snow crunched and squeaked beneath his feet. *Hard to be stealthy with all that crunching going on.* Small pools of light surrounded each streetlight, so Flynn stayed in the shadows as he made his way toward the prison.

High concrete walls topped with concertina wire surrounded the grounds. Guard towers with high-intensity spotlights, machine gun emplacements, and snipers loomed above. The gulag seemed unassailable. Flynn hid behind some shrubbery and waited for something to happen. He stomped his feet and rubbed his arms to generate some internal body heat. *Harper had better be right about the day and time.* His arms and legs grew numb, and he wasn't sure how much longer he could stand the bitter cold.

And then something strange happened.

All the lights illuminating Polar Owl blinked off for a few seconds. Then they came back on and blinked off again. The silhouettes in the guard tower bustled about frantically while the lights flickered like a failing fluorescent bulb, and then went black and stayed black.

A distant whirring sound broke the silence. It grew in volume to a deep, resonant rumble. Flynn recognized the rhythmic beat of a helicopter rotor. He turned toward the incoming roar but saw no navigation lights. The reverberation of the blades grew louder and sharper as the whop-whop-whop punched the air with each rotation. A brief, blinding light flashed. Flynn squinted as the bird launched two missiles. He tracked the fiery exhaust as they shot across the dark sky, zipping over his head. Flynn turned to run as they collided with the high concrete wall. The shock wave blasted him off his feet. He landed face down in the snow. A wave of intense heat washed over him. Flynn pushed himself upright and turned. The wall crumbled, blown wide open. One of the guard towers crashed down. A 30mm autocannon shredded the other towers as the attack chopper circled the compound.

Flynn's ears rang with the aftermath of the explosion, so he didn't hear the four black Sentinel Armored Rescue vehicles trundle to a stop just outside the breach. But he saw them in the moonlight. Black-suited commandos in tactical vests, helmets, and night-vision goggles poured from the vehicles.

Kalishnik likely led the charge.

The helicopter hovered right above him. The beat of the blades and the rush of wind caused the cold to bite even harder. The autocannon continued to thunder. The rotor wash kicked up snow as the Russian-made Night Hunter helicopter touched down. Two dozen commandos entered the breach in the wall.

. . .

A powerful explosion shook Bettina awake. She hurried to her cell door to call to Dankworth, and was shocked to discover him standing in the corridor. He pulled open her cell and shouted, "They unlocked the doors!"

"Who?"

"Who the bloody hell knows?"

"What was that boom?"

"I don't know, but it was a big one."

The other prisoners in solitary pushed past them, hurrying down the corridor. Someone had set them free. Bettina had an idea who. She followed the other prisoners. Dankworth trailed after and shouted, "Maybe we'd be safer inside our cells."

"Are you kidding me?"

"We don't know what's out there!"

"You'd rather stay here and wait for them to lock us up again?"

"That might be the better course of action."

"We have to find out what's happening!" Bettina hurried forward, leaving Dankworth behind.

He picked up his pace and shouted, "Do we? *Really?*"

As they made their way out of the solitary cell block and into the outside exercise area, the shouting, screaming, and gunfire intensified. Bettina stopped to decide which way to go. Dankworth caught up with her, grabbing her arm, out of breath. "I really think we should go back!"

Prisoners clashed with jailers, fighting with anything they could get their hands on. A few grabbed assault weapons from fallen guards. Bettina hit the snow as bullets whizzed overhead and ricocheted off the walls. *Dankworth isn't wrong. Even if we do escape, where would we go?* Dressed as they were, they wouldn't survive the cold for more than a half an hour.

．．．

The four commandos guarding the helicopter and the armored rescue vehicles focused on the breach in the prison wall. That was where they expected the threat to come from. The shouts and gunfire inside were cacophonous and covered Flynn's approach. He snuck up behind a guard and took him down with a chokehold, then stripped him of his helmet, body armor, night-vision goggles, and weapons. Flynn took out each guard in succession. The fourth saw Flynn dispatch the third. Flynn shot him in the knee before he could raise his weapon. Down he went. Flynn quickly disarmed him, sat on top of him, and choked him into unconsciousness with an armbar.

Flynn scrambled to his feet as someone shouted something to him in Russian. He spun around. The helicopter pilot aimed a pistol at his head. "*Do svidaniya, pindosy!*"

A gunshot rang out. The pilot staggered and fell face down in the snow.

A furious Caitlyn ran towards him.

Flynn smiled at her resourcefulness. "How'd you get free?"

She punched him in the jaw, knocking him flat on his ass. "I keep a knife in a sheath on my ankle, you idiot!"

Flynn rubbed his jaw. "Well, thank goodness you do."

Caitlyn pulled Flynn to his feet, and he immediately swept hers out from under her. As Caitlyn crashed to the ground, Flynn hurried through the breach in the wall. She shouted after him. "Flynn! *FLYNN!*"

Bedlam reigned inside. The guards were no match for the night-vision-wearing commandos. The chopper had taken out all the guard towers, and now that the prisoners ran free, they quickly overwhelmed their tormentors and torturers.

He had to find Bettina. *But how?* Flynn shouted over the screaming mob. "Bettina! *Bettina!*"

The mob of prisoners pushed past him to escape, knocking him off his feet, and nearly stomping him into the icy ground. He fought to get upright and regain his footing, but the flood of bodies kept pushing him back.

A faint female shriek pierced the air. *Bettina?* Flynn called to her. "Bettina! *Bettina!*" He listened hard, hoping to hear her over all the clamor and chaos. Finally, she cried out again.

Flynn followed her screams into one of the barracks. He shoved his way forward, past the mob of cheering, laughing prisoners, and found her on the cold floor. Two prisoners held her down, while a third struggled to pull down her pants. She kicked and bucked as a beaten and bloody Dankworth, held back by two hulking brutes, fought to free himself and shouted, "Let her go! *You let her go!*"

Flynn flipped up his night-vision goggles and tossed a flashbang into the far corner of the room. He turned away, squeezing his eyes shut and plugging his ears. The grenade detonated. A blinding flash and deafening blast disoriented and momentarily staggered him. Flynn fought the nausea as he pushed through the blinded and stupefied prisoners.

He took hold of Bettina's hand and pulled her to her feet. Tears streaked her dirty face. Her lower lip trembled as she pulled up her torn pants. Dankworth stumbled about, deaf and blinded by the flashbang.

Flynn grabbed him by the arm and Dankworth tried to fight him off. "It's me! It's Flynn! It's *Flynn!*"

Recognition dawned on Dankworth's face and he went limp. "I tried to stop them. I tried to help her."

Flynn dropped a smoke grenade and dragged them both across the compound.

When the effects of the flashbang faded, it finally dawned on Bettina who had rescued her. "Flynn?"

"We need to hurry!"

"Hold it." Dankworth bent forward and blew chunks.

Flynn dragged him along anyway and dropped another smoke grenade to obscure their escape. The thick white smoke only added to the pandemonium in the courtyard. Prisoners stampeded to freedom through the open gates. Some fled in prison buses. Others escaped on foot. Flynn directed Bettina and Dankworth in a different direction.

"We're going the wrong way!" Dankworth screamed. "Where the hell are you taking us?"

"To freedom!" Flynn shouted.

When they approached the breach in the wall, Flynn noticed five of the night-vision-wearing commandos escorting Ivanov in the same direction. The biggest of the commandos turned to look directly at them.

Kalishnik.

He aimed his finger at Flynn and shouted something in Russian. Flynn raised his weapon as they all raised theirs. Four against one. Caitlyn was right. Flynn might have just led Bettina to her doom.

With a thunderous growl, a Sentinel Armored Rescue vehicle cleared the breach and crashed into Kalishnik and his three commandos, sending them flying.

Caitlyn shouted from the driver's side window. "Come on! *Come on!*" As the commandos tried to stand, she backed over two of them and knocked down Kalishnik again. "*You coming or what?*"

Flynn, Bettina, and Dankworth hurried inside the vehicle. Kalishnik, now on his knees, opened fire. But the Sentinel's bulletproof glass and heavy-duty armor deflected every shot. Caitlyn floored it in reverse and slammed into him for a third time. The tires spun on the ice and snow until the Sentinel found purchase and propelled them through the gap in the wall.

Bullets pinged off the ballistic glass armor. Flynn looked back. Kalishnik stumbled after them, firing wildly.

Dankworth couldn't believe it. "That's one determined wanker!"

"You have no idea." Flynn peered out the window. Flames consumed the other three Sentinels as well as the helicopter. Caitlyn was never one to take half-measures. The fuel tank on the helicopter exploded, and the shockwave rocked the Sentinel.

Flynn rested his hand on Caitlyn's shoulder. "I suppose I should thank you."

"Don't mention it."

"You really went above and beyond."

"No, really. Don't mention it. *Ever again.*"

Chapter Twenty-Five

The hair-raising ride to Salekhard took forty-five minutes on a snow-swept two-lane highway covered with patches of black ice. Because the all-wheel-drive Sentinel ARV had massive steel-studded snow tires, they only slid off the road twice. Flynn checked behind to make sure they weren't being followed and scanned the skies for attack helicopters. Ten minutes outside of Salekhard, he spotted something in the twilight sky through his night-vision goggles. A drone moving at high speed. Probably sent by someone on Kalishnik's team to blow them off the road.

Flynn climbed up into the turret behind the PKM machine gun. Even with the scarf wrapped around his head, the icy wind bit into his skin. Having studied drones extensively on YouTube, Flynn identified the IAI Mini HARPY; a kamikaze drone that detonates on impact. It can fly as fast as 148 kilometers per hour. Flynn had trouble zeroing in on it. Fifty yards out, he finally made contact. The drone exploded. Flynn felt the heat of the fiery blast lighting up the night.

. . .

A chartered jet waited for them on a freshly plowed runway at Salekhard Airport. Flynn and the others climbed aboard. Within minutes, the Hawker 900XP was in the air. The bedraggled group arrived at Helsinki-Vantaa Airport in Finland five hours later. Caitlyn had arranged for a hotel as well. Knowing Flynn's predilection for luxury accommodations, she booked them all rooms at the Radisson Blu Plaza Hotel.

Flynn and Caitlyn's room had two twin beds. She was clearly still upset with him. Flynn couldn't blame her, tying her up the way he did. But if he hadn't, Bettina wouldn't be alive. Caitlyn had to see that. Even though he knew she would never admit it. Caitlyn had a stubborn streak a mile wide.

Without a word, she headed to the bathroom to shower first. Flynn offered to join her. She just glared at him. Fifteen minutes later, she came out wearing a white terrycloth robe, her filthy clothes stuffed in a hotel laundry bag. Flynn showered alone and let the hot water pummel away the Siberian cold that still chilled him to his bones. He skipped his usual cold rinse and wrapped himself in a similar robe.

They left Kharp in too much of a hurry to retrieve their luggage, so Caitlyn sent out their muddied and bloodied clothes to be laundered.

Flynn slept in the altogether and awoke to find Caitlyn fully dressed, looming over him. "They're waiting for us down in the Bistro."

"Who?"

"Bettina and Dankworth. I laid your clothes at the foot of the bed."

"Already back from the laundry?"

"I'll meet you downstairs."

"Are you still peeved with me?"

"Peeved? No. I'm fucking furious." She left and slammed the door.

Flynn winced as he climbed from the bed.

●　　■　　●

Flynn found the lot of them at a table in Bistro Vilho. Breakfast was buffet-style, and Flynn was famished. He went through the line and filled his plate with black bread, smoked salmon, ham, a variety of cheeses, and scrambled eggs. He joined their table to find a double espresso waiting.

Bettina immediately reached out and put her hand on Flynn's. "I ordered you a coffee. I know how much you hate tea."

"Thank you."

"No, *thank you*. Without your help, we never would have made it out of there alive."

"Without *Caitlyn's* help, you mean. She's the one who saved the day."

Caitlyn took a bite of toast and grumbled something unintelligible.

Duncan Dankworth stared at his bowl of muesli and spoke without looking up. "I do appreciate what you both did."

Flynn sipped his espresso. "I'm sure you'd do the same for me."

Dankworth glanced briefly at Bettina and then Flynn. "I tried to stop them from taking her, but there were so many. Too many."

"I could see that." Flynn put down his cup. "But you fought with ferocity."

"And failed to protect her."

"Not for lack of trying. You put yourself in harm's way and that took great courage."

Dankworth reacted to the compliment by blushing and looking back down at his muesli. "I tried."

"We all fought like hell and lived to tell the tale. Thanks to Caitlyn."

"I was never there," Caitlyn said.

"Of course you were. You saved the day," Dankworth insisted.

"Flynn saved the day. All I did was charter a flight and get your sorry asses out of Russia."

Dankworth shook his head. "We all saw what you did."

"We didn't see a damn thing and that's what we have to testify to," Bettina explained. "Caitlyn needs plausible deniability."

"Ah, I see," Dankworth replied. "*Of course.* As ex-CIA, you can't be seen participating in that kind of paramilitary adventure."

"And this is the last we'll talk of it," Caitlyn said.

Dankworth nodded. "Of course."

"When we're finished here, we have an appointment at the American embassy." Caitlyn glanced at Dankworth. "MI6 will be represented there as well."

Flynn finished his coffee. "If that's the next thing on our agenda, I'm going to need another double espresso. And perhaps something stronger."

■ ■ ■

The American Embassy in Helsinki resided in the Kaivopuisto district with nine other embassies. The neighborhood included the beautiful, sprawling green space known as Kaivopuisto Park. Crowded with runners, walkers, bench sitters, and picnickers, it butted right up against the Gulf of Finland.

Caitlyn had been to Helsinki once before while working as a senior analyst at Accenture. In truth, that high-powered career served only as her cover story. Her greater allegiance was to the CIA, who'd recruited her out of Stanford. Her actual job was to investigate money laundering by international drug dealers and terrorist organizations.

The embassy itself, built in the 1950s, was protected by high stone and wrought-iron walls topped with concrete bald eagles at regular intervals. US Marines manned a vehicle access point equipped with anti-ram barriers and other modern security measures. An embassy security officer met them at the front door and led them to a large conference room where a number of important-looking people waited.

A fit, severe-looking woman in her forties sat at the head of the conference table. "I'm Special Agent Gunville, the FBI Legat assigned to the embassy here in Helsinki." She gestured to the balding and rather rotund man next to her. "This is Mr. Morrissy. He's with the CIA."

Caitlyn nodded to them both.

Gunville continued. "Ms. Runkle is the Deputy Chief of Mission for the State Department. Mr. Osgood is the defense attaché, and Mr. Simms is a team leader with MI6. First, we want to express our heartfelt thanks and admiration for a job well done. The bigwigs in Washington were at first irritated that you didn't inform them of your mission, but it's hard to argue with success. Ms. Valentine, was this *your* operation?"

Caitlyn shook her head. "This was all Mr. Flynn. I simply arranged transportation to Finland after the fact. To be honest, I agree with the bigwigs. Breaking two Americans out of a Russian gulag seemed foolhardy, if not downright foolish. I actually tried to dissuade Mr. Flynn, but he was quite determined."

Ms. Runkle interjected with her own observation. "You were right to try to dissuade him, Ms. Valentine. This could easily have created an international incident. The fact that the Russians want to keep this quiet is the only thing preventing that from happening."

The CIA's Mr. Morrissy broke in with a baritone voice. "Mr. Flynn, perhaps you can explain how you broke two prisoners out of one of the most secure penitentiaries in the world?"

Flynn shrugged. "I knew that Oleg Ivanov had arranged for a small army to free him from prison. I just piggybacked on his plan. I took advantage of the chaos to free Ms. O'Toole-Applebaum. Mr. Dankworth sabotaged Ivanov's escape helicopter. He then stole a Sentinel for our use and set fire to the rest."

The MI6 team leader regarded Dankworth with a new level of respect. "That was quick thinking, Dankworth."

A stunned Dankworth nodded. "Um…yes…well…we needed a way out, and I knew the danger Ivanov's escape would…engender, and…you know…I just…well…"

"Mr. Dankworth is being modest," Flynn said. "Without his rapid-fire resourcefulness, none of us would be here today."

Bettina nodded along with Caitlyn.

Dankworth basked in the recognition.

Agent Gunville smiled at Duncan Dankworth with newfound admiration. "Looks like you're the man of the hour."

"I do try to do my best," Dankworth mumbled.

Flynn pointed a pencil at Agent Gunville. "What about Ivanov? Do you know if the Russians recaptured him?"

"We're not entirely sure," Mr. Simms from MI6 replied. "The Russians never confess to their mistakes, and wouldn't want the world to think that a man like Mr. Flynn could make a mockery of their security apparatus."

"However, Ivanov isn't exactly a shrinking violet," the CIA's Mr. Morrissy pointed out. "If he did escape, I'd expect he'd let the world know. Though indirectly, since Putin continues to pose quite a threat."

Flynn nodded. "I concur with that assessment. Ivanov has an ego to rival Putin's. If he made it out, we'll likely know soon."

Mr. Simms from MI6 locked his eyes on Flynn. "Was Harper Sinclair your trusted source? Was she the one who provided you with that necessary intelligence?"

"She was."

"And do you know where she is?"

"I do."

Morrissy straightened up in his chair. "Would you mind sharing that information with the rest of us?"

"I would. Though the CIA's plan to turn her over to Putin in exchange for Bettina and Duncan created a considerable lack of trust. Let me talk to her. Perhaps I can convince her to come in."

"Tell us where she is and you won't have to convince her."

"Mr. Morrissy, I appreciate your point of view, but she is clever and has considerable resources. More importantly, she doesn't trust you."

Simms from MI6 interjected with a smile. "But she *does* trust Mr. Flynn. Which is why we put him on this project in the first place. MI6 would like to fly Mr. Dankworth and Mr. Flynn to London for a more robust debriefing. From there, they can return to California and convince Miss Sinclair to come in from the cold."

"Sinclair's on US soil?" Morrissy growled. "This should be a CIA operation."

"But she came to us. Not you. This is a joint operation agreed to by the highest levels of our respective governments. Let's not muck it up by being impatient."

Morrissy fumed. "We need to be there at the debriefing."

"Of course."

"I gotta be honest, Simms. I'm not enjoying your snippy tone."

"Well, we have that in common, then."

The diplomat, Ms. Runkle, swooped in. "It's settled then. Mr. Flynn will accompany Agent Dankworth to London. The President has requested that Ms. O'Toole-Applebaum join him at the White House for a press conference. Would that be all right with you, Ms. O'Toole-Applebaum?"

"Absolutely." Bettina didn't lose her cool, but her eyes gleamed.

Morrissy glared at Simms. "Do you object to us flying Ms. Valentine to Langley for our own debriefing?"

"Not at all. She's one of yours," Simms said.

"Well, I object," Caitlyn snapped. "I no longer work for the CIA, and I had nothing to do with that prison break. Unless you intend to charge me with something, I'm flying to Switzerland first thing tomorrow morning."

Morrissy sneered. "Would you *like* us to charge you with something?"

"You can try, but you people already locked me up once on trumped-up charges. Do it again and I will sue your collective asses off. I have the best defense lawyers in D.C. lining up to represent me free of charge. So, if I were you, I would tread lightly, Mr. Morrissy."

■ ■ ■

Flynn asked the hotel concierge for a dinner recommendation, and he sent them to *Ravintola Kosmos*. The restaurant opened in 1924 and was still run by the Hepolampi family four generations later. As they entered the storied establishment, the wood-paneled walls and vintage décor created a cozy atmosphere that the Finnish called *tunnelma*.

Flynn, always adventurous in his gastronomic endeavors, ordered the slightly salted reindeer with balsamic cloudberries and *celeriac* cream as a starter, with fried Baltic herring and mashed potatoes for his main course. Caitlyn went for the Chateaubriand and fried duck liver with herb-seasoned potato fritters. Bettina had trouble finding a vegetarian entrée and settled on the mushroom patties with beetroot and bean ragout. Duncan, a picky eater with a touchy stomach and a nut and shellfish allergy, didn't like any of the appetizer choices and ordered the wiener schnitzel with mashed potatoes.

Flynn selected a celebratory bottle of champagne for the table. After one glass, Duncan looked a little tipsy. After two glasses, he began laughing for no good reason. He pointed at

Flynn and leaned on the table, dipping his elbow in his mashed potatoes. "Thank you."

"For what?"

"For not throwing me under the bus. For making me look good in front of my team leader."

"We're all in this together, aren't we?"

"I'm sorry I judged you so harshly. You acquitted yourself quite well when the chips were down. You seem to thrive under pressure, while I, on the other hand, do not do well in high-stress situations."

"Perhaps because you haven't had the practice."

"You just have so much…confidence."

"I wasn't born with it. Believe me. At one time, I was much like you. Apprehensive, insecure, and totally lacking in self-esteem."

"That's hard to believe."

"It's true. Confidence is one of those things you have to work at. What's the saying? Fake it 'til you make it?"

Caitlyn looked at Flynn hard. "There's such a thing as *too much* confidence."

"Nonsense," Flynn replied. "You know what Theodore Roosevelt said?"

"Who?" asked Duncan.

"The 26th President of the United States. He went from being a sickly, four-eyed milquetoast to leading the Rough Riders in the Spanish-American War. He said, 'Believe in yourself and you're halfway there.'"

"Halfway where?"

"To believing in yourself."

"But how?"

Flynn smiled. "By letting go of fear and going balls to the wall. Churchill said, 'Courage is going from failure to failure without losing enthusiasm.'"

"So, I should fail enthusiastically?"

"Exactly."

"But I just have so much…self-doubt. So much…" He whispered the last word. "Dread."

"When people list the things they are afraid of, do you know what's always at the top of the list?" Flynn raised his eyebrows and set his champagne flute down.

"Dying?"

"You would think so, but no. Public speaking. They're most afraid of public humiliation. They'd rather face death than embarrassment. Well, I say bollocks to that. You can't live in fear of what other people think of you. You need to live shamelessly and without regret. Fortune favors the bold."

"It's always worked for me." Bettina grinned.

Caitlyn nodded. "And as much as I'd rather not…I have to agree."

Flynn caught Caitlyn's eye. "Are you sure you don't want to come with us to London tomorrow?"

She shook her head. "I need some time alone. Time to figure things out."

"What things?"

"Everything."

To fill the awkward pause in the conversation, Flynn pointed to his plate. "Would anyone like to try a bite of fried herring? Duncan?" He cut off a piece and forked it onto Duncan's plate.

Duncan scowled, pierced it with his fork, and lifted it to his mouth. "What if I hate it?"

"Then you'll know you don't like herring. But what if you do like herring and don't know it? What if it turns out to be the best thing you've ever tasted?"

"What if I'm allergic to it?"

"What if you're not?"

Duncan steeled himself, opened his mouth, and inserted the herring. He bit down and chewed as he looked around the table.

He spat it out and wiped his tongue with his napkin. "It's kind of fishy."

"Well, it is a fish, but by taking that chance, you've broadened your horizons and bravely stepped into the unknown."

"I did, didn't I?"

"And you didn't die."

"Not yet."

"Well, no one lives forever. But if you're never willing to take a chance, you're not really living at all, are you?"

Chapter Twenty-Six

Claridge's opened its doors in 1854, but really rose to prominence when Queen Victoria visited the hotel to meet with her friend, Empress Eugénie of France. The original structure was demolished in 1893, and the new owner commissioned the architect of Harrods to build an elegant seven-story hotel that still stands to this day. The hotel was expanded and the décor changed in the 1920s to an art deco motif with an elegant, mirrored lobby and leaping deer lamps. During the Second World War, Claridge's became a haven for exiled royalty and heads of state. Often, callers would ring the hotel, asking to speak to the king, and the operator would reply, "Which one?" Right after the war, many of Hollywood's biggest stars would stay at Claridge's. Katharine Hepburn was regularly admonished for breaking the dress code. Ladies weren't allowed to wear trousers in the lobby. So, Miss Hepburn chose to use the staff entrance instead.

When Flynn tried to enter MI6 headquarters at Vauxhall Cross the previous year, they'd blocked his way and even threatened him with arrest. At the time, he assumed they didn't want him to blow his carefully constructed cover as a psychiatric patient in an American mental hospital. But one year later, they welcomed him with open arms.

Flynn admittedly found the details foggy, but when he left London approximately twenty years earlier, MI6 had been in a much older building. The men who ran the place were all ex-military. Tough-minded, unsentimental men who showed no emotion other than aggravation. A stark contrast to the perky, warm, friendly, female deputy director who ushered Flynn and Dankworth into her office for their debriefing. She was Dankworth's immediate superior's superior. She told Flynn to call her Kathy before directing them to comfy chairs across from her desk. Her assistant Peter brought Dankworth a cup of tea and Flynn a cup of coffee. It was all very amiable and relaxed.

Kathy smiled at Flynn. "We are very grateful you rescued our friend and colleague, but as I'm sure you realize, the wider world can never know what you did."

"Of course."

Kathy turned to Dankworth. "Simms told me your part in the escape and, I must say, I'm quite impressed. You rewarded my faith in you and redeemed yourself. After this mission is concluded, I see a very bright future for you here."

Dankworth looked at Flynn with surprise before offering Kathy a grateful smile. "Thank you, Mum."

"But for that to happen, you both need to complete your original mission." Kathy leveled her gaze at Flynn. "I understand you know where Harper Sinclair is hiding, but refused to give up that information to the CIA. They actually considered arresting you and subjecting you to enhanced interrogation. But we intervened. The CIA can be ham-fisted about such things.

"You're the only one Miss Sinclair trusts. Without you, we fear she may disappear. I believe you were simply trying to protect her and, in so doing, gain her confidence. That is admirable. But now it's time for you to bring her in and retrieve the intelligence she promised us. We will protect you and we will protect her, but only if she gives us what we need."

"I'm sure she'll be glad to hear that, Kathy." Flynn caught a gleam in Kathy's eye. She held his gaze a moment longer than necessary, indicating an unmistakable hint of something more than professional admiration.

"We will fly you and Agent Dankworth to California tomorrow morning. The flight is top secret because we don't want the CIA tailing you to Ms. Sinclair's location and cocking everything up. This evening, I want you to hit the town and enjoy yourselves. The CIA will shadow you. We want them to. You'll return to your hotel at the end of the evening. Early the next morning, a decoy team will lead the CIA on a wild goose chase while we fly you out on a military transport plane. They won't know you've left the country until it's too late. By then, you'll be in Los Angeles."

Dankworth nodded. "I appreciate your faith in me, Mum."

"But please do not bungle this, because if you do, there's no way I can protect either one of you."

■ ■ ■

Dankworth would have rather stayed at his modest flat in Bromley, but the deputy director made it quite clear that she wanted him to stay with Flynn. The American insisted on paying for Dankworth's stay at Claridge's, and this time Dankworth didn't argue. Grateful billionaires had paid Flynn handsomely for his services in the past, and he obviously had unlimited resources. He might be delusional, but he was far from stupid. In fact, he was everything Dankworth was not. Charming. Courageous. Resourceful. Accomplished. He had underestimated Flynn every step of the way and had paid dearly for that mistake.

Claridge's was possibly London's poshest hotel. The suite Flynn secured for them was one of the most luxurious. At six times the size of Dankworth's flat, the Royal Suite lived up to its name. It had two large bedrooms decorated with all the pomp of the Victorian era. A gold Gilbert and Sullivan grand piano presided over the elegant living room.

Flynn ran his hand over the piano. "Gilbert and Sullivan themselves likely stayed in this very suite." He glanced at Dankworth. "Care for a cocktail?"

"It's a little early, isn't it?"

"Nonsense. It's time to get this party started. But pacing is important. Oscar Wilde said, 'Everything in moderation. *Including* moderation.'" Flynn opened the minibar and popped the top on a split of champagne. He poured them each a flute and tapped his glass against Dankworth's. "I'm going to shower before dinner. I've heard the restaurant here is excellent."

Dankworth sipped some champagne. The bubbles made him burp. "Sorry."

"No reason to be sorry."

"On the contrary, I owe you an apology for how I treated you when we first met. I misjudged you, Mr. Flynn. I insulted you and didn't appreciate your competence and capabilities."

"I misjudged you as well, and please, call me James."

"If you call me Duncan."

"Of course."

"And even though I treated you abominably, you came to my rescue and risked life and limb to save me."

"Well, to be honest, I was there for Bettina, but I wasn't about to leave you behind. After all, we *are* on the same team."

Duncan nodded. "I know that now. And I'm sorry I didn't treat you with the respect you deserved."

"Well, that's all behind us. Going forward, neither one of us will make that mistake again."

Flynn offered his hand and Dankworth shook it, marveling again at the power of his grip. He could have easily crushed his hand, but held back because he had no need to prove his dominance. A wave of emotion bubbled up as Dankworth realized he'd rarely been treated with that kind of deference from someone so formidable. If Flynn could believe in him, perhaps he could start believing in himself.

. . .

Since Flynn abandoned his luggage back in Kharp, he needed to replenish his travel wardrobe. He made a stop at Hackett on Savile Row and brought Duncan along as well. The lad did not dress to impress, and the outfit he decided on for the evening was less than inspiring. His baggy khakis, ill-fitting button-down shirt, and clunky brown loafers had to go. Times had changed, and standards of dress had sadly devolved. Dapper was now a dirty word. Casual, frumpy, and dowdy were now the order of the day. Flynn, however, believed in the maxim, *Dress like you've made something of yourself, even if you haven't.* Clothes might not make the man, but the wrong ones can sure make a man look like a muppet.

Flynn wanted to buy Duncan a more fitting outfit for the evening. The sales associate selected something a little younger and hipper than the Prince of Wales cashmere suit Flynn had purchased. A blazer in dark gray, a white cotton poplin shirt, slim-fit herringbone chinos, and black leather Oxfords.

They both fit right in at the Fumoir bar. A popular watering hole for the smart set since 1929. Flynn stood belly up to the black marble bar, ready for a memorable night on the town.

Duncan, standing right next to him, stood a little taller and exuded a bit more confidence as he sipped his mojito. Flynn kept to his tried-and-true vodka martini.

Shaken. Not stirred.

Two beautiful women watched them from across the room. A tall, slender blonde and a buxom brunette. They both seemed somewhat familiar to Flynn, though he couldn't quite place them. The blonde looked at him as if she knew him. When she caught his eye, she offered a dazzling smile. Flynn nodded and smiled back. She poked her friend and pointed at Flynn. Within seconds, they headed in his direction.

Flynn immediately assumed they were honeypots sent to seduce them. What better way to keep tabs on them than with high-priced prostitutes? Flynn remembered an operation the CIA ran in the 1960s. Operation Midnight Climax lured in enemy agents and plied them with psychedelic drugs. The assumption was that post-coitus, they would reveal all their secrets while high on LSD. Could this be Operation Midnight Climax 2?

The tall blonde moved with the grace of a dancer. She covered the small room in five quick strides. The brunette had shorter legs and a voluptuous body that bounced as she brought up the rear. The blonde's long, straight hair fell past her shoulders. A sprinkle of freckles on her nose and a polished RP accent gave her an aristocratic air. "Are you James Flynn?"

"I am, but no thank you."

"Excuse me?"

"I know who you are and what you do and why you're here and what you want."

At that, Duncan casually turned and nearly fell off his stool. He pointed at the blonde and Flynn pushed his finger down. The agent's eyes widened and his jaw dropped when he noticed the buxom brunette just behind her.

The blonde seemed amused. "What do you think I want?"

"I think you want to take advantage of me."

"That's a distinct possibility." She offered Flynn her hand. "I'm Ava."

Flynn took it and made a show of lightly kissing it. "A pleasure."

"And this is my friend, Kate."

"Kate Mulligan." Duncan blurted. "I loved your last movie. And yours too, Miss Davenport. *Tangled Lies* was even better than *Fatal Temptation*."

Ava turned to Duncan. Flynn thought the young MI6 agent might faint. "Thank you. That's very nice of you to say."

"Duncan. I'm Duncan. Dankworth."

Flynn reassessed the situation. He may have misjudged their intentions. "So you're actresses?"

"Two of the biggest movie stars in the world," Duncan gushed. "Both have been nominated for BAFTAs *and* Academy Awards."

"Impressive."

Ava turned her attention back to Flynn. "Not compared to the amazing things you've accomplished."

Kate nudged Ava to one side as she moved closer. She dressed far more provocatively than her blonde friend. Duncan laser-focused on her heaving cleavage. "Eyes up," Flynn whispered.

Duncan immediately raised his gaze to Kate's huge blue eyes.

Her accent was a little less posh than Ava's. "Now that you know we're not hookers, would you gentlemen like to join us?"

Duncan tried to reply, but nothing came out of his mouth.

Flynn picked up his drink. "Thank you. We would love to."

They followed the ladies back to their booth. Ava squeezed in next to Flynn, and Kate scooted next to Duncan. Flynn ordered another round of drinks. For the ladies as well. Duncan, blushing and slightly sweaty, had to steady his trembling hand when he sipped his mojito. Kate rested her hand on Duncan's thigh and leaned close, her bare shoulder touching his, her luscious lips inches from his ear. "And what do you do, Duncan?"

"I...I'm...I work for...well, I—"

"MI6," Flynn said.

Duncan's eyes went wide. "What? Whoa. No. We're not supposed to—"

"Reveal we're international super spies? I would say that cat's out of the bag."

Kate's huge blue eyes widened as she pressed herself against him. "MI6? Seriously?"

"I can't really say," Duncan mumbled.

Kate's voice grew breathy. "Are you here on a mission?"

"I can't really say."

Flynn nodded. "He's following proper protocol, which is why he can't tell you he recently helped me free an American journalist from a Russian gulag."

Ava grinned. "Are you talking about Bettina O'Toole-Applebaum?"

"We can't really say," Duncan said more forcefully. He shot Flynn a glare.

Ava looked delighted. "The Guardian said a deal was struck, but it sounds like it was you two who struck."

"I can't really say," Flynn replied playfully.

"But you've already said enough, haven't you?" Duncan snapped.

"We'll have to ask you two ladies to stay mum about this. Official secrets act and all that," Flynn insisted.

Kate and Ava both offered close-mouthed smiles and pretended to zip their lips.

Duncan downed half his mojito and wiped the sweat from his forehead with the sleeve of his suit. Kate took his clammy hand and kissed him on the cheek. "Thank you for your service, Duncan."

Duncan nodded and blushed as Ava offered Flynn a mischievous grin. "So, what's the secret mission?"

"Nothing secret about it," Flynn said. "We're just here for some R&R."

"A night on the town?"

"Exactly."

"So, you're not here to meet anyone?"

"I believe we already have."

Kate snuggled closer to Duncan. "Real-life spies. How exciting."

"We only play pretend," Ava said. "To come across the real thing is quite thrilling."

"It's just what we do," Duncan said, finally getting into the spirit of things. "Nothing special."

"Exactly," Flynn added. "Simple civil servants keeping the world safe from those who would do it harm."

Ava rested her hand on Flynn's knee. "Would you two be interested in joining us this evening? Escorting us around town. Keeping the paparazzi and riffraff at bay?"

"Us join you?" Duncan squeaked.

"Unless you have something better to do," Kate said.

"No, not me. Nope. Uh uh. We're just, you know…no."

"What were your plans for this evening before you met us?" Ava asked.

Flynn shrugged. "Dinner. Drinks. A bit of gambling, perhaps."

"Have you ever been to Les A?"

"I have indeed," Flynn replied. "A member once brought me there as a guest. It's quite the exclusive club."

Ava smiled. "One that I happen to belong to. And exclusive as it is, I'm able to avoid that riffraff I alluded to earlier."

Flynn turned to Duncan. "How does that sound to you?"

Duncan was too flummoxed to actually get a word out. Instead, he just nodded.

"Brilliant," Ava said. "I'll text my driver, and off we go."

Les A was the perfect place to avoid the prying eyes of the CIA. They couldn't enter without a membership and would have to reconnoiter the front door instead. As Ava texted, Flynn noticed a couple at the bar with eyes on them. A man and a woman. Both fit and in their thirties. When they caught Flynn's glance, they immediately looked away. Were they CIA? Or simply hotel guests astonished to see two movie stars?

Ava scraped back her chair and stood. "Everybody ready?"

Chapter Twenty-Seven

At Flynn's suggestion, they dined at No. 6 Hamilton Place. The elegant interior mirrored the art deco design at Claridge's. The cuisine matched the nationalities of Les A's most frequent and profligate gamblers. The restaurant boasted Arabic, Chinese, and classic European dishes on the eclectic menu. Kate proposed they make a meal out of appetizers. They shared hummus, baba ganoush, lamb kafta, dim sum, and crispy spring rolls. The ladies ordered champagne cocktails. Duncan mimicked Flynn by ordering a vodka martini.

Ava raised her glass. "Here's to those who wish us well, and those who don't can go to hell."

"Damn straight," Kate laughed.

Flynn sipped his martini and set it down. "Fame is indeed a double-edged sword."

"Guess you never expected to get famous, huh?" Kate asked.

"No, I did not." Flynn replied, "In fact, I find it to be quite an impediment."

"As do I." Ava put down her drink. "I can't just be a fly on the wall anymore. I used to love to people-watch and eavesdrop on what they said. How they moved. How they spoke. It was part of my process. And then I got famous."

"You get good tables in restaurants, but that's about it," Kate grumbled.

"Don't get me wrong. I love my fans." Ava picked up a crispy spring roll. "I wouldn't be able to do what I do without them. But sometimes, I just wish I could disappear. I wish I could walk into a pub and not have everyone watching every move I make. It's exhausting."

Duncan took a sip of his martini and made a face. "Yeah, I don't think I'd like that. I prefer not to draw attention."

"Which makes you the perfect spy." Flynn clinked his martini glass against Duncan's. "You are quite inconspicuous."

"Though sometimes it can be irritating when you can't get someone's attention. Like cab drivers. Or bartenders. Or those hand blowers in bathrooms. I can never get them to turn on. Even they don't seem to see me."

"Sounds like heaven," Ava said.

"Not to me." Kate grinned. "I like the attention. That's why I became an actress. When people don't recognize me, I get a little anxious."

"Well, no worries in that department," Ava said. "Every eye in the place is on you."

"And you," Kate laughed.

Ava sighed. "I just have to stay Zen. Stay focused on the moment and who I'm with." Ava put her hand on Flynn's.

Kate smirked. "Better watch it, James. If some random paparazzi gets a shot of you two being lovey-dovey, you're going to be a hundred times more famous than you already are."

"In for a penny, in for a pound." Flynn turned his gaze to Duncan, shyly hiding behind his drink. "Speaking of pounds, I'd like to front you ten thousand of them."

Duncan's eyes went wide. "Ten thousand pounds? For what?"

"For a bit of gaming. I know you wouldn't gamble your own money, but if you expect to get the full Les A experience, you need to dip your toe in the water."

"That's okay. I'll watch you."

"Nonsense. You can't always be an observer. Sometimes you need to get into the thick of it."

"No, thanks."

"I'll coach you. Last time I was here, I won two hundred and fifty thousand pounds. I think I can risk ten thousand to show you how to turn it into much, much more."

Kate grinned and put her hand on Duncan's knee. "Come on. It'll be fun!"

Duncan blushed and drained the rest of his martini, squinching up his face from the taste.

. . .

Duncan felt a little loopy as he entered the elegant casino and marveled at the opulent décor. Dark paneled walls with gold wainscoting and high ceilings with massive crystal chandeliers. The soft burgundy carpeting helped muffle the sound, creating a quiet and more elegant atmosphere. Not that Duncan had much experience with casinos. In point of fact, this was the first casino he'd ever stepped foot in.

When Flynn asked Duncan which game he wanted to play, he picked the only casino game he had any experience with. Blackjack. He'd played it with his Uncle Ned when he was a kid and rarely won. His hypercompetitive uncle would pound bottles of Guinness and smoke countless fags and regularly beat Duncan out of his meager allowance. Duncan would cry, and Ned would laugh and browbeat him about how important it was to be a good loser. Over time, Duncan became an excellent loser.

A total loser.

A complete and utter loser.

Duncan's bowels clenched as he sat at one of Les A's blackjack tables between Kate and Ava. Ten thousand pounds in plaques were neatly piled by his right elbow.

Flynn stood just behind him. "Ready to have some fun?"

"Um…"

Flynn patted him on the shoulder. "Can I buy you a drink?"

"I'm actually still feeling a little nauseous from that martini."

Kate nudged him with her elbow. "Open your mouth."

"Excuse me?"

"Stick out your tongue."

"What?"

"Just do it."

"Why?"

"Why not?"

She gently grabbed him by the nads and he opened his mouth with surprise. She tossed some kind of tablet into his gob. He started to choke. Ava handed him her Cosmopolitan. Duncan drank half to wash the tablet down, his eyes watering, still coughing.

The dealer, an attractive thirty-something Asian lady, finished shuffling the cards and addressed the table. "Place your bets, please."

Kate and Ava each bet a hundred-pound plaque. Duncan bet the minimum. A ten-pound plaque.

The dealer dealt herself a five. Duncan received a jack and a five. Kate held firm with a ten and a queen. She waved away a hit and the dealer looked at Duncan. Duncan stared back. He knew she expected him to do something, but he wasn't sure what exactly.

Kate nudged him. "You want a card?"

"Do I?"

Flynn leaned in. "I thought you said you played this before?"

"I'm feeling a lot of pressure here," Duncan mumbled.

"No worries. Win or lose, it's just about having fun."

"But I'm *not* having fun."

The dealer caught Duncan's eye. "Sir?"

"Yes."

"Yes what?"

"Tap the table if you want another card." Kate demonstrated. "If you don't, wave them away." She demonstrated again.

Duncan waved the dealer away. Ava tapped the table. She received a six for a total of twenty. Duncan realized that six would have given him twenty-one. "Shit," he whispered.

The dealer dealt herself a second card. A queen. And another. A nine. She busted. Duncan won with a fifteen. He felt a rush of power and adrenaline as he reached for his winnings.

"Use the reverse Martindale method," Flynn said.

"The reverse what?"

"Martindale. With that method, you double your bet every time you lose. The theory being eventually you'll win everything back."

"What if you run out of money?"

"Then you don't win everything back."

"What if I just keep taking my winnings and bet the same bet every time? What's that called?"

"That's a variation of the Paroli system. Double your bet after each win, but return to the original bet after each loss."

"That sounds reasonable."

"Yes, you can win with that system, but you won't win big, and if you're not going big, why go at all?"

The dealer dealt herself a king, Kate a four and a seven, and Duncan two eights.

Kate tapped the table and got a three. She tapped again and busted with a jack.

A painful gas bubble tried to claw its way out of Duncan's bum. He concentrated on keeping his cheeks squeezed together as Kate nudged him with her elbow. "Split," she whispered.

"Hmm?"

"Sixteen is a terrible hand, and two eights make a great split," Flynn whispered.

"How do I do that?"

"Set them side by side and bet another twenty pounds."

"That's forty pounds?"

Flynn rested his hand on Duncan's shoulder. "The dealer's showing a six. Since each deck has sixteen face cards and tens, odds are the dealer has a sixteen and will bust on the next draw."

Duncan squeaked out a high-pitched toot and doubled down. He took a hit on each hand and received a ten on one and a seven on the other. He stood on the eighteen, but hit the fifteen and turned it into a twenty-one.

Ava had blackjack.

The dealer busted.

Duncan grinned and let it all ride. He won again. And again. And doubled down on his three-hundred-and-twenty-pound bet. When he began the game, his intestines were in knots, but the more money he won, the more they relaxed. The same with his sphincter. He let out a few more trumps and toots, and for some reason just didn't care. Not what people thought. Not what anyone thought. He just kept doubling down until he had twenty thousand pounds in plaques piled up all around him.

Flynn tapped him on the shoulder. "Now might be the time to step away."

Duncan answered Flynn with an extended fart and a shake of the head. "Not while I'm on a winning streak."

Duncan felt strangely euphoric; his usual anxiety and self-consciousness suddenly replaced by irrational confidence and exuberance. *This must be how Flynn sees the world. Is this what insanity feels like?* If so, he decided he needed to lose his mind more often. Did Kate slip him some kind of hallucinogenic? Is that what that tablet was? Everything suddenly seemed so vivid.

He ran his fingers over the felt on the table and then Kate's milky white thigh. So unbelievably soft and silky. She smiled at him, and her smile lit him up inside and filled him with such indescribable pleasure. In that moment, he realized how much he loved her. And Ava. And Flynn. Duncan felt a deep, boundless, all-encompassing love for everyone.

Even himself.

Even himself.

His soul left his body as he floated above his corporeal form, rising towards the ceiling, an ethereal being of pure energy and love.

The dealer's words brought him back to Earth. "Would you like to let it ride, sir?"

Duncan couldn't think of the words to express what he was feeling. Instead, he just nodded, and the dealer dealt more hands, and Duncan continued to play, and the pile of plaques grew taller and taller.

Flynn whispered, "I think it might be time to cash in."

"Have you lost your faith in me, Flynn?"

"Of course not."

"*Then there is no cashing in.* Luck is like a river. Once you're in the flow you must let it take you wherever it wants to go."

"Duncan—"

"No, don't you see? I'm now part of the eternal stream of creation that connects every soul in the universe."

Duncan could feel a crowd surrounding him as he continued to let it ride until towers of ten-thousand-pound plaques teetered all around him. A megalopolis of money that stretched to the heavens.

His bowels no longer bothered him. His intestines ceased to be twisted. He had somehow reached a perfect state of transcendent bliss and knew that he never had to keep anything trapped inside again. He could finally let go of all the fear and anxiety and shame and worry and painful gas. He no longer had to be mortified by his physical self. He could finally let go.

Finally, let it blow.

Loud and long and proud.

Everyone backed away from him, likely in awe of what he had become. A being of pure light. A massive ball of burning gas. A human-sized sun. He felt untethered to gravity and this plane of existence. He felt himself floating as the universe welcomed him as the pinnacle of perfection.

Chapter Twenty-Eight

Methylenedioxymethamphetamine, commonly known as ecstasy, molly, or MDMA, was first synthesized by the German pharmaceutical company Merck in 1912. They patented it in 1914, but the medication largely went unexplored. At that point, a rival German company, Bayer, had a hit with Heroin, the brand name for diacetylmorphine, which they marketed as a non-addictive substitute for morphine. In the seventies, MDMA was marketed as a means of enhancing communication during psychotherapy. It created a sense of euphoria, boosted energy, enhanced sociability, and intensified sensory perception. In the 1980s, it became the party drug du jour. In 1985, the DEA classified MDMA as a Schedule 1 controlled substance, lumping it in the same category as cocaine and heroin. Not surprising, since heavy and prolonged use could lead to neurotoxicity, long-term anxiety, depression, and psychological dependence.

Flynn knew Duncan needed to sober his arse up. Whatever Kate slipped him had sent him into an altered state. He surfed some kind of psychedelic wave when he toppled backwards off his stool and landed flat on his back. Flynn lifted him upright and helped him to the men's room as the casino staff gathered up his winnings. He splashed cold water on Duncan's face and sat him on a toilet in a stall. He grinned at Flynn and grabbed his hand and held it against his face.

"You feeling okay?" Flynn asked.

"I feel perfect."

"You seem a little buzzed."

"Thank you."

"For what?"

"Everything."

Flynn nodded and sighed. "Do you think you can walk?"

"I think I can fly."

Flynn took Duncan to the elegant Library Bar and ordered him a double espresso. He drank it down in one long chug. Flynn realized too late that caffeine probably wasn't the best choice for someone already high on ketamine or MDMA or whatever the hell Kate had dosed him with.

Dankworth's eyes were wide, and his grin manic. "How much did I win?"

"At your peak, half a million pounds."

"*Half a million pounds*?!"

"But then you let it ride and lost it."

Duncan looked devastated. "All of it?"

"No, a few ten-thousand-pound plaques had fallen on the floor. Which we found when you fell off your stool. The casino wrote you a check."

"I need it! I need to go back. I need to let it ride."

"That streak ended when your arse kissed the floor. But forty thousand pounds is nothing to sneeze at."

Flynn pulled out the check and handed it to Duncan. He held it with both hands and bolted to his feet. "I'm rich!"

Flynn waved him back down. "Richer than you were. That's for sure."

"And you're the reason why. You helped me find my way past that paralyzing fear that filled me with such dread."

"There's a book by a man named Dale Carnegie that I read when I was just a lad. He said 'Take a chance! All life is a chance. The man who goes farthest is generally the one who is willing to do and dare.'"

"Like you!"

"Like anyone who achieves anything. A lack of confidence is crippling. Conquer that and you can conquer the world."

Duncan threw his arms around Flynn and hugged him tight. Just then, Kate and Ava came rushing in with matching grins. Flynn suspected they had indulged in the same illicit pharmaceutical that Kate fed Duncan.

"We want to go dancing," Kate said.

"I've never been," Duncan replied.

"You've never been *dancing*?"

"I've always been too afraid."

"Afraid?"

Kate looked nonplussed. "Of what?"

"Of looking like an ass clown."

"And now?"

"Now I don't bloody care."

■　■　■

Flynn eyed the long line of hip, beautiful twenty-somethings that snaked down the street from *Cirque Le Soir*. Ava's limo pulled right up by the front doors. Those at the head of the line stared daggers at the tinted windows. But that all changed when Ava and Kate climbed from the car. The mood shifted from frustration to adulation as people shouted their names and yelled out how much they loved them.

"*Ava! Hey!*"

"*It's Kate Mulligan!*"

Kate grinned and waved as a massive bouncer lifted the velvet rope, and she and Ava and Flynn and Duncan headed through the front doors of *Cirque Le Soir*.

Flynn nearly collided with a mime as Duncan rushed forward, full of reckless enthusiasm.

"Oh, my God!" Duncan pointed at the trapeze artists flying overhead and banged into a stilt walker who staggered sideways and nearly fell on a fire eater. A beautiful burlesque dancer suspended in a cage shook her booty to the beat of the hip-hop artist performing on stage.

A multicolored light show throbbed with that same beat as all the party people tripped the light fantastic. Neon glowed everywhere as purple, aqua, and crimson spotlights lit up dominatrix dwarfs, nearly naked dancers, bearded ladies, and leather-clad sword swallowers.

Duncan pointed and shouted out the names of the various celebrities he saw shaking their moneymakers. "Miley Cyrus! Leonardo DiCaprio! Wait? Is that *Scarlett Johansson*?"

Kate grabbed him by the arm. "Be cool, Duncan! Be cool!" She pulled him onto the dance floor and shook her booty with abandon. Duncan tried to match her sultry gyrations, but moved more like a man trying to stay upright in the throes of an epileptic fit; jerking and twisting and twitching as if a mad puppeteer randomly and angrily yanked his strings.

Ava shouted in Flynn's ear. "How do I compete with that?"

"How do *I*?"

Ava laughed. "How about a drink?"

"Excellent idea."

They made their way to their private table in the roped-off VIP area. A server appeared. "Ava, hi."

"Hey, Kelly. Can we get a bottle of Dom Pérignon?"

"You got it."

As Kelly headed for the bar, Flynn regarded Ava with amusement. "You must be a regular."

"It's always good to make friends with the servers."

"I agree."

"And assistants and executive secretaries and doormen."

"Be nice to the people you meet on the way up, because you'll see them again on the way down?"

Ava nodded. "But it's more than that. Life's hard enough as it is. Why be a jerk if you don't have to? Why not just be nice to people?"

"I agree."

"I've met more than my share of entitled assholes in this business. They surround themselves with fawning parasites and believe the rules of civility and common decency don't apply to them. That's why I like Kate. She hasn't lost touch with who she was. Who she is. And it's not just true of movie stars. I've met a lot of rich tossers who think they can do or take whatever they want. I can't tell you how many asshole producers hit on me when I was coming up."

"Happened to a friend of mine."

"I know. Chloe Jablonski."

"You've met?"

"We have. We shot a movie together last year. She told me all about you. How you saved her from her tormentor."

Flynn spat the name with disdain. "Goldhammer."

"That's quite a story."

"He won't be bothering anyone ever again."

"A jerk and a bully. Just like Kate's ex."

"Abusive?"

"Physically *and* emotionally. He's one of the biggest stars in the world, so he gets a free pass."

"Are they divorced?"

"Separated. But he just won't let her be. He sleeps with anyone he wants, but if she goes anywhere near another man, he loses his shit. Makes him absolutely crazy."

Flynn glanced over to see her dancing with Duncan.

"He constantly has her followed. That's why I wanted to go to Les A. That cheesy private detective he uses couldn't follow us in there. And if he tailed us here, he's probably still waiting in that queue wrapped around the block. Even if he makes his way to the front, no way are they letting that ugly numpty in here."

Flynn had noticed a car following them after they left Les A. He assumed it was the CIA.

Kate came rushing up to their table, breathless and sweaty, a big smile on her beautiful face. She grabbed Ava's champagne and downed it in one go.

Ava refilled Kate's flute and filled a new one for herself. "You're schvitzing like a pig."

Kate gave her a hug and Ava laughed and recoiled. "Get off me!"

"You love it! Admit it!"

Seconds later, Duncan arrived looking equally sweaty and uncharacteristically happy. He grinned like a bloody idiot. Flynn was glad to see it. Duncan wasn't much of a smiler. In fact, he usually looked miserable and somewhat constipated. Flynn playfully punched him in the shoulder. "You busted a few moves out there."

"I know, right? Katie seems really into me."

"Why wouldn't she be?"

"Because I'm me and she's…she."

Flynn glanced at her. The actress' sexy, happy demeanor suddenly changed to abject terror.

A booming voice thundered across the club. "Kate Mulligan!"

The music came to a thudding stop, as did all the laughter and fun. Dead silence pervaded the massive club as dancers and party people stepped aside, creating a path for one of the largest men Flynn had ever seen.

He stood six foot six, but was nearly as wide as he was tall. He wore a suit that could barely contain his massive musculature. Flynn recognized him from his action films, but seeing him on screen was one thing, seeing him in the flesh was quite another. Ruggedly handsome with piercing blue eyes, a bald head, and a chiseled jaw, Jericho Stone crossed the room with all the grace of an angry bear, exuding power and charisma and unbridled fury.

He grabbed Kate's arm. Duncan stepped between them and put his hand on Stone's gargantuan chest. "Unhand her, sir."

"Who the fuck are you?"

"I told you to unhand her. I won't say it again."

Stone dwarfed him in every way, yet Duncan stood his ground, resolute and seemingly unafraid. An evil smile crinkled Stone's face. He released Kate and stepped closer to Duncan. She scurried behind him and cowered.

Stone poked Duncan in the chest. "This woman is my wife."

"And yet you treat her abominably. She isn't your property. She's an independent human being who deserves respect."

"Do you have any idea who I am?"

"Jericho Stone. I've seen your films, and at one time I was a fan. You always play a hero, but you're no hero at all. You're a bully. An arsehole. A coward."

"What did you call me?"

"You heard me. You might play a hard case in the movies, but you fight bad guys who are paid to lose. You've been pretending to be a tough guy for so long you actually think you are one."

A few of the party people laughed. A vein throbbed in Jericho's forehead.

"You're purposely trying to piss me off, aren't you? You *want* me to hit you. You're not trying to protect her. You're here for a nice payday. Well, think again, you twat. You want to stop me? Go ahead. But you're gonna have to make the first move." Jericho pushed past Duncan and clamped his hand on Kate's dainty wrist. She cried out in pain as he pulled her after him.

Duncan tried to grab Jericho's arm, but it was so large he couldn't get a grip. Flynn considered stepping in, but Duncan grabbed the half-empty bottle of champagne and tried to crack

Jericho in the head with it. Not being tall enough, he instead smacked him in the back. Jericho hardly noticed as he dragged Kate across the floor past the horrified party people. An angry Duncan chased after him and threw the bottle as hard as he could. It clunked off the back of Jericho's head and shattered on the ground. Jericho didn't even flinch.

But he did stop.

Duncan launched a foot between his legs, smacking Jericho directly in the balls before losing his balance and falling flat on the floor.

Jericho turned, wrenching Kate around with him. "You all saw it," he shouted. "The little bugger attacked me. Multiple times."

Duncan scrambled up and came at him again, launching another kick. Jericho caught it with his left hand and lifted Duncan off his feet. The MI6 agent fell back and banged his head on the dance floor. Jericho stomped him in the groin and glanced around at all the lookie-loos, shouting, "Are you not entertained?"

Duncan grabbed his gonads and grunted in pain. He rolled over into the fetal position to protect his injured man parts.

Kate tried to get away, but Jericho twisted her wrist until she screamed. No one in the place lifted a finger to help her. None of the patrons. None of the bouncers.

No one.

Jericho jerked her towards the door and found someone standing in his way. Someone taller and broader than the little man who just tried to defend Kate's honor.

"Out of the way!" Jericho boomed.

"I don't think so," Flynn replied.

"This is a fight you don't want."

"I'm not letting you take her, and if you try, you will regret it."

"There's always some would-be badass in every fucking bar who thinks he can take me down." Jericho let Kate go. "Well, come on, tough guy. Have at it. I'll give you the first punch." He pointed to his chin. "Take your best shot. But you better take me out. Because if you don't, I'm going to break your neck and both your bloody legs!"

Flynn executed a perfect *kansetu geri*, a lateral kick to the side of the knee. The loud crack echoed through the silent club. Jericho collapsed like a Jenga tower.

He lay on the floor, screaming bloody murder. "You broke my goddamn knee! What the fuck did you do to me?"

Flynn didn't answer him. He just helped Duncan to his feet with the aid of Kate and Ava.

Jericho continued to shout. "I will fucking kill you! You hear me! And that bitch too! You're all fucking dead! Every single one of you!"

Flynn left Duncan to walk over to Jericho. He bent down and said, "You play a hard man in the movies, but I don't play. I have a license to kill. If you ever threaten or intimidate or hurt Kate or Duncan or any of us ever again, I won't hesitate to use it. I will end you. It won't be quick and it won't be pleasant. Do you understand me?"

Fear replaced fury as all the bluster left Jericho Stone.

"Do you understand me?" Flynn repeated.

Jericho nodded.

"Good."

· · ·

By the time they reached Claridge's, Duncan felt a tad better. The crippling agony in his nether regions had faded into a dull, throbbing ache. He still dealt with the effects of whatever drug Kate slipped him, and for that he was grateful. The whole way to the hotel, she was solicitous and nurturing.

Kate proposed a nightcap at Fumoir. Duncan agreed to join them. Anything to help numb the pain. They arrived in time for last call. Duncan ordered a margarita on the rocks.

Kate sidled up next to him in the booth, pressing herself up against him and whispering in his ear. "Thank you."

"For what?"

"For standing up for me."

"Not very successfully."

"I disagree. That was very brave of you."

"I just couldn't bear to see him treat you like that."

"Jericho's quite intimidating. No one else had the nerve to confront him."

"Flynn did."

"Only after you slowed him down."

"I tried my best."

"If he dragged me home, he would have beaten me bloody."

Duncan shook his head. "He's the worst kind of bully."

"I've always been attracted to arseholes. I guess it's what I grew up with. But I think I can break that pattern with you."

"Excuse me?"

"You're sweet and gentle, but you're no pushover. You're no coward."

"I don't like bullies."

"Would you come upstairs with me?"

"Upstairs where?"

A smile. "Where do you think?"

"You mean-"

"Yes. That is, if you're not afraid."

"Afraid?"

"Of Jericho."

"I don't think we need to worry about him."

"So, you're interested?"

"Of course I'm interested. But to be perfectly honest, my twig and berries are a bit banged up."

"I can kiss them and make them better."

"You can?"

She grinned and took Duncan by the hand. "Ava? Flynn? Duncan and I are going to call it a night."

Ava raised an eyebrow. Flynn did the same.

Kate led Duncan from Fumoir and up the lift to the luxurious suite she shared with Ava.

. . .

Flynn finished his martini and kissed Ava on the cheek. "I'm going to call it a night as well."

"Would you like me to join you?"

"I would indeed, but unfortunately I can't."

"Of course you can."

"As beautiful as you are and as much as I'm attracted to you, I'm in love with someone else."

"It's Caitlyn Valentine, isn't it? I read the article about you two in *Rolling Stone*. She is impressive."

"She is indeed. Though at the moment we're on the outs."

"Yet, you still want to be true to her."

"I do. I'm sorry."

"Don't be. I think that might be the most romantic thing I've ever heard." She kissed Flynn on the cheek. "Thank you."

"For what?"

"Everything."

Chapter Twenty-Nine

Duncan Dankworth opened his crusty eyes as someone jostled him awake. He looked up into Kate Mulligan's heart-shaped face.

"Duncan?" She jostled him some more and lightly slapped him. Then slapped him harder. "*Duncan?*"

"Hmm?"

"Are you okay?"

Duncan slowly took in his surroundings and marveled at the fact that a stunningly beautiful movie star, a woman he had spent an inordinate amount of time fantasizing about, gazed down at him wearing nothing but a smile. Anxiety and agitation overwhelmed whatever confidence and self-assurance he had the previous evening. His memories of the night before were a confusing jumble. A Technicolor blur. Did he really bed this exquisite goddess? And why was she slapping him in the face?

"Duncan, say something."

"Good morning."

Her face lit up with a grin. Those huge blue eyes of hers broke his heart. "Someone's here for you."

"Who?"

"Your friend, Flynn."

Whatever illicit pharmaceutical she gave him the night before left him groggy as hell. He couldn't focus or put two thoughts together. "Who?"

"He says you need to go."

"Go where?"

"Flynn's waiting for you in the other room."

"Have to pee."

Duncan sat up with Kate's help and staggered to the bathroom. He stood swaying and peeing for what seemed like forever. He was still peeing when Kate opened the bathroom door and tossed his clothes inside.

Tottering back and forth, he struggled to pull up his pants. Eventually, he managed to get his entire Savile Row outfit back on. Though the white cotton poplin shirt looked considerably more rumpled, and the black leather oxfords were sticky with some unknown spillage.

When he exited the bathroom, he found Kate now wearing a hotel robe and sitting on the edge of the bed. She approached him with a warm smile and wrapped her arms around him.

"You really let loose last night."

"I did?"

Her voice, hoarse from screaming over all the loud hip-hop, house, and RnB at Cirque Le Soir, was now a sexy growl. "Oh, yeah, you did."

Her amorous intent kicked his anxiety up to a ten. An ominous rumble rocked his guts. "I don't remember."

"Well, I do, and we're going to have to do it again."

"Okay, then."

"But first you and Flynn need to go save the world."

"We do indeed."

She took his hand and led him to the door. Out in the fabulous living room of the Georgian-decorated suite, Flynn enjoyed coffee with Ava. Duncan wondered if Flynn too spent the night.

Flynn grinned and bolted to his feet. "You ready?" He pointed at Duncan's crotch and Duncan blanched and looked down to see his shirttail poking from his open fly.

Duncan zipped up. "I am now."

"I want to thank you ladies for an incredible evening. Once we make the world safe for king and country, we will return.

.   .   .

Flynn and Duncan met with the MI6 extraction team in a maintenance area next to a service elevator. The decoy team bore a strong resemblance to Flynn and Dankworth, and mimicked their gait and dress. While the decoy team left by a side door and entered a waiting limousine, MI6 had the actual Flynn and Dankworth wear disguises. Flynn wore the flowing robes of a modern-day Arab prince, and Duncan dressed as his wife in a gray burqa. Duncan protested, but only briefly, before he and Flynn were led down a secret corridor that led to a hidden elevator that took them to an underground garage of another hotel a few buildings away. There they climbed into an armored Rolls-Royce limousine that whisked them off.

The drive to RAF Northolt in West London took a little under an hour. They boarded an air transport and headed for the Canadian Air Force base in Goose Bay, Newfoundland. After refueling, they flew to CFB Comox in British Columbia. No longer dressed as husband and wife but in RAF uniforms, the last leg of the journey landed them at Whidbey Naval Air Station in Washington State. There they changed back into their civvies. A ferry ferried them to Seattle, where they boarded a private jet operated by MI6 that flew them to Van Nuys Airport in Los Angeles, thereby bypassing customs and immigration.

.   .   .

Harper Sinclair couldn't remember ever being this relaxed. Wearing a borrowed bikini and sun hat, reclining in a chaise lounge and slathered in sunscreen, she sipped a mojito and enjoyed the view from Alessandra Bianchi's back deck.

Alessandra reclined on the chaise next to her, but she didn't wear a bikini. Instead, she was covered head to toe in UPF 50+ protective wear. Chic wide-legged pants in white, a long-sleeved hooded tunic in light gray, and a stylish sun hat that kept her face in the shade.

Harper enjoyed the slight cooling breeze and smiled at her famous friend. "You're bundled up from head to toe."

"I rarely ever wore bikinis. Mainly in the movies. Or sometimes in Cannes or Saint-Tropez in my younger days. I have very fair skin, and the sun is not my friend."

"I bet you could still rock this bikini."

"No one wants to see an eighty-one-year-old woman in a bikini, *amore mio.*"

"I disagree."

"Those days are done for me. I have no yearning to be an object of desire and no need for another man in my life. I am happy on my own and have no wish to compromise."

"I get that. I am tired as hell of having other people tell me what to do and how to live."

"And with Flynn's help, you may never have to again."

"Witness protection may not be much better. I'm still going to have to play a part. Pretend to be something I'm not."

"We all play pretend. You're as much an actress as I am. Maybe more of one. The stakes for you are much higher than they ever were for me. But play enough parts and, after a while, you lose who you are. For years, I played the sex symbol. The movie star. But that was never me. Not until I found the real me did I find the love of my life. Philip fell in love with my true face. Not the sex goddess, but the skinny little girl from Italy with all her flaws and insecurities. He fell in love with the inner me, and I loved him for that. And so, so many other things."

"You miss him."

"I do. I miss many of my friends who have shuffled off this mortal coil. But that is why I so relish making new friends." She reached over and patted Harper's hand. The doorbell rang and Alessandra grinned. "That must be James."

. . .

Duncan Dankworth struggled with car sickness from their drive through the Santa Monica mountains. MI6 supplied them with a rented BMW that hugged the hairpin turns and allowed Flynn to navigate Malibu Canyon Road at a ridiculous speed. Duncan would have appreciated the scenery if he hadn't felt like spewing. But somehow, he managed to keep it together and now they found themselves in front of an incredible beach house in the fabled Malibu Colony.

Who does Flynn know who lives here?

That question was quickly answered when a genuine movie star answered the door. She appeared much older than she did in her many movies, but she still stood tall and regal and devastatingly beautiful.

Flynn and Alessandra Bianchi embraced like long-lost friends.

"James, it's so good to see you."

"You too, my dear. You look as ravishing as ever."

"Oh, please."

"Duncan Dankworth, meet Alessandra Zimmel."

Duncan couldn't hide his astonishment. "Zimmel?"

"My married name," Alessandra said.

Duncan tried to reply with something witty, but nothing came out. His brain completely locked up. Not a single word or thought traversed the empty space in his head, so Flynn picked up the thread of the conversation. "This is where you say it's a pleasure to meet you."

"It is," Duncan sputtered. "A pleasure. To meet you."

Alessandra touched him on the shoulder. "It's a pleasure to meet you too, Duncan. It's perfectly okay to be flustered, but that'll pass once you get to know me. Would either of you two gentlemen care for a cocktail?

"I would love one," Flynn replied. "Duncan?"

"Huh?"

"A cocktail?"

"Uh huh."

· · ·

Flynn stepped out on the deck to find Harper sunning herself on a chaise in an itty-bitty vintage bikini on loan from Alessa. It fit her perfectly. Flynn fought to keep his libido in check. This transaction needed to be all business, and he couldn't let her obvious charms distract him from that. Though clearly that was her intention.

Caitlyn didn't think the woman could be trusted, and Flynn agreed. But he needed her and would do whatever was necessary to get what he wanted. It was the kind of duplicitous dance he had done before, charming and seducing women for information, leverage, and hard intelligence. He didn't enjoy doing it, but it was part of the job and he was good at it.

Flynn sat on the chaise next to Harper. Alessandra brought him a vodka martini. "Thank you, Alessa. For this. For everything."

"Alessa's the best." Harper sat up and crossed her long legs. "She's been so kind to me."

"And courageous to put herself at risk like this. Now it's your turn to do the right thing."

"Your government wanted to sell me out."

"As all governments do," Flynn replied. "Which is why I took away Putin's bargaining chips. Now you can get what you need by giving them what they need."

"Witness protection?"

"Miranda Jacks assured me it's still on the table. And I'll be there to make sure they don't renege on the deal."

"Why would they care what you have to say?"

"Because I know what they've been up to. I know where all the bodies are buried. And I just rescued a Pulitzer Prize-winning journalist who would be more than happy to tell that story."

"So, you're saying I'm going to have to trust you?"

"Isn't that why you contacted MI6 and asked for me? Because you believe in me?"

Harper offered him no answer to that and no expression. "I don't trust anyone. Not completely. But I trust you a tiny bit more than I trust them."

"Where's the thumb drive then?"

"At Bob's Berry Farm in Anaheim."

"The amusement park?"

"Yep."

"That's an enormous place."

"You want the exact location?"

"I do. Can you write it down for me?"

"I can. But I won't. And if I catch any whiff of the FBI or MI6 waiting to swoop in, I will shut this shit down. Once we have an agreement that is signed and notarized, they'll get the names and locations of every Russian sleeper agent operating in North America and Western Europe."

"You have a solicitor?"

"Of course I do. I'm not half-assing this. I want the proper protections in place before I hand anything over to anyone."

Flynn nodded. "Understandable."

Alessandra returned with a fresh mojito for Harper and another one for herself. "James, I'm happy to give you some of Philip's clothing if you need it. I still have a few of his firearms as well. As a strong proponent of the Second Amendment, Phil had quite the arsenal, as I'm sure you remember."

"Thank you, Alessa. I appreciate the offer and, to be honest, I could use some additional clothing and firepower."

"Just take what you need. Knowing my Phil, he would have bent over backwards to help you. I'm just sorry you two never got to meet. He would have enjoyed your company as much as I do."

"I don't doubt it. Philip and I were clearly cut from the same cloth."

. . .

Flynn picked out a few outfits for the road. He needed something casual for a day at Bob's Berry Farm. He selected a dark gray polo shirt, khakis, chukka boots, and a black leather jacket.

As most theme parks now had metal detectors and high-powered security teams, they wouldn't be able to carry weapons into the park. Instead, he selected two to leave in the car. A Walther P5 and a Remington 870 pump-action shotgun. Duncan didn't want a gun, but Flynn insisted and picked him out a Browning Hi-Power and a holster to go with it.

"Better safe than sorry," he said.

Chapter Thirty

By the late 18th century, pleasure gardens like Vauxhall Gardens drew enormous crowds with their hot air balloon ascents, concerts, and fireworks displays. A wave of innovation created mechanical rides like steam-powered carousels. Chicago's World Columbian Exposition in 1893 married entertainment and engineering and featured the first Ferris wheel. Pleasure resorts like Coney Island in Brooklyn expanded the concept and constructed one of the very first roller coasters. In the 1950s, Walt Disney bought up orange groves in Anaheim and created the biggest theme park of them all: Disneyland.

At 3 a.m., Harper climbed from bed, tiptoed into the bathroom, closed the door, and placed a call.

Kalishnik answered on the second ring. "*Da.*"

"I served Flynn up to you on a silver platter. How is it he's still walking around?"

Kalishnik replied in Russian. "He had help."

Harper kept her side of the conversation in English. "That's hardly my problem. I did what was asked. Multiple times now. I deserve to be paid the money that was promised to me."

"You get paid when we kill Flynn."

"That was *not* our agreement."

"I disagree. Where are you?"

Harper hesitated. She didn't want to put Alessandra in danger. Sending Kalishnik to her beach house would mean the elimination of everyone. All witnesses. Harper was ruthless, but not *that* ruthless. "Flynn's not with me."

"Do you know where he is?"

"I know where he *will* be."

"Tell me."

"How do I know you won't mess it up again?"

"Last time he knew I'd be there. This time he won't. We will take him by surprise, and he won't know what hit him."

"Bob's Berry Farm. I don't have an ETA yet, but when I do, I'll text you."

"You're taking him to a farm?"

"An amusement park. In Anaheim. They have metal detectors, so you won't be able to bring weapons inside."

"I'll hit him outside then."

"There's an MI6 agent with us as well. Duncan Dankworth."

"Then he will die too."

．　．　．

Arseny Kuznetsov's father died in the invasion of Dagestan during the second Chechen War. All Russian men are required to serve in the military for one year, but Arseny didn't wait to be conscripted. He enlisted. His intention was to join the GU Spetsnaz. The selection process was rigorous, and very few made the cut. Arseny impressed his superiors with his fitness, marksmanship, and his unrelenting, cold-blooded determination to destroy the enemies of the Russian Federation. He completed missions in the North Caucasus, Syria, and Crimea, and in 2020 was recruited by Russian military intelligence to join GRU Unit 29155. They serve as the GRU's special operations team tasked with the abduction and elimination of spies, traitors, and foreign agents all over the world.

Dressed in a wetsuit, Arseny piloted a fishing boat off the coast of Malibu in the dead of night. He commanded a team tasked with the abduction of the sleeper agent turned traitor.

Nadya Lipovsky now called herself Harper Sinclair. Arseny didn't know what she did to deserve her fate, but he didn't care. The reasons why weren't his concern.

An asset deeply embedded at MI6 told him where to find Lipovsky. As the Malibu Colony was home to some of the most famous people in the world, the mission wouldn't be easy. A gated community protected by a team of guards—not fat rent-a-cops, but retired combat veterans. The easiest approach would be from the sea.

At 3 a.m. a waxing moon hovered low on the horizon, illuminating the whitecaps with a luminescent glow. The light breeze created minimal swell. Matvey dropped anchors at both the bow and stern. Leonid looked pale and seasick as he loaded a dry bag with two pairs of night-vision goggles and two semi-automatic pistols fitted with silencers. Arseny's dry bag included bolt cutters, lock-picking tools, zip tie handcuffs, and a metal case with five syringes filled with a fast-acting sedative.

Anchored five hundred feet from the coast, they made their way to Malibu Beach with paddleboards. No one would see them as suspicious. Surfers and paddleboarders were common on that stretch of beach.

After dragging their boards up the sand, Arseny and Leonid hurried towards the house. Matvey stayed behind with the boat and watched their progress through his binoculars.

Some of the beachfront houses were massive. Many had motion-activated security lights or cameras or both. Their cold wetsuits, dripping with seawater, hid their thermal signatures long enough to avoid tripping any devices. They reached the shadowy area under the deck, where they checked their weapons and put on their night-vision gear.

Arseny cut the phone lines and disabled the alarm system. Leonid fastened a suction handle to a window and used a glass cutter to create a hole for him to reach inside. He unlocked the latch and raised the window. Silently, they entered the house.

Their instructions were to abduct Lipovsky and kill or subdue anyone who interfered with them. They would take her back to the boat and then to a warehouse in Ventura, where a GRU interrogation team waited to extract whatever information they could get from her. As an *illegal*, she was highly trained and would not be easy to subdue. Killing her was not an option. That would constitute mission failure. And Arseny had never failed a mission.

Arseny searched the house with his night-vision goggles, listening for any telltale sounds. Something scuffled behind him. He turned to find a small, elderly Pomeranian looking up at him. The diminutive animal growled and bared its tiny teeth. Arseny drew his silenced pistol and took aim.

Suddenly, the lights came on, blinding Arseny and Leonid. As he ripped off his night-vision goggles, the Pomeranian clamped onto his ankle. A door swung open behind him. Two tiny darts punctured the skin on the back of his neck. Before he could turn, 50,000 volts locked up every muscle in his body. The Pomeranian popped off his leg and bounced off a wall. Arseny lost his pistol and fell to the floor. Leonid stumbled over him, blind, as someone smacked him in the head with a fireplace poker. Arseny reached for his fallen pistol as another jolt of 50,000 volts sent him down a dark hole.

■　■　■

Flynn pulled the zip tie handcuffs off the belt of the intruder Alessandra had tased and secured his hands and legs. He then zip tied the intruder that Harper had hit with the fireplace poker. Not that either one was going anywhere anytime soon. Both were out for the count.

Peanut wandered in a daze, bumping into walls. Alessandra scooped her up and held her close. "Oh, my poor baby. I'm so sorry. Are you okay?"

She squeaked out a bark and licked Alessa's face.

"Oh, good. I'm so glad."

Harper found the case of syringes in the dry bag and examined the vials. "Propofol."

Flynn nodded. "Apparently, they wanted to take you alive."

"Let's put this to good use, then." Harper extended their unconscious condition by giving them each a dose that would keep them out for at least four more hours. They then dragged them into Alessandra's four-car garage.

Harper covered them with a canvas tarp. "This is a GRU team. Unit 29155."

Duncan angrily paced. "How the hell did they find us?"

"My guess is MI6," Flynn said. "Since they can track our vehicle, they have our location."

Duncan sputtered. "What are you saying? MI6 has been compromised?"

"Is that so hard to believe?" Flynn replied. "After all, it's happened before. Philby. Burgess. MacLean."

Harper nodded. "It's not safe here."

Flynn concurred. "They were wearing wetsuits, so they came by sea." He headed into the living room with its view of the ocean and opened the French doors. From the deck, he headed down the stairs to the beach. The sun had yet to rise, and the cool early morning air carried the salty tang of the sea. The Santa Monica mountains rose behind him and the endless Pacific stretched forever into the distance ahead. A few fishing boats bobbed on the horizon. One of them likely belonged to the assault team.

The beach itself was virtually empty save for an elderly man walking his dog, a few early morning runners, and the pint-sized sandpipers chasing the retreating waves. When Flynn returned, everyone was in the kitchen eating pancakes. Save for Duncan Dankworth, who claimed he was too nervous to eat.

"Don't be a git," Flynn told him. "You need to fuel up. You don't want to run out of gas just when you need it most."

"I never run out of gas. Especially when I'm stressed."

Flynn joined them at the table and tucked into blueberry pancakes and a rasher of thick-cut bacon.

Harper carried her empty plate to the sink. "We really gotta go."

"I'm ready when you are," Flynn said.

"Me too," Duncan added.

Alessandra grinned. "Just let me grab my wrap, and I'll be ready as well."

Harper sighed. "Not a good idea, darlin'."

"Why not?"

"It's not safe," Dankworth said.

"Is it any safer here? There might be more of them out there for all we know."

Flynn nodded. "I agree. You should come with us. And since you're coming along anyway, would you mind if we borrowed your Phantom?"

"Of course not."

"Once we're on the road, I'll call the FBI and let them know about our uninvited guests."

Harper shrugged. "They can pick them up, but they won't get anything out of them. And you better not tell them where we're going."

"I wouldn't think of it."

Flynn put the Walther P5, the Remington shotgun, the Browning Hi-Power, and the assault team's weapons and Russian-made night-vision gear into a duffel bag and loaded it into the Phantom's trunk. At 9:00 a.m. they headed for Anaheim. Flynn called the Los Angeles office of the FBI and left a cryptic message for Miranda Jacks. Something about a surprise waiting for her at Alessandra Bianchi's beach house.

The drive took two hours through morning rush hour traffic, and when they arrived at Bob's Berry Farm, the parking lot was already packed. They were directed to a lot a short distance away, left their weapons in the trunk, and hoofed it to the main entrance.

Chapter Thirty-One

Kalishnik found a bench from where he could monitor all the arrivals from the overflow parking lot. To fit in with the other tourists, he wore cargo shorts, New Balance running shoes, a Chicago Cubs baseball cap, and a large Hawaiian shirt over a bellyband holster that held his Lebedev pistol. But he wouldn't be shooting Flynn today. Instead, he would poison him with Novichok, per Ivanov's instructions. He would inject the nerve agent subcutaneously with a ring designed for just that purpose.

At first, Flynn would have difficulty breathing as the muscles around his heart and lungs spasmed. Nerve signals to other muscles would be disrupted, causing violent convulsions. He would shit and piss his pants and vomit his guts out. His last moments alive would be excruciatingly painful, but Kalishnik would be gone by then, having melted away into the crowd.

Putin poisoned more than a few enemies with Novichok in the past. Political rivals. Suspected double agents. Former spies. Using that method would immediately implicate the Russian dictator in Flynn's death. Worldwide condemnation would follow. Then massive economic sanctions. Soon after that, his spy networks in the US and the UK would be rounded up and arrested. He would be humiliated on the world stage.

Bit by bit, Ivanov would strip away Putin's power by turning the Russian people and his paid lackeys against him. He would use his army of hackers to loot his riches and reduce Russia's infrastructure to rubble. And Kalishnik would stand with him as he took power and replaced Putin as the savior of Russia.

But first Flynn must die.

Kalishnik would have to get close to the lunatic to inject the poison, but that shouldn't be a problem with the crush of the crowd. Flynn, Harper, an elderly woman, and a small Indian man stood in line at one of the ticket booths. Kalishnik assumed the Indian was the MI6 agent.

Kalishnik favored a more direct approach. He would have preferred beating Flynn to death with his bare hands, but Ivanov wanted something that put the blame squarely on Putin. So Kalishnik would have to kill him with poison.

Like a woman.

Kalishnik stepped to the rear of the line that Flynn and his companions waited in. He slowly moved forward, jostling past other tourists waiting patiently to reach the ticket kiosk.

"Hey!" A fireplug of a lady in her sixties grabbed Kalishnik by the back of his shirt. "Where do you think you're going, bucko?"

Kalishnik leveled his terrifying eyes at the lady. He had done this many times to intimidate would-be rivals and discourage witnesses from testifying, but this time his killer glower held no power.

"Get in line like the rest of us," barked the lady.

"My friend is up ahead."

"So what? You're just going to cut in line?" The lady had a raspy smoker's growl and some kind of East Coast accent.

"I'm not cutting in."

"What am I? Blind? Wait your damn turn."

Other people in line, encouraged by the lady's fearlessness, joined in.

"You heard the lady!"

"Wait your turn!"

"Don't be a dickhead!"

Kalishnik shrugged her off, and now another lady, a Black lady, shorter and wider than the first, turned around to stare him down. "You better not be cuttin' in front of me!"

"Please, my friends are waiting for me." Kalishnik tried to push her out of the way, but with her size and low center of gravity, she was immovable.

"Get your goddamn hands off me!"

Now the first lady came to the defense of the second lady. "Are you putting your hands on her?"

The Black lady gave Kalishnik a shove. He stumbled back into the first lady.

"Touch me again and I will lay you out!" She raised a rather large purse.

Kalishnik balled his hands into fists, but saw two security guards heading in his direction.

"Learn some frickin' manners!" yelled the first lady.

Not wanting to create a scene and attract Flynn's attention, Kalishnik backed down. He held up his hands, palms out. "I'm sorry. Excuse me. *Sorry.*" Stepping out of the queue, he headed for the back of the line.

The walk back took five minutes, and when he turned around, Flynn was gone. *Where did they go? Were they already inside?* He couldn't let them get away. He'd have to pay his way in and scour the park for them. Kalishnik stood on his tiptoes, hoping to glimpse Flynn leading his band of misfits into the park. He considered following without a ticket, but the security guards continued to eyeball him.

"*Blyat!*"

.   .   .

While the fishing boat lightly rocked back and forth in the swell, Matvey watched the house with his binoculars. Arseny and Leonid had yet to return with the traitor. Matvey couldn't raise them on the radio. He had a hard decision to make. Head back to Marina del Rey, where they rented the boat, or swim to the beach and find out what happened to them.

Soon after Arseny and Leonid had entered the house that held the traitor, lights blinked on inside. Ten minutes after, a man stepped out onto the deck and scanned the horizon. He seemed to gaze directly at Matvey. He went back inside, and after a time, the sun rose higher in the east.

Thirty minutes passed. Matvey tried to raise them again before finally deciding to paddleboard to shore. More people populated the beach now, a few dog walkers, a handful of runners, and a half dozen surfers. Matvey dragged his paddleboard up the sand and left it next to Leonid and Arseny's. He walked towards the house, scanning the windows, looking for signs of life. Ducking between the properties, he found the open window his squadmates used to enter the house.

He landed lightly inside and listened for movement. Hearing a low growl, he pulled his pistol and turned. A diminutive dog bared its tiny teeth. He heard no other voices or movement and carefully searched room by room. The small dog continued to dog him, growling and snarling every step of the way.

He couldn't find anyone anywhere. Finally, he poked his head into the garage to discover Arseny and Leonid secured with their own zip tie handcuffs. He unsheathed his Korshun fighting knife and cut them free.

Arseny was apoplectic and Leonid looked unsteady, the hair on the back of his head caked with dried blood.

"We have to follow! They went to a berry farm!" Arseny sputtered. "Bob's Berry Farm."

Leonid teetered to one side and held on to a shelving unit to steady himself. "I think I might have a concussion."

Cars squealed up outside. Matvey peered through a small window in the garage door. Men and women in blue FBI windbreakers climbed from three black SUVs. "Time to go."

They hurried through the house, out the French doors, and down the deck onto the beach. Without slowing down, they grabbed their paddleboards and headed for the surf. Matvey looked back to see the FBI on the deck, but by now he and his squad looked like just another trio of water sports enthusiasts.

∎　∎　∎

FBI Agent in Charge Miranda Jacks noted signs of a struggle. She found the shredded zip tie handcuffs and gaffer tape on the floor of the garage, along with a puddle of dried blood. Whatever surprise Flynn left for her to find was no longer there. She suspected a GRU hit squad, but clearly they had underestimated Flynn. They always did. Though he claimed he had a license to kill, Flynn never killed anyone. At least not intentionally. He must have subdued them, but someone freed them.

And now Flynn was on the run. Probably with Harper and possibly that fearful little MI6 agent. Alessandra Zimmel was missing as well. *Could she be with Flynn?* A rented BMW sat in the driveway and, according to the DMV, all of Alessandra's cars were there except for one. A Rolls-Royce Phantom.

With only three Rolls-Royce dealers in Los Angeles, it didn't take long to track down where Alessandra purchased hers. Miranda quickly ascertained that the Rolls came with LoJack anti-theft protection. She used the law enforcement interface to ascertain the location of the car.

Bob's Berry Farm.

She contacted the FBI's Tactical Helicopter Unit and requested transportation for her and her team to Anaheim.

∎　∎　∎

Flynn had never been to a theme park before. He'd read about them and seen them on television and in the movies, but the real deal was not what he expected. Hordes of large tourists in shorts and T-shirts fruitlessly tried to control screaming mobs of manic children hopped up on sugary soft drinks and candy. He watched with alarm as the little ones darted about like hyperactive rats. Flynn couldn't remember ever seeing a place more out of control and chaotic. And that included the prison riot at Polar Owl.

The entranceway to the park looked like a cross between a carnival midway and a rustic Wild West town. Barkers barked at people to play their rigged carnival games, while others lured them to booths that sold all manner of junk food. Sunburnt sightseers crammed churros, corndogs, and cotton candy into their gaping cakeholes. The smell of all that fried food mingled with the sickly sweet coconut scent of sunscreen created in Flynn an urge to flee.

Harper handed him a churro. Without thinking, he took a bite. The fried dough dusted with cinnamon and sugar somehow comforted him. It also elicited a distant memory. A memory so faint it almost seemed like a dream. He was ten when he lost his parents in a climbing accident in the French Alps. Or at least that was what he always believed. But in that moment, in that memory, his father wasn't Scottish and his mother wasn't Swiss. They were Americans, and they lived in Burbank. They'd brought him to Bob's Berry Farm for his tenth birthday. And they loved him. His parents loved him.

And then they were gone.

Killed not in a climbing accident, but in a car accident on the way back home from Bob's Berry Farm. The crush of metal echoed in his ears. The screams. The terror. Grief grabbed Flynn by the throat and nearly took him to his knees. He dropped his churro and stumbled to a bench, his head swimming as he plopped down.

Harper sat next to him. "Are you all right?"

"Right as rain."

"Then why are you crying?"

Flynn wiped the tears off his face. He had no answer for her. *"I'm fine."*

Harper touched his cheek and held his gaze. "Talk to me."

"There's nothing to say." He looked away. The humiliation overwhelmed him.

"Let's just sit here then."

Flynn felt sick. Had to be that churro. All that sugar and grease. He could still taste the cinnamon on his lips. He fought to bury his angst and reignite that spark of confidence that somehow went dark. He turned his attention outward to quell the pain that squeezed his heart.

Dancehall girls in skimpy outfits stood outside the Tumbleweed Saloon and crooked their fingers at overwhelmed fathers, luring them in with the promise of cleavage, cold beer, and air conditioning. The Cactus Creek blacksmith pounded horseshoes with a hammer, the rhythmic clanking keeping time with the clippety-clop of horses pulling the Cactus Creek Stagecoach. Native Americans in native dress pounded tom-toms while dancing and chanting and singing in a circle. A long line of travelers waited to enter an outdoor theater that looked like a frontier fort. Flynn scanned a sign advertising some kind of Wild West show.

Alessandra smiled at him with concern, and Dankworth scarfed down a corndog.

Harper touched his elbow. "How are you feeling?"

"I'm fine."

"Ready to go find that locker?"

Flynn nodded. The disturbing hallucination that masqueraded as a memory faded into something unsubstantial as he remembered who he truly was and why he was here. "Let's do it."

Flynn, Dankworth, and Alessandra followed Harper under a large wooden archway that led to an expansive area with thrill rides, kiddie rides, and roller coasters. Everything seemed vaguely familiar. The Sea Serpent Swing. Geronimo Falls. Crazy River Rapids. The Jungle Rumble Roller Coaster. The clatter it made as the cars roared by brought up another distant memory that Flynn violently tamped down. He had to stay focused on the job at hand and push those false memories away. Flynn had suffered endless traumas, saving the world countless times, and the resultant PTSD played tricks with his mind. The stakes were too high to let those demons get in his way.

Harper tapped him on the arm. "Flynn?"

"Yes?"

"Are you sure you're okay?"

"I'm tip-top. Just point the way."

She pointed towards a sign a distance away atop a sheltered area that said *Lockers*.

Chapter Thirty-Two

Novichok means "newcomer" in Russian and applies to a group of advanced nerve agents developed by the Soviet Union in the 1970s and 1980s. These fourth-generation chemical weapons were developed under a Soviet program codenamed Foliant, an attempt to circumvent chemical arms control. Certain variants are five to eight times more toxic than VX nerve agent and sarin and are difficult to identify. They act by blocking messages from the nerves to the muscles, causing death by cardiac arrest or asphyxiation. Considerably more lethal than the typical poisons used in Agatha Christie mysteries.

The prominent vein in Kalishnik's temple throbbed ominously as his blood pressure skyrocketed. Fighting his way in wasn't an option, so he waited in that endless line. The idiot manning the booth had to be brain damaged, as each tourist took forever to buy their stupid tickets. Sweat trickled down his back and soaked the armpits of his festive Hawaiian shirt. He thumbed the ring that would deliver the fatal dose of nerve agent. Jewelry that small rarely sets off metal detectors, but even if it did, it wouldn't be deemed suspicious. Not that Kalishnik needed a weapon to dispatch Flynn. He fought for Russia in the Olympics as a heavyweight boxer. He trained in Systema and Brazilian Jiu-Jitsu. He could snap Flynn's neck or crush his skull with his bare hands if necessary. Not that it would be. Not after injecting him with a fatal dose of Novichok.

Kalishnik studied the colorful map he picked up at the ticket booth and searched for the symbol that indicated where the lockers were located. He found two places. One near a video game arcade and another beneath a giant roller coaster. He pulled out his phone and texted Harper's burner. *Where are you?*

When she didn't immediately respond, he headed for the lockers near the video game arcade. On the way, he spotted the Cactus Creek Knife and Gun Shop. Inside, he found six-guns, hunting knives, sheriff's badges, cowboy hats, and copies of the US Constitution. The guns were fake, but the knives were real. He bought himself a twelve-inch Bowie knife with a staghorn handle. He wouldn't need it for Flynn, but if he were identified, he might need it to fight his way out. His phone vibrated as he exited the shop. A text from Harper.

Heading for the lockers near the Jungle Rumble Roller Coaster.

■　■　■

Once Arseny, Leonid, and Matvey returned to Marina Del Rey, the ride to Anaheim in their rented Ford Taurus took a little over an hour. Their instructions now were to let the traitor retrieve the thumb drive. Then take it from her and liquidate her in no particular order. This time, they wouldn't let Harper or Flynn get the upper hand.

To that end, they slipped into the backstage area of the Outlaw's Revenge Stunt Show. In the dressing room, they found enough western wear for all of them: hats, boots, black leather dusters, and gun belts. The six-shooters and lever-action rifles only fired blanks, but there was a nice selection of throwing knives with leather bandoleers that held six at a time.

Arseny loved westerns. *The Magnificent Seven. The Good, the Bad, and the Ugly. The Wild Bunch.* But his favorite had to be *Tombstone* with Kurt Russell as Wyatt Earp. He would play cowboy for a day and take out that traitor. Each Russian put on a Stetson, strapped on a six-gun, and a bandoleer of throwing knives. Arseny stopped in front of a full-length mirror to check himself out. He liked what he saw and drew his six-gun, spinning it on his finger before aiming at his image.

He shouted like Kurt Russell playing Wyatt Earp in Tombstone (if Kurt Russell had a Russian accent and a voice two octaves lower). "So, run, you *svoloch*! And tell the other *svoloches* I come to get them! And Hell comes with me! You got that, you *kozyol*! *Hell comes with me!*"

■ ■ ■

A helicopter landed on the roof of the Orange County FBI office. Miranda and her team jumped out and joined six special agents assigned to the Orange County office. They left in three black unmarked SUVs and drove the six miles to Bob's Berry Farm, parking near the security office.

Miranda could have called in SWAT but didn't want to create widespread panic or alert Flynn and Harper that they were on to them. Which is why they wore street clothes and not FBI windbreakers. Miranda knew the head of security at Bob's Berry Farm. A retired FBI agent from back in the day. He sent out text messages, complete with pictures, to every security officer walking the grounds.

Miranda's team then spread out over the park while Miranda joined her former colleague in the massive security control room. The control room itself looked like something you'd see at NORAD or NASA. Every square inch of Bob's Berry Farm was under constant surveillance. It was only a matter of time before Flynn revealed himself. He couldn't help himself. Miranda just hoped she could find him before his enemies did.

■ ■ ■

Harper knew she was being watched. She kept it casual, nonchalantly looking around, hoping to find the strike team before they struck. Training and experience had given her a sixth sense when it came to counter surveillance. Perhaps she was reacting to all the security cameras. They were everywhere.

She glanced at Flynn. *What the hell is wrong with him? What made him freeze like that?* His usual confidence just disappeared, replaced with fear and unbelievable sadness. He was broken, and yet she still arranged for someone to murder him. He trusted her and she deceived him. That betrayal weighed on her. She had to let it go. Her conscience was getting in the way, and if she wasn't careful, it would get her killed.

Flynn caught her staring. She offered him a smile.

He raised a quizzical eyebrow. "What?"

Harper shrugged. "I don't think I properly thanked you."

"For what?"

"For rescuing your friends and preventing Putin from using them as a bargaining chip. If not for you, I'd likely be on my way to Siberia."

"I'm sure you would've done the same for me if the situation was reversed."

Harper had no answer for that. She focused on leading Flynn, Alessandra, and Dankworth into the covered area with the lockers. Key in hand, Harper found the right locker and opened it. Inside, a small envelope sat crinkled and lonely at the bottom. As she pocketed it, she caught sight of Kalishnik out of the corner of her eye.

▪ ▪ ▪

Kalishnik removed the cover of his ring, revealing the tiny needle that would deliver the nerve agent and end Flynn once and for all. He caught Harper's eye. They traded a glance. *What's that look? Is she feeling guilty?* Suddenly, she lurched off. Flynn hurried after her. The elderly woman and the MI6 agent hustled to keep up.

So did he.

A gunshot rang out. The crowd panicked and ran, revealing a cowboy standing in the center of the street. He shouted a challenge to another cowboy just up the way.

"End of the line, Billy Bob!"

Harper and Flynn stood between them as the crowd parted.

"Don't think so, partner. Nobody's faster than me!"

Both cowboys had Russian accents. Kalishnik found that puzzling.

"Skin that smoke wagon and see what happens!"

"You calling me out?"

"I'm calling down the thunder!"

Flynn and the others stood transfixed as the cowboys dropped their fake guns and reached for their throwing knives. They launched them simultaneously, both spinning through the air in Harper's direction. Flynn stepped in front of her and, with lightning reflexes, snatched one knife right out of the air. The other, however, buried itself in Flynn's shoulder. He staggered backwards and fell as Harper dove for cover behind a barrel.

The cowboys advanced. Harper had nowhere to hide. Kalishnik considered trying to save her but decided it was none of his business. Instead, he turned to Flynn. But the lunatic no longer lay on the ground. He was gone.

Blyat! Where the hell did he go?

That question was soon answered by the rattle of a stagecoach as it thundered between Harper and the cowboys. Flynn, holding the reins, shouted, "Time to go!"

The Russian cowboys ran towards the stagecoach as Harper, Alessandra, and Dankworth piled inside. Flynn snapped the reins. The horses rumbled away, leaving the Russian knife flingers in the dust.

Kalishnik had to admire the bastard. But only for a second before he chased after the departing stagecoach. He couldn't let Flynn get away again.

. . .

Blood poured from the knife wound in his shoulder, but Flynn didn't have time to stop and staunch the bleeding. He snapped the reins to get the horses to gallop faster. People screamed and jumped out of the way. He grew lightheaded, but steeled himself to stay conscious.

Harper shouted to him from inside the coach, but he couldn't hear her over the thundering hooves and rattling wheels. He glanced back. The knife-flinging cowboys fell farther behind. When he turned forward, the panicked crowd ahead ran and dove to get out of the way.

One young woman pushing a pram stood frozen, her feet rooted to the ground. Flynn couldn't get around her without trampling scores more. So, he pulled back on the reins as hard as he could. The horses quickly halted, kicking up dust. He pressed his hand over the wound in his shoulder and jumped to the ground, crashing down on his side. Dankworth and Harper helped him up and hurried him along.

The cowboys kept coming.

. . .

Harper scanned the crowd for Kalishnik. Flynn saved her yet again, but she couldn't afford to be sentimental. Kalishnik would kill Flynn whether or not she helped him. That was unavoidable. No point in delaying the inevitable. Flynn was badly injured. Blood seeped down his arm and over her hand. She should let him go and save herself. That was the only logical thing to do.

She looked at him. He looked at her. She took in the pain, strain, and determination on his face and let him go. Flynn stumbled and fell, dragging Dankworth down with him.

She ducked into the Cactus Creek Blacksmith shop and grabbed a ball-peen hammer off a bench. The blacksmith looked askance and raised his voice in protest, but Harper swept his legs out from under him. She searched the crowd for the cowboys. A handful of security guards fought to quell the stampeding mob. She glanced back at Flynn as Alessandra and Dankworth struggled to get him back on his feet.

That was when she saw Kalishnik. Shoving panicked tourists out of the way, he zeroed in on Flynn. Harper could have fled and joined the unruly horde heading for the exits. It would have been the smart thing to do. The only thing to do. Instead, she ran in Flynn's direction, cocked her arm, and let the hammer fly. She aimed for Kalishnik's giant pumpkin-shaped head but miscalculated and hit him in the sternum instead. It staggered him back, but the blow didn't stop him or take him out. So, she kept running and launched herself into the air, planting a flying sidekick squarely in his chest. Kalishnik staggered back but stayed on his feet. Harper came at him again.

"What are you doing?" he shouted in Russian.

Her only answer was a sidekick to his kneecap. He absorbed the blow without buckling and grabbed her by the throat. Harper struggled to break free using her Systema training, but the bastard had a grip like a steel vise. She couldn't breathe. Her strength ebbed. Just before she lost consciousness, a knife spun towards her through the air. She twisted and turned. Kalishnik pivoted to follow and caught the spinning knife in his massive trapezius. Harper pulled free as another knife buried itself in his deltoid.

Kalishnik roared like a bear and turned to confront his attackers. The cowboys let loose two more throwing knives. One plunged into Kalishnik's thigh, and the other buried itself in his chest. Kalishnik sank to his knees as the two cowboys drew their last blades and cocked their arms.

She spotted Flynn a second before he tackled her. The twin spinning blades flew over them both and impaled a panicky park mascot.

Clucky Cock-A-Doodle-Doo caught both knives in his rear end and ran off, howling more like a coyote than a chicken. He flattened Dizzy Duck and Gobble Wobble before running hell for tail feathers out of harm's way.

Harper tried to scramble to her feet as the killer cowboys pulled out two hand axes and pressed forward. Flynn put himself between them, prepared to protect Harper once again, when both Russians were blown off their feet by multiple gunshots.

"FBI!" shouted Miranda Jacks.

Miranda advanced with her Glock. Four other FBI agents flanked her with their own weapons. A dozen terrified Bob's Berry Farm security guards followed from a safe distance.

She glanced at Flynn on the ground, his hand pressed against his bleeding knife wound, his face pale. He pointed with a finger dripping blood. "Kalishnik," he whispered.

Kalishnik staggered off with four knives sticking out of him.

Miranda recognized him immediately. "Arrest that man!"

Special agents surrounded the enforcer and, for a split second, Harper thought he might resist, but Kalishnik raised his hands and put them behind his back so they could slap handcuffs on him.

■   ■   ■

Flynn's head rested in Alessandra's lap as Duncan Dankworth pressed hard on the would-be agent's wound to staunch the bleeding. He worried for his friend. Dankworth didn't have many friends. For all his misgivings, Flynn treated him with respect. He encouraged Dankworth and saw the best in him. And now Flynn had sacrificed himself yet again to save someone else. Flynn was more courageous than anyone Dankworth had ever met. Maybe that was because he was mentally ill. But perhaps his fearlessness had nothing to do with madness and everything to do with his innate decency, fortitude, and gallantry. Some commentators had compared Flynn to Don Quixote. But Don Quixote tilted at windmills, not international supervillains intent on world domination.

Alessandra patted Flynn on the face to keep him conscious. "Are you okay?"

"I don't think I am."

Dankworth squeezed his arm. "Help is on the way."

Flynn winced with pain. "We *are* that help, and we have done what we must to save the day." He offered Dankworth a wan smile before shutting his eyes and falling silent.

"Flynn? *Flynn?*"

The paramedics arrived to take over. Alessa and Dankworth left Flynn in their capable hands. The FBI interrogated Harper Sinclair and Dankworth and wandered over to join the scrum.

"You need to stop holding out on us," Miranda insisted.

Dankworth interrupted before Harper could answer. "Do I need to remind you that Ms. Sinclair is an MI6 asset?"

"I understand that," Miranda said. "But she is on US soil, which gives the US government a vested interest in this case."

"This was all settled at that meeting in Helsinki. Your government and my government came to an agreement. MI6 has official command and control of this asset *and* this mission."

"That was before a GRU hit squad brought violence and chaos to Bob's Berry Farm and put hundreds of American citizens in danger."

Duncan nodded. "Fair enough, but we still need to work together on this." Duncan turned his attention to Harper. "What's in the envelope you took from that storage locker? Is that the thumb drive?"

Miranda glared at her. "I want to see that envelope."

Harper sighed and handed it over.

Miranda looked inside and lost her neutral, non-regional accent and professional demeanor. "A *key*? Where's the damn thumb drive?"

"It's behind the door this key opens," Harper said.

Miranda sputtered with anger. "Are you going to tell us where to find that effing door?"

"Absolutely. Once we sign all the paperwork legally committing the Justice Department to putting me in witness protection."

Chapter Thirty-Three

The Indian Removal Act of 1830 led to the expulsion of Native Americans with settlements and burial mounds near the Fox River. Five years later, James and Hezekiah Gifford established the town that became known as the butter capital of the world, and eventually gained fame as the largest manufacturer of fine watches in the United States. The brothers named the town after a Scottish folk tune. Over the years, the modest municipality spawned quite a few famous sons and daughters. Five navy admirals, a Nobel Prize winner, two Academy Award winners, a General Motors CEO, and Earl "Madman" Muntz all hailed from Elgin, Illinois.

Harper Sinclair struggled to remember her new name as she drove her Ford Focus into Elgin. She had a hard time keeping it top-of-mind. Perhaps because it was so close to her previous made-up name.

She said it aloud in an attempt to lodge it in her brain. "Hanna Sadler. Hi, I'm Hanna. Hanna Sadler. Hanna. Sadler." She ditched her syrupy Southern accent for a Midwestern one. More Minnesota than Chicago. She repeated a particular series of phrases to cement that accent in her mind and mouth. "Gosh darn it. You betcha. Geez Louise. Oh, for cripe's sake. I'm just gonna scoot right past ya there. I make a mean Jell-O salad."

Before driving to Elgin, she dyed her natural blonde hair a mousy brown. She wore brown contact lenses and large red plastic glasses. Ugly, oversized clothes concealed her slender, shapely form. She wanted to avoid attracting attention. To blend into the background. Make herself invisible. At least that's what her handlers at the US Marshal Service's Federal Witness Protection Program recommended she do. They created a new identity for her with a new social security card, driver's license, and address in Elgin, Illinois.

The rented townhouse sat in a brand-new housing development, built over what used to be a cornfield. They would fund her living expenses until she established herself. Even then, they'd still provide a modest stipend. A far cry from the ten million dollars Ivanov promised her for setting up Flynn.

In the end, she cursed herself for letting her conscience get in the way of common sense. Of course, Ivanov wasn't someone she could trust. He could have easily stiffed her and ordered Kalishnik to liquidate her as well. For now, the enforcer rotted in a federal supermax. Though Ivanov would likely put his considerable resources towards freeing his former right-hand man. If that day ever came, Harper had no doubt that Kalishnik would hunt her to the ends of the earth. No Witness Protection Program participant who followed the rules and guidelines set forth by the US Marshal's Service had ever been killed while under active protection.

But there was a first time for everything.

Harper found the Illinois countryside flat, dull, and boring as hell. She passed by a number of new housing developments, all equally insipid and cookie-cutter. She finally found her own townhouse complex. The Commons at Fox Creek. Since she didn't have the opener for the underground garage, she parked in the visitor's lot and made her way to her new address. One half of a duplex.

Sprinklers sprinkled, keeping the well-manicured lawn lush and green. Small shrubs and even smaller trees lined the yard. Harper couldn't imagine a blander, more personality-free place. Or Hanna couldn't. *Not Harper.* "Hanna. Hanna Sadler. Sadler. *Hanna Sadler.*"

The front door of her townhouse was unlocked. Inside, she found her case officer waiting in the kitchen, sitting in the breakfast nook, eating a burger from Hardee's. Scott Johnson was tall and balding. He had the broad shoulders and softening middle of a former athlete. He held up a Hardee's bag. "You hungry? I bought an extra burger just in case."

Harper shook her head. "No, thanks."

Johnson pointed to a binder on the kitchen table. "All your documents are in there. Birth certificate. Driver's license. Social Security card. I established a bank account for you. The ATM card and passcode are in there too. Your medical insurance card. The keys to your mailbox. What else? Oh, yeah, I arranged a couple of job interviews for you at Woodfield Mall. At Blaze Pizza, Subway, and Wetzel's Pretzels."

"You do realize I have a PhD from Caltech?"

"Harper Sinclair has a PhD from Caltech. Hanna Sadler dropped out of North Hennepin Community College."

"Are you shitting me?"

"Once you're gainfully employed, feel free to start looking for another job. Nothing too high profile, though. The object is not to attract attention."

"Got it."

"Yeah, I'm not sure you do. But if you follow the rules and all the proper protocols, no one will ever find you."

She pointed at some ketchup on Johnson's face. "You got some stuff on your—"

He dabbed at his face with a napkin.

"Other side." He dabbed again and missed. "A little higher."

More dabbing.

"There you go."

"You still need to sign your pledge."

"Didn't I do that?"

Scott slid a piece of paper over to Harper's side of the table. "No, you didn't."

She looked it over and reread the phrase that gave her pause the last time she didn't sign it. Number seven on the list. *Be a good person and live a normal life.* Harper had no idea what that meant. She had never been a good person *or* lived a normal life. She wasn't exactly sure how to do either one. She signed it anyway. Mainly to get Scott Johnson off her ass and out the door.

She slid the paper to him. "Are we done here?"

Scott nodded. "We're done."

"*Good.*"

"If you need anything, you have my number."

Harper just stared at him until he gathered his things and headed for the exit. "Don't try to white-knuckle this. I'm here to help."

He stepped outside and turned to say something, but she slammed the door in his face.

■ ■ ■

Harper went to a local Jewel-Osco supermarket and picked up some groceries. She returned to her new home, nuked a frozen pizza, and plopped herself on the couch to watch TV. Her townhouse came furnished. She wondered if Scott Johnson did the decorating. The décor matched his drab personality.

"Sadler. Hanna Sadler. I'm Hanna Sadler, gosh darn it. You betcha. Geez Louise." She took a bite of pizza and burned her mouth on the molten cheese. "*Goddamn it.*"

She soothed her burnt mouth with a cold beer and flipped through the channels to find something to watch. *MILF Manor* on TLC. *When Sharks Attack* on National Geographic. *Beat Bobby Flay* on The Food Network. Then the face of a person she knew popped up on the screen.

Alessandra Bianchi.

She starred in the spy film that made her an international sex symbol. Stunningly beautiful, she stood on a beach in the warm glow of the setting sun; her clothes ragged, her face smudged, her hair perfect, and her gaze resolute. Breaking millions of hearts the world over. The movie didn't end with her sitting on a couch in a frumpy disguise, watching TV and eating pizza. Reality never matched the movies. But Alessa turned out to be every bit a hero. It broke Harper's heart that she wouldn't ever be able to contact her again. Alessa showed her so much kindness.

She flipped the channels again only to find another familiar face.

Miranda Jacks.

It looked like some kind of press conference. Harper unmuted the sound as Agent Jacks approached a podium. "Morning, everyone. My name's Miranda Jacks, and I'm the Special Agent in Charge of Counterterrorism at the FBI's Los Angeles field office. I'm here today with Kurt Daniels, Special Agent in Charge of Counterintelligence, and Deputy Attorney General Albert Carver. We are here to announce the arrest of forty-two Russian nationals charged with espionage against the United States. Each one was operating deep undercover and masquerading as a US citizen.

"We are just one part of an international effort that has arrested and charged Russian sleeper agents operating all over the world. That said, the investigation is ongoing and some suspects are still at large. A joint task force comprised of local, state, and federal law enforcement agencies is currently in the process of hunting them down. At this point, I'll turn this over to US Deputy Attorney General Carver."

A short, stocky, stern-looking man with glasses approached the podium. "Good afternoon. And thank you, Special Agent Jacks for the extraordinary work you and Special Agent Daniels have done on this investigation. The Department of Justice will not tolerate these kinds of threats to our institutions, our corporations, or our citizens. The cases unsealed today take place against a backdrop of malign activity from the Russian Federation that includes espionage, murder, and unceasing efforts to steal sensitive US technology and national security secrets from…"

Harper muted the sound. An electrical frisson of fear raised the hairs on the back of her neck. The FBI made no mention of her or Flynn, and that was purposeful. That was to protect them. But there was no protecting her from Putin. Russia's President for Life would know who was responsible for decimating his intelligence capabilities. She knew he would spare no expense to hunt her down and make an example out of her.

Without the ten million Ivanov promised her, staying alive would be much more difficult. Saving Flynn was maybe not the best decision. She let sentimentality get in the way of self-preservation. Though in the moment, she couldn't let Kalishnik kill him. Flynn had somehow rekindled the tiniest ember of a conscience that long lay dormant in her moribund soul. She was sure her GRU training had removed any trace of human feeling. But then again, maybe her resurrected humanity had more to do with Putin than Flynn. Perhaps that stupid war he started and the slaughter of her beloved brother was the real catalyst that reanimated her cold, dead heart. Flynn simply saw the good in her, even if she could no longer see it in herself. He never doubted that she was a decent human being, despite all evidence to the contrary.

Before she met Flynn, she couldn't understand how someone like Caitlyn Valentine could've fallen in love with him. To fall for someone as delusional as Flynn seemed equally, if not even more, delusional. But there was something about him. Something so pure and true and decent and hopeful.

Much to her surprise, tears welled up in her eyes. She unlocked her phone and stared at a picture of her brother. A scan of a photo from when they were children. She was ten, and he was eight. They stood together against the world. She loved him and she protected him. But she couldn't save him from Putin and his vainglorious war. She took solace in the fact that she found some small measure of justice by striking back at the man who sent him and so many thousands of other young men to slaughter.

It broke her heart that she couldn't protect him.

But maybe she could still protect Flynn.

■ ■ ■

Duncan Dankworth waited in the anteroom outside his immediate superior's superior's office. He had a bombshell to present to Kathy, and the anxiety it created aggravated his IBS to no end. Her upper-class twit of an assistant, Peter, regarded him with his usual contempt. As if Duncan were something disgusting he found stuck to the bottom of his Crockett & Jones loafer. The resultant pressure caused him intense discomfort. He struggled to keep an errant trump from escaping his bum.

The phone on Peter's desk buzzed. He picked up and looked at Duncan. "She's ready for you now."

"Perhaps you should join us."

"Excuse me?"

"To take notes if necessary."

A sneer. "Why would that be necessary?"

Kathy poked her head out the door. "Duncan?"

Duncan bolted to his feet. "Hi, Mum. I asked Peter to join us. I thought it might be helpful to have someone take notes."

"Fine. But quickly. I have a call with the Home Secretary in ten minutes."

Duncan followed Kathy into her office. Peter joined them with a pad. She motioned for Duncan to sit. He took the chair across from the desk. Peter sat on the couch a short distance away with his usual look of barely veiled disdain.

When Duncan didn't immediately begin, Kathy prodded him. "You said this was important?"

"It is, Mum. I believe I've ferreted out the Russian mole."

Peter smirked at that.

Kathy raised an eyebrow. "And how exactly did you do that?"

"No one but you knew we were in Malibu."

Her face grew pink. "Are you accusing me?"

"No, Mum, of course not. But I went through the records to see who might have been monitoring the location of the rental car Flynn and I were driving."

"Why would I need to monitor the rental car location? You told me where you were."

"And you told no one else?"

Irritated. "Of course not."

"I just wanted to make sure you didn't ask Peter to check on the rental car location."

"I already told you I didn't."

"But the records reflect that Peter *did* check on the rental car location. He also knew about the rendezvous in Solvang."

Peter sprang to his feet. "You can't be serious!"

"A deeper dive into Peter's phone records uncovered a series of texts to a number in the US."

"So what? I have a cousin there. Living in Los Angeles!"

"Is he a member of Unit 21955? Because the texts were sent to a burner phone found on one of the assassins."

Kathy hit her intercom. "Security to my office."

Peter bolted for the door. Duncan tripped him. He hit the floor hard,and scrambled to his feet, racing from the room.

Duncan and Kathy followed to find him face down on the ground, his wrists zip tied behind him by two heavily armed members of the protective security staff.

Kathy offered Duncan a grateful smile. "I never did like that insufferable prat."

Chapter Thirty-Four

Miguel wore his dinner proudly. Mashed potatoes, Goldfish cracker crumbs, and peas decorated his chubby two-and-a-half-year-old face. He flung peas at Flynn and laughed every time one bounced off his head. "Peas!" he shouted. "*Peas!*"

Alyssa looked horrified. "I'm so sorry."

"Apparently, he's not especially keen on peas." Flynn picked up an errant pea. He tossed it back at Miguel. It bounced off his nose and landed in his mash. Miguel buried his nose in his plate and when he lifted his head, the whole plate stuck to his face.

"I think he's done with dinner." Alyssa peeled off the plate and wiped his face with a damp sponge. Miguel squirmed and struggled and flailed as she lifted him out of his high chair. She carried him to the nursery, leaving Flynn and Sancho alone to finish their meal.

Sancho had picked the bangers up at a UK specialty store in Burbank. He'd developed a taste for pub food when he and Flynn visited London the previous year. He grilled them on his barbecue and made the mash himself. The sweet peas were from a can. They washed down the meal with bottles of Black Toad Dark Ale.

Sancho opened his mouth to say something, but no words emerged. Whatever he wanted to communicate, he couldn't quite work up the nerve to say it. Flynn gave him time to find his courage, but when that courage wasn't forthcoming, Flynn patted his old friend on the hand. "Are you all right?"

Sancho shrugged. "I guess I'm feeling a little guilty."

"For what?"

"For not coming with you to break Bettina out of prison."

"Don't be ridiculous. First of all, I didn't ask you to come."

"Why? Why didn't you?"

"Because that mission wasn't sanctioned by anyone. Not MI6. Not the US government. It worked out in the end, but to be honest, I was lucky. It could have gone tits-up at any time."

"You make your own luck, dude. You always have."

"I appreciate that. But Caitlyn wasn't wrong. I could have ended up in a Russian gulag or worse. And the last thing I wanted to do was put you in harm's way again. You're a father now. You have responsibilities. A son who depends on you. That's the only reason I didn't call on you."

"Okay, I get that, but you need to know I have your back. You're my *hermano* from another mother, man. I wouldn't even be here if not for you. I definitely wouldn't have Alyssa and Miguel in my life."

"I'm sure that's not true."

"I am." Sancho drained his beer and set the bottle down. "So, with Kalishnik in prison, you think Ivanov will call off the dogs?"

"Let's hope so." Flynn reached for his beer and flinched. A bandage covered his upper pectoral and shoulder. The throwing knife had sliced through muscle and nicked a rib, but luckily missed his lung and major arteries. Recovery was slow and painful as hell.

"Where are you gonna go? You need to find someplace safe."

"There is no such place. I wanted to retire and leave it all behind. That's why I took Caitlyn to Switzerland. But as much as I tried to let the past go, it wouldn't let *me* go. My enemies are determined to have their revenge. I can either wait for them to come for me or I can come for them."

"So, you're not going back to Switzerland?"

"I'm not sure what the point would be."

"To work things out with Caitlyn."

"I think that ship has sailed."

"She loves you, *mano*."

"She wants me to be someone I'm not. I wish I could accommodate her, but I'm just not ready to hang up my hat. I thought she understood that. I thought we were on the same path. Evidently, I was mistaken."

"So, you're just gonna give up on her?"

"It's she who has given up on me."

Sancho shook his head. "You two have been through too much to just walk away."

"I agree." Alyssa stepped back into the kitchen and turned on the water for tea. "If you want Caitlyn in your life, you need to fight for her."

"Fighting does seem to be the one thing we're good at," Flynn said.

"That's because you two care about each other."

"I understand what you're saying, luv. I do. But I'm probably better off on my own."

Alyssa looked exasperated. "*You are infuriating.*"

"Caitlyn would agree."

■　■　■

Duncan Dankworth did not like being the center of attention. That kind of scrutiny elevated his anxiety and aggravated his IBS. The ceremony took place at St. James's Palace. Duncan clenched the muscles in his pelvic floor to keep a loud squeaker from escaping his bum. It was such a glorious moment; Duncan didn't want to ruin it with an errant trump. Every year, at an annual ceremony, King Charles handed out medals, ribbons, and citations to members of Britain's intelligence agencies who showed exceptional bravery, gallantry, and leadership during active operations.

Duncan stood with four other fellow agents and looked out over a small crowd of government officials and colleagues. No family members, friends, or press were invited, as the operations each agent participated in were classified as top secret. Duncan could only ever reveal this honor to those who also held top secret clearances.

As King Charles approached, a severe stab of gas pain threatened to double Duncan over. He stood strong, however, even as the sweat dripped down his forehead and into his eyes. When he saluted the king, he surreptitiously wiped away the perspiration and let go with a tiny, high-pitched squeaker.

The King raised an eyebrow but gave nothing else away as he said, "It is with great honor and profound respect that I present you with the George Cross. Your courage and selflessness in the face of extreme danger exemplify the highest ideas of valor and service. This award is a testament to your extraordinary courage and commitment. Thank you for your exceptional service."

The King pinned the medal on Duncan's suit. The small audience applauded long and loud enough to cover a lengthy, glorious, thunderous fart. Duncan caught the eye of an attractive female colleague in the crowd, someone who had never even acknowledged his existence before. Jennifer Fairfax-Wells. The youngest daughter of a second-tier peer in the British aristocracy. She offered him a warm smile. Duncan reciprocated with a manly nod.

Beyond this medal, he also received a promotion. From Officer to Senior Officer. Of course, Duncan couldn't tell his family or friends about that honor either. But none of that mattered. The important thing was that he knew. He had looked danger in the face and hadn't flinched or turned away. He found his courage, and for that he had Flynn to thank. James saw something in Duncan that even Duncan couldn't see.

And now everyone saw it.

Even the King of England.

Chapter Thirty-Five

The Metropolitan Detention Center in downtown Los Angeles holds both male and female inmates prior to and during court proceedings. It opened in 1988, just two blocks from the U.S. District Courthouse, and sported a unique design for a federal prison. There weren't bars or cells, but housing units with ballistic glass windows. It looked more like a high-rise office building than a prison, though MDC Los Angeles was classified as a high-security facility. The most dangerous and violent prisoners were held in their own cells. Those considered slightly less dangerous were assigned a roommate and held in marginally larger accommodations.

Kalishnik bottled up his cold fury as he sat in the central dining hall and ate his sliced meat sandwich on white bread. Some of his fellow inmates included serial killers, gangbangers, and Islamic terrorists. There was also a porn producer charged with sex trafficking minors. Most of the inmates assumed he was Russian mafia and kept their distance. Even the two *sicarios* from the Cali Cartel gave him a wide berth.

Three new arrivals changed that dynamic. Kalishnik could tell they were GRU the moment he saw them. Word spread about the Russian hit squad soon after they arrived. They were recently released from the infirmary as Flynn and Harper had apparently kicked the crap out of them. He watched as they walked through the cafeteria line and filled their trays with food.

Unit 29155 clearly wasn't what it used to be. This new generation didn't have the same level of commitment. Though that wasn't entirely their fault. A fish stinks from the head down, and those who now led the unit clearly didn't know what the hell they were doing. These stupid *glupyets* let themselves be taken alive. That never should have happened. Of course, Kalishnik was taken alive as well. But then he had a reason to live. He knew Ivanov would spare no expense to get him out.

The three-man hit squad made a beeline for Kalishnik's table. If he wasn't exactly a friendly face, at least he was a Russian face. And Kalishnik felt the same way. At one time he *was* them. Ex-Spetsnaz and GRU.

They sat across from him. The biggest of the three offered his hand and addressed Kalishnik in Russian. "I'm Arseny. That's Leonid, and that ugly son of a bitch is Matvey."

Kalishnik nodded. "I'm—"

"Kalishnik. Of course, we know who you are. You won the bronze medal in the fucking Olympics. You are Spetsnaz. Just like us. But you made good. Made money. You are what we all hope to be one day."

"Locked up in prison?"

"That's just temporary. For you. For us. They won't keep us here long."

Kalishnik shrugged. "How very optimistic of you."

"More realistic than optimistic. And while we're here, I propose we watch each other's backs."

"You don't see me as an enemy?"

"Why would we?"

"I work for Ivanov. Putin wants Ivanov dead, and since you work for Putin, wouldn't that make me your adversary?"

Arseny shook his head. "Not until Putin puts a target on *your* back."

"What happens if he does?"

"Then we'll kill you or you'll kill us. But no reason to worry about something that has yet to come to pass."

"I agree."

Matvey opened his sandwich and pulled out the thin slice of greenish lunch meat. "What kind of meat is this?"

Kalishnik shrugged. "Better not to know."

Leonid scowled and put down his sandwich.

"It's settled then," Arseny said. "You watch our *zhopy* and we'll watch yours. That way none of us will end up in a sandwich."

. . .

Oleg Ivanov bought himself a new superyacht after Flynn blew up his last one. *The Fancy* was now at the bottom of the Mediterranean. His new superyacht, berthed in Bali, was even more extravagant than his last one. And, like *The Fancy*, he named it after another famous pirate ship.

The Jolly Roger measured one hundred and fifty-eight meters from stem to stern. He had extensive security measures installed, including advanced radar, sonar, and thermal detection systems, jamming and disruption devices, water cannons, anti-piracy nets, armor plating, and an anti-missile defense shield. Thirty ex-special forces operatives served as his security team.

This time, he wasn't taking any chances.

Bali didn't have an extradition treaty with either the U.S. or Russia. If you had riches, you were welcome. Even though his ex-wife stole his company and much of his cash, he still had over a billion dollars hidden in accounts all over the world.

He turned the yacht's grand ballroom into a war room where he could monitor the activities of his enemies, his vast holdings, and his remaining businesses. From there, he plotted his revenge. On Putin. On the U.S. government. On his ex-wife, Anya.

And on James Flynn.

Kalishnik sat rotting in a federal prison in Los Angeles. But not for long. Ivanov financed a dream team of attorneys to secure his release. In the meantime, he hired an army of assassins to hunt down Flynn and end him once and for all. Ivanov still intended to frame Putin for Flynn's murder. Since Flynn helped Harper expose Putin's entire worldwide spy network, many would now easily believe that Putin wanted Flynn dead.

Revenge was now the organizing principle of his life. Every setback and challenge only served to inspire his ultimate ambition. Global dominance. Total world hegemony. That was his true destiny.

Once he held sway over every human being on Earth, Caitlyn Valentine could not deny him. She would realize the horrible mistake she made in rejecting him and beg for his forgiveness.

She would beg.

Chapter Thirty-Six

After an eleven-hour flight from LAX and a two-hour train ride from Zurich, Flynn arrived at Interlaken Ost Station. He slept little on the plane and fought the exhausted, floating sensation of jet lag. He cabbed to the flat he and Caitlyn shared in a newer building on the north shore of Lake Brienz. Sancho and Alyssa were right. He owed Caitlyn one last chance. If he wanted to be with her, he would have to fight for the privilege.

Flynn took the elevator to the top floor and headed to his door. He slid his key into the lock to discover it no longer worked. He wiggled it around. He rattled the knob. *Did she change the locks?* He knocked on the door, and then knocked harder. He pushed the doorbell and knocked again.

"*Kommen! Kommen!*" came a gruff voice on the other side of the door.

Who could that be?

The door opened and a stooped elderly man glared at Flynn. "*Was willst du?*"

"Do you speak English?"

"English. Yes."

"Who are you?"

"Who are *you?*"

"I live here."

The old man poked Flynn in the chest with a bony finger. It hurt like hell as he was still recovering from that knife wound. "*I* live here."

"Where's Caitlyn Valentine?"

"Ah, yes. She moved."

"Moved?"

A tiny elderly lady shuffled up with a walker. *"Wer ist das?"*

"Er sucht Caitlyn Valentine." The old man pointed at Flynn. "English."

"She moved," the lady said.

Flynn already felt weird from the jet lag. This wasn't helping. "Where'd she move?"

The lady held up a finger. *"Warten."* She shuffled off.

Flynn looked back at the man. "Do you know where she moved?"

"Wait. My wife is getting her address."

Flynn waited impatiently. The woman did not move quickly. Eventually, she returned, shuffling back ever so slowly with a tiny scrap of paper in her hand. She handed it to her husband, who handed it to Flynn, who unfolded it and checked the address. It was local. "When did *you* move in here?"

The old man shut the door in Flynn's face.

The address was just a few blocks away. He decided to walk and discovered a smaller, more modest place on a busy street without a view. Two burly men loading a truck on the street stared at him as he brushed past. One had a fat lip, a swollen eye, and toilet paper shoved up his nostrils. Flynn noted it as suspicious and hurried inside. He took the stairs two at a time and rapped on the door. It creaked open, unlocked.

He entered the flat to discover it in complete disarray. The dining table was overturned. Broken crockery covered the floor. *Is that blood?* In the kitchen, a single cup and dish sat in the sink. He found an open suitcase on the floor of the bedroom and recognized Caitlyn's clothes hanging in the closet. Rumpled blankets covered the bed, and toiletries circled the sink in the tiny bathroom. But he saw no sign of Caitlyn.

He glanced out the window. The two moving men stared up at him. They immediately jumped into their truck. Flynn rushed out the door and down the short flight of stairs. The truck started pulling away. Flynn didn't break stride as he wrenched open the passenger door, reached inside, and tore the passenger out of his seat. He grabbed onto Flynn as he fell, taking them both to the ground.

Flynn's stitches ripped. The sharp, searing pain in his shoulder took his breath away.

The driver stopped the truck and jumped out as Flynn grappled with the passenger. The man was powerful, but even with one good arm, Flynn managed to flip him over and press his face into the concrete. He twisted the man's arm back, causing him to cry out in pain.

Two burly hands grabbed Flynn by his shirt and threw him to the ground. Flynn kicked straight up, catching the driver between the legs with the heel of his shoe. The driver staggered and grabbed his groin as the passenger started pummeling Flynn. Flynn grabbed the passenger by the shirt, pulled him close, and clamped his teeth onto the man's nose.

A foot caught Flynn on the side of the head. The driver again. Flynn rolled to his side and then to his feet to square off against both of them. Blood covered the passenger's face and the driver clutched his junk. Both looked reluctant to engage again.

Flynn's chest wound pulsated and throbbed. Blood soaked his shirt. His head swam as he started to wobble.

A police car pulled up. Two officers jumped out.

The driver and passenger shouted to the officers in German, pointing at Flynn. Flynn shouted over them. "Whatever they're saying, they're lying! They're liars! They've kidnapped Caitlyn Valentine! Check the truck! They have her in their truck!"

Flynn pointed at the truck.

The officers approached the back of the panel truck and the driver opened the doors. Flynn looked inside. Boxes and furniture, but no Caitlyn.

"She's in there! She has to be! She's probably drugged and unconscious in one of those boxes."

The driver and the passenger shouted in German. The police pushed Flynn up against the truck. They frisked him and handcuffed his hands behind his back, ripping open his wound. Blood flowed as he sank to his knees.

"No, no, no! You don't understand! You have the wrong man! It's them! They're the ones! They have her. They…they…" He pitched forward and slammed into the cement with his face.

• • •

Sancho awoke with a start. The room was dark. A soft hand caressed his face. "Sancho?" Alyssa whispered.

"Hmm?"

"Miranda Jacks is on the phone."

"What time is it?"

"Late." She handed Sancho his cell phone.

Sancho sat up and put his feet on the floor. "Hello?"

"Sancho? It's Miranda. It's about Flynn."

"Is he okay?"

"He's fine. But he was arrested."

"Arrested?"

"In Switzerland. Apparently, he assaulted two moving men. They sent him for a psych eval and determined he was delusional and a public menace."

"Jesus."

"I got a call from the US embassy in Bern. They're deporting him."

"When?"

"Now. They're putting him on a plane as we speak. Do you think you could pick him up at LAX?"

"I guess. Sure. Jesus."

"I promised the embassy that once he arrived in the States, he'd be sent to a psychiatric hospital for an evaluation. Can you make that happen?"

"I'll take him to City of Roses. When does his flight get in?"

"Late this afternoon."

"Did he hurt anyone?"

"Not seriously, but the Swiss are pretty strict about foreign nationals committing any kind of crime. He won't be able to return to Switzerland for fifteen years."

"Have you talked to Caitlyn?"

"We can't find her. Flynn claims she's been kidnapped."

"What do the Swiss think?"

"They think he's crazy."

. . .

Sancho waited at LAX and watched the faces of all the travelers as they exited from customs and immigration into the arrivals area. Flynn looked terrible. Exhausted and pale and miserable as hell. He had scabs on his face, his shoulder was bandaged, and he exhibited none of his usual *cheerfulness*. The energetic crowd buffeted him as he made his way out.

Sancho felt a twinge of guilt for encouraging him to go back to Switzerland. Clearly, Caitlyn was gone when Flynn got there. As usual, he came up with some crazy theory to explain why she wasn't there. He obviously couldn't deal with being rejected again, so he went to his usual tried and true. He did the same thing the last time she dumped him. This time, though, Sancho felt partially responsible.

He caught Flynn's eye and met him halfway. "Hey, *mano*, it's good to see you. How was the flight?"

"Exhausting."

"Let's get you out of here."

After collecting his luggage, they headed to the Aston Martin Flynn gifted him six years ago. Flynn sat uncharacteristically quiet as they left the airport. Sancho decided he was probably just tired. But he looked so dejected. So goddamn sad. Sancho reached over and patted Flynn on the knee. "Dude, you okay?"

"They took her, Sancho."

"Who?"

"Caitlyn. They took her. I wasn't there. Once again, I failed to protect her."

"Who took her?"

"I don't know. I have so many enemies. It could have been any of them. Ivanov. The Army of God. Goldhammer."

"I'm sure she's fine."

"Why would you say that?"

"Because she usually is. She's tough as hell. She's probably just lying low."

"They took her. I know they did."

Sancho sighed. Better to humor him than deny his delusion. "We'll get Miranda Jacks to look into it. She can call Duncan Dankworth at MI6. He can probably get Interpol involved."

"I should have been there."

"You can't be everywhere, man. You need to rest up. Heal up. Get your strength back."

Flynn shook his head. "They think I'm crazy. That's why they deported me. I tried to tell them it was just a cover story. That I'm not really a mental patient, but they refused to believe me."

■　■　■

Sancho arranged for Flynn's readmission to City of Roses. The head psychiatrist, Dr. Michaels, resisted at first. Flynn had slept with his wife back in the day, and caused all kinds of trouble. But Sancho played on his ego. *No one knows his case like you do. If anyone can help him, it's you.* The head nurse at City of Roses worked on Michaels as well. Nurse Durkin was once Flynn's arch nemesis, but now she actually felt some sympathy and possibly even affection for him.

Many of the patients who'd been at City of Roses for years had great fondness for Flynn. Upon his return, he was greeted like a conquering hero. The activity room buzzed with excitement as many of Flynn's friends and fellow patients converged on him. Quentin, Flynn's former roommate, greeted Flynn with a welcoming salute.

The elderly, self-proclaimed genius inventor shouted, "Wait until you see my latest creation!"

Three-hundred-pound ex-gangbanger Ty grinned when he saw Flynn. "Look who's in the house!"

Former 1940s pinup girl, Doris Frawley, shuffled over with her walker, batting her eyes and vying for Flynn's attention with Mary Alice, a big-boned, fifty-something, freckled-faced lady with intermittent explosive disorder. Mary Alice grinned and shouted with the raspy voice of a three-pack-a-day smoker. "I knew you'd be back!"

Sancho watched as all the adoration buoyed Flynn's spirits.

He took Flynn to check in with Dr. Michaels. His secretary, Miss Honeywell, offered Flynn just the hint of a smile as she pushed the button on her phone/intercom. "Mr. Flynn's here to see you, doctor."

"Send him in," said a taciturn voice.

"Honeywell, I must say, you look quite fetching today."

"He's waiting for you, Mr. Flynn."

"Sometimes I think you're the only one who really understands me."

"No one understands you."

She went back to typing as Flynn and Sancho entered Dr. Michael's office.

"It's good to see you, sir."

Michaels pointed Flynn and Sancho to the chairs facing his desk. "Please have a seat."

Sancho sat. Flynn remained standing. "Did someone brief you on the situation?"

"The situation is this. You'll be kept on a very short leash. You need to follow the rules, and you need to do what I say. I will not tolerate any inappropriate behavior. We're here to help you, but for that to work, you need to want our help."

"Of course, I want your help, sir. I know I can't do this alone. This time, we will do this as a team. You have my word."

"I'm gratified to hear that."

"Caitlyn Valentine has been taken. By whom, I don't know, but I do know she's in great peril. They are using her to get to me, so I will gladly avail myself of every resource you can offer."

Dr. Michaels sighed, rolled his eyes, and glared at Sancho. "Nurse Perez, Mr. Flynn is now your responsibility. Keep him in line. Is that clear?"

Sancho nodded. "Crystal."

▪   ▪   ▪

Three hours later, Sancho sat in the outdoor courtyard and watched the nurses watching Flynn execute a strenuous karate kata the best he could with one arm in a sling. Sweat glistened on his bare chest and shoulders as he snapped front kicks and spinning back kicks and struck multiple stances, turning and moving with power and precision, shouting a loud *kiai* with every blow.

He was in training mode, determined to turn himself into a lethal and unstoppable force. Flynn ignored his pain and shrugged off his fear and insecurity by jettisoning reality. But maybe that's what all heroes did. Dismiss the obstacles stacked against them. Ignore the fact that they can die. Let self-deception lead them into the line of fire so they can overcome seemingly insurmountable odds.

Or die trying.

ACKNOWLEDGEMENTS

Books are like magic to me. For a short time, I can escape into other people's lives, visit places I've never been, real or imagined, experience incredible adventures and become a cynical, world-weary private eye, a world-class villain, a plucky ten-year-old, an insecure teenager, or an unstoppable hero. This year, in particular, I've really needed that escape. So, I want to start by thanking all the authors who transported and inspired me. They are far too numerous to list here, but I do want to acknowledge Ian Fleming and Miguel de Cervantes Saavedra. Their timeless heroes helped to inspire the creation of Flynn.

Next, I want to thank all the fans of Flynn's adventures who have written reviews on Amazon and Goodreads, and those who have reached out to me online or in person at conferences. Your enthusiasm and support inspire me every day. I love knowing that I've transported you, just as my literary heroes have transported me.

I also want to thank my brilliant editor, M.J. Moores, and my intrepid literary agent, Darlene Chan.

I'm incredibly grateful to the friends and fellow writers who generously gave their time to help shape my early drafts, offering insightful notes, brilliant ideas, and unwavering support. In particular, I want to thank Dwight Holing, Richard Procter, Cam Torrens, Tom McCaffrey, Gary Gerlacher, Karen K. Brees, and Gojan Nikolich.

I also want to thank Victoria Gerken and the team at Podium Audio as well as the brilliant actor who brings Flynn (and everyone else) to life in the audiobooks, Chris Ciulla.

Thank you to Reagan Rothe and the whole team at Black Rose Writing.

My siblings, Mike, Lisa, and Lynne, my Uncle Sandy, and my Cousin Neenie, are always there for me, and I am so grateful to have them in my life.

Finally, I want to thank my wife, Kim, and my son, Jakob, and his wife, Charlotte. I don't know what I would do without their love and support.

ABOUT THE AUTHOR

Haris Orkin is a novelist, playwright, screenwriter, and game writer.

His play, *Dada,* was produced at The American Stage and the La Jolla Playhouse. *Sex, Impotence, and International Terrorism* was chosen as a critic's choice by the L.A. Weekly and sold as a film script to MGM/UA. *Save the Dog* was produced as a Disney Sunday Night movie. His original screenplay, *A Saintly Switch,* was directed by Peter Bogdanovich and starred David Alan Grier and Vivica A. Fox.

He is a WGA Award and BAFTA Award nominated game writer and narrative designer known for *Command and Conquer: Red Alert 3, Call of Juarez: Gunslinger, Company of Heroes 2, Tom Clancy's The Division, Mafia 3, Dying Light, Evil West, Resident Evil: Shadows of Rose.*

www.harisorkin.com

NOTE FROM THE AUTHOR

I was a shy, skinny, bookish, bespectacled, and insecure twelve-year-old living in the suburbs of Chicago when I first realized what I wanted to be when I grew up. I wanted to be Alexander Mundy in *It Takes a Thief*.

I wanted to be Illya Kuryakin in *The Man from Uncle*. I wanted to be part of the Mission Impossible team. I wanted to be Jim West, Derek Flint, and Matt Helm. I wanted to be James Bond.

Those men had no fear. They knew karate and could scuba dive and rock climb and skydive and ski and shoot the eye out of a flea at fifty yards. They were confident in any situation and were comfortable in their own skin. I think that was the biggest wish fulfillment fantasy of all for an awkward pre-teen struggling through puberty and that's what inspired James Flynn and his adventures.

At twelve I was terrified of girls. I was always picked last in gym class. I lived a life of perpetual embarrassment. In hindsight, that's probably how most twelve-year-olds feel, but at the time, I didn't know that. So I started lifting weights. I became a gymnast. I boxed. I studied karate. I became a rock climber and learned to ski and scuba dive. I even studied in London for a year and traveled the world.

But I never did become an international super spy. Instead, I became a screenwriter and game writer, creating wish fulfillment fantasies for other nerdy twelve-year-olds. Thank you for indulging in my fantasies. I hope you enjoyed the journey. I do believe Mr. Flynn is just getting started.

Please connect with me on Bluesky and Facebook and feel free to ask me anything. This is a two-way conversation.

~Haris Orkin

NOTE FROM THE PUBLISHER

Word-of-mouth is crucial for any author to succeed. If you enjoyed *The Spy Who Hated Me*, please leave a review online—anywhere you are able. Even if it's just a sentence or two. It would make all the difference and would be very much appreciated.

Thanks!

We hope you enjoyed reading this title from:

www.blackrosewriting.com

Subscribe to our mailing list – *The Rosevine* – and receive **FREE** books, daily deals, and stay current with news about upcoming releases and our hottest authors.
Scan the QR code below to sign up.

Already a subscriber? Please accept a sincere thank you for being a fan of Black Rose Writing authors.

View other Black Rose Writing titles at www.blackrosewriting.com/books and use promo code **PRINT** to receive a **20% discount** when purchasing.